Prologue

25th December 2011.

I was lying on my front in a hospital bed and two prison officers were sitting by the door fiddling with their mobile phones. A saline drip fed into a cannula on my right arm. In my left hand I was holding a circular tube with a button on top which, when I pressed, delivered a dose of morphine. This was enough to keep about fifty percent of my pain at bay but only for, what felt like, a few minutes.

Every so often a nurse would come in, take my blood pressure and temperature and stick some device on the end of my finger. I noticed from her badge that her name was Beryl Butler. She never spoke to me but on this, perhaps her fourth visit, she had wished both the prison officers guarding me a merry Christmas.

As she was waiting for the readings to come through, she spoke to them.

"They told me this is that famous police officer who did that murder. Is that right?"

Off to the side, a voice replied:

"Yeah, that's right."

"What exactly happened to him?" The nurse asked.

"He was jugged. Another prisoner poured boiling water mixed with sugar over his head." The voice replied.

"He was lucky, it went down his back." The nurse replied.

I didn't feel very lucky. The pain was overwhelming.

"The papers said he was highly decorated for bravery?" The nurse asked.

"Not anymore; it's been rescinded. There's a photocopy of the letter from the Queen going around the prison."

"The Queen?"

"Well, her private secretary or someone. It was his formal notification that he is no longer entitled to wear the medal or use the initials, Q, something, something." One of the officers replied.

"I saw some woman on the T.V. last week, reckoned he was innocent. I think it was his mother. She's started some campaign for a retrial." The nurse said.

"Yeah, I saw that too, but I think she's chasing a lost cause. I saw a programme about the case a couple of months ago. They interviewed the original detectives and the victim's daughters. They found his DNA at the scene. You can't really argue with that." A second voice said.

"Bang to rights, then." The nurse remarked, as she started to take the various medical instruments off my body.

"I'm innocent." I muttered.

I know it didn't matter what two prison officers and a nurse thought but I wanted them to hear me.

The nurse leaned forward and shone a small light in each of my eyes.

"I'm innocent." I repeated, speaking slightly louder.

I blinked.

"It makes a change from the usual PS overdose." The nurse observed, as she started to write in my file.

PS stood for psychoactive substance and usually referred to as spice, a type of synthetic cannabis. There was barely a day that went by when one of my fellow prisoners wasn't taken to hospital suffering from the effects of a PS overdose.

"He's a strange one, that's for sure. Quite frankly, if the cons want to jug him, it's almost impossible to stop them. As an ex-copper, he's even more hated than the paedophiles or grasses." The first voice said.

I groaned in agony.

"The woman on the telly yesterday, she said she'd offer like a hundred thousand pounds for any information that would prove his innocence". The nurse said.

I hadn't seen the news article to which the nurse was referring, but I knew the woman was Mrs M. I had been living with Mrs M when I was arrested for the crime, right up until I was sentenced. She was my friend, and the mother of my old colleague, WPC Dawn Matthews, who'd been murdered by the IRA back in 1983.

"Who knows what goes through the minds of these people." The first officer replied.

"I don't envy you your job." The nurse replied.

"Oh, I couldn't do *your* job." The first officer replied.

"I'm innocent." I said again, but my eyes were closed now, and I could feel myself drifting off into another morphine induced sleep.

I heard the nurse walking away from my bed towards the door.

"I'll tell you what, you two." She said.

"Go on?"

"I hope he is guilty. I really hope he did it."

"That's a strange thing to say, nurse."

"Because if he is innocent, that man must be living in a place worse than hell."

Chapter 1

One year earlier – December 2010

I used to think being a Detective Sergeant was the best rank to be but I was wrong. I had now been a Detective Inspector for three years and my only regret was that I'd not taken promotion earlier. The thing was, as a DS people were always checking up on you. You don't realise it at the time, but they are. It's their job. As a DI however, you are afforded a level of trust. I think it's an officer thing, probably derived from the military. No one asks you what you're doing, no one makes sure you are where you say you are. Life is therefore a lot more laid back.

I got promoted when I was working for the Assistant Commissioner on a case in Portugal and when that ended, he took me onto his team as a kind of Deputy Staff officer. The work was boring, and I implored him to find me another interesting project. I had more leverage than most Detective Inspectors because he was having a relationship, actually an affair, with Mrs M. As a result, I got a series of projects. The first was to assist preparations for a public enquiry; the second was to research and make out a case for a legal extension to the maximum time a terrorist suspect could be held without charge; the third, by far the most interesting, was to make arrangements for the Deputy Chief of the New York Police Department to undertake a three-month secondment to the Met.

The Deputy's name was Vince Elflain and it was my responsibility to find him somewhere to live; provide him transport; pull together a meaningful, interesting and informative itinerary so, in the three months he was with us, he could get a comprehensive understanding of the Metropolitan Police.

I'd arranged a day flying over the capital with India 99; three night duty's on Brixton's area car; a day with the River Police at Wapping; a visit to Hendon Training School, three days shadowing a murder squad DCI and a week shadowing the DAC for Counter Terrorism. He was invited as a guest to every Management and Finance Board during the three months. As a bit of fun, I'd also arranged a guided tour the Houses of Parliament, a back lot tour of Buckingham Palace and a private visit to the Tower of London. For each of these events, well except the Management Boards, I had to accompany him.

Finally, I had to take him to Bramshill College, wherever that was, so he could observe a Senior Command Course; the one Chief Superintendents have to pass before they can attain ACPO rank.

I'd spent weeks liaising with his Personal Assistant in New York and from her I gleaned that once Vince had completed his trip to the Metropolitan Police, a reciprocal offer would be extended to a senior officer in the MPS. I knew exactly what would happen, I'd do all the work for his visit and in return someone who hadn't, but who held a similarly exalted rank, would be invited to visit New York. Still, I decided to make Vince my new best friend in the hope that he would feel obligated to extend the return offer to me.

This explains why, at nine o'clock one gloomy January morning, I was waiting in Arrivals at Heathrow Terminal 3 with a rather poorly hand-made sign in my pocket that read 'Vince Elflain' in badly coloured black lettering.

The Delta flight from JFK had only just landed so I got myself a coffee and settled down to do the Telegraph crossword. Sitting immediately in front of me was a white lady in her early forties with two children, both boys, in their early teens. I was genuinely struck by her beautiful hair, long, fair and layered – she looked like she'd just walked out of a salon.

The three of them possessed a nervous tension and the woman kept getting a brush out and applying it with precision and purpose to the boys' hair. Every time she did so, they got more and more irritated.

In the end, I couldn't resist and tapped very gently on her right shoulder. She turned around.

"You really wanted girls, didn't you?" I enquired.

I smiled broadly and tilted my head to one side.

She laughed out loud.

"Is it that obvious?" She asked.

I nodded.

"I thought about changing them but what can you do, apparently they're for life and not just for mini rugby morning."

"I've got two girls; trust me, when they get older, you'll be really pleased you had boys."

She went to turn around.

"Can I just say one more thing? Something I've never said to a strange woman before."

She didn't say anything, but I took her silence as consent.

"Your hair is absolutely amazing. You look like you've just stepped out of a Vidal Sassoon salon."

Her face burst into a smile.

"I have; well Nicky Clarke actually, about ninety minutes ago. And he actually did me himself." She replied, checking her watch.

"Well, whoever you're meeting, is a very lucky man."

"It's my husband. He's been working in the States for the last six months. We're all terribly excited to see him again."

"Well, you look gorgeous; I'd be bursting with pride if you were my wife and I was meeting you at the airport." I said.

"What a nice man you are. Are you waiting for someone special?"

I shook my head.

"No, it's a work matter. I'm meeting someone from New York who's coming to work with my company for a few months. I've never met him before." I replied.

"A company. I'd have thought you were a policeman – you've just got that confident air about you."

I smiled and pulled my warrant card out of my back pocket.

"I knew it." She replied.

I laughed.

"Do you know that many Old Bill?" I asked.

"None. You just had that look, that *je ne sais quois*." She said, suddenly bursting into a strong guttural French accent.

"I don't know what that means." I replied, in all honesty.

"Very funny, very clever Mr Plod." She replied.

There was a sudden commotion as her children spotted their father and my new friend stood up.

"Nice nearly meeting you." I said.

She fished into her coat pocket, handed me a calling card without saying a word, and was off, walking into a turbulent sea of people.

I thrust the card into my jacket pocket and checked my watch. I needed to find a toilet and then stand amid the numerous drivers, with my sign.

Chapter 2

Deputy Chief of the NYPD was a tall, smart black male in his early forties with a completely bald head wearing an immaculate Hugo Boss dark grey suit. He could have been straight out of a Hollywood movie.

As we drove into London, I learned a little about my new colleague. He was divorced, with three children and lived 'up state' in a town called Westchester, apparently about an hour from Grand Central Station. He had joined the police from college where he'd graduated with a degree in Law. Apparently, he'd received a scholarship which had meant his student loan was minimal.

"Where will I be staying?" He asked.

"I've found you a flat in Belgravia. It's one of the flats owned by the Met which they give to their really senior officers. It's very central, which will be perfect. Ten minutes' walk from Scotland Yard and Victoria station. Have you been to London before?" I asked.

"No, this is my first trip abroad." He replied.

"What? You mean anywhere outside the States?" I asked, incredulously.

"Sure. Most Americans don't travel much, not when Florida is only a short plane flight south. Why would ya? What with the threat of terrorism, too. Look at those attacks last month in Milan and Paris. Very worrying. Will I be safe in Bell, Bell, Ravia?"

"Belgravia, Vince. Yes, you'll be safe. We Londoners are used to bombs. We had the Blitz in the Forties and the IRA in the Seventies and Eighties, and the Muslim extremists more recently. We very much take it in our stride."

"The cops at the airport, they had guns, right?" Vince asked.

I nodded.

"But you're not carrying, are you?"

"Good god, no." I replied.

"What about your colleagues? What about him?"

We were in heavy traffic on the A4 into London and Vince was pointing at a uniform PC who was walking along the pavement."

"No, he won't be armed." I replied.

"How in god's name do you protect the public, if you can't even protect yourself?" He asked.

"We just do." I responded, coolly.

"You're on duty now, right?"

I nodded.

"No piece?"

"Nope"

"Any personal safety equipment at all?"

"Nope" I replied.

"What happens if you see a robbery? Here, now, right in front of us? Would you intervene?"

"Of course." I replied.

"How? By getting yourself shot?" He asked.

"Well, it probably won't be an armed robbery. More likely a knife, we call them muggings."

Vince smiled and shook his head in disbelief.

"It's a culture thing. In England, a member of the public's rights outweighs a police officer's rights, every time."

"Shocking" He replied.

"Last year we had an Internal Investigations case. This guy had a big argument with his wife and ended up on the roof of his house. NYPD attended. The perp was drunk and drinking from a crate of Bud. When he finished one, he would lob it towards the street below. The officers got up on an adjacent roof and started to open a dialogue with him. He chatted to them but when he finished his next bottle of Bud, he threw the empty bottle towards the officers. It fell short and wide. The first officer, Bret Leondowski, drew his weapon and shot him dead."

"Jesus Christ you're kidding!" I replied.

"Internal Investigations cleared him. The perp had used lethal force and the officer responded. No further action. Welcome to the good old U S of A, buddy." Vince said.

"In England, the officer would have been found guilty of murder and sentenced to prison for life." I replied.

"Then this is one fucked up country." Vince responded.

I felt a degree of anger. This may be a *'fucked up country'* but it was my fucked up country. With that said, I kind of agreed with him. I bit my lip.

"Do you have an internal investigations department?" Vince asked.

"It's called the Directorate of Professional Standards. But there is an Independent Police Complaints Commission, who oversee all serious matters, like deaths in custody and police firearms discharges." I replied.

"Can I meet with both of those departments, please, buddy?"

"Of course. Otherwise, are you happy with the itinerary?" I asked.

"Yeah, but I'll take another look this evening; there might be a couple of things we can drop."

"Vince, let me ask you, so that I can make sure I can help you as best I can. Exactly what is the purpose of your visit? What are you trying to learn, or gain?"

"I want to identify what you do better than us and then take that home and implement it."

"So, you're going to disarm your entire Police Service." I said, jokingly.

"Do you know what buddy, while I doubt it, I come with an open mind. If in three months' time, I think it's a better way to police a large city, then, hell, yes, I'll propose it."

I nodded.

I was impressed with Vince. He was certainly a stereotype of a NYPD senior officer, but he had a manner about him which balanced confidence with friendliness. When I glanced at him a few moments later, I realised that he'd fallen asleep. The effects of the red-eye were starting to take effect, which was a shame, because we were about a hundred yards away from his Belgravia flat.

Chapter 3

Looking after Vince Elflain was a pleasure, and for a while, I almost forgot I was a Detective Inspector in the Metropolitan Police. I became a driver, grocery shopper, diary secretary, bodyguard, travel agent, translator, private secretary, tour guide, restaurant critic, confidant, and drinking companion.

I quickly grew to like Vince and to trust him. It was interesting because the most critical he ever was, was during that first journey from Heathrow when he was obviously tired and not quite thinking straight. Through him, I also met the most senior officers in the Met, and in most of these meetings, I was allowed to sit quietly in the corner making notes.

Life was easy, and I felt like I was on a sabbatical from proper policing, which was a real pleasure after twenty-eight years at the front line.

I also got to view the organisation I loved through somebody else's eyes. This was incredibly refreshing and even more revealing. What did I see? A police service remarkably accepting of criticism and refreshingly willing to listen and change. A police service that had lost the respect of the younger generation and which, as a direct result, had largely lost control of the streets. A detective and forensic capability that was world leading. And finally, and perhaps worst of all, a Management Board comprising of highly ambitious, self-centred senior officers who were constantly leaking to the press and running their contemporaries down with the intention of advancing their own careers. At least that was what Vince saw. When he explained his rationale for coming to such a conclusion to me during the many long hours we spent sitting in London traffic, I was mesmerised and at the same time more than a little unsettled.

I was careful not to probe, or to ask Vince questions which would put him in an awkward situation, but one particular Friday about halfway through his visit, I put such sensitivity to one side.

He'd been at Management Board all day. Management Board is the single most important meeting in the Metropolitan Police. It is the mechanism through which the organisation of forty-eight thousand employees is run. Attendees at Management Board include only the very senior operators: the Commissioner and the Deputy; the four Assistant Commissioners; the Chief of Staff; and, the Heads of HR, Finance, Communications, and Legal Services (all civilian roles). These eleven people *are* the Metropolitan Police.

"I used to work with Kitty Young. We were PCs together at Stoke Newington back in the early eighties." I said, in anticipation of initiating a response.

"She's the black Deputy Commissioner, right?" Vince replied.

I nodded.

"She's invited me to a meeting of Emu. What is that?" He asked.

"It's the Association of Ethnic Minority Officers. Are you going to go?"

"Of course." He replied.

"I've given her your email address to make the arrangements."

"Great" I replied, with as much enthusiasm as I could muster for anything to do with that woman.

"I won't be allowed to accompany you on that visit." I said.

"Of course you will." He replied.

My plan to get Vince talking about Kitty Young, and when I say *'talking'* I actually mean *'slagging off'*, didn't appear to be working. Should I give the subject one last poke or just let it go? But before I could say another word, Vince took the decision away from me.

"I think AC Young thinks she should be the next Commissioner."

"Rumour was that she went for it last year when she was still only a Deputy Assistant Commissioner, but she lost out to the former Deputy, our current Commissioner. I think she's likely to get the next one but that'll be four or five-years' time, if she can be bothered to wait that long when she has the mother of all pensions awaiting her when she retires. What are your thoughts?"

"She's bitter. She's quite disrespectful to her colleagues and she even made reference to her publishing a book about her life in the police and the impossible hurdles she's risen above. Is that allowed, while she's still serving?" Vince asked.

"They usually wait until they retire. That might mean that's what she has in mind. I don't think the Job would be too impressed if she published her book now. But, hey, what do I know, buddy?"

I smiled.

"When you told her I was looking after you, did she say anything about me?" I asked.

"Yeah, she referred to you as Nasels."

"My nickname is Nostrils. Not Nasels, but close enough."

"Nostrayls" Vince replied, placing a deep hard 'aye' sound as the second syllable and giving the whole word a very cockney twang.

I laughed out loud.

"You ever had a nickname?" I asked.

"Nigger" He replied.

I immediately felt very uneasy. No one used that word, ever! Well, apart from the odd black rapper.

"Gosh, really?" I replied.

"Buddy, I grew up poor, really poor. I grew up in Harlem in the sixties and seventies. It was a tough land. At eight, I was adopted by a white family, my family. They were fantastic but I went to a predominately white school - hence the nickname."

"Did it hurt?"

"All nicknames hurt."

I didn't agree but I wasn't going to tell him that, it would just sound too argumentative when he was discussing what was clearly a sensitive subject.

"Were your adopted family better off, then?"

"No buddy; they were as poor as they come but they lived on the lower West Side which was mainly first and second-generation Italian immigrants. That's how I ended up as the only nigger in a sea of spics. After a few years, they started calling me coconut, you know brown on the outside, white inside. I was great at sports, that always helps, and I am proud to say the first from my school to be awarded a scholarship to Columbia."

"You did alright in the end, then?"

"Yeah, for a nigger." He replied, a wide smile on his face.

"You've been here, what, six weeks? Is the Met racist?" I asked.

Many years ago, I'd had a similar conversation with a black colleague, DC Colin Harte, who was a good friend. What he told me that day, that the Met was racist, had stuck in the back of my conscience ever since and I was keen to know, but also a little nervous to learn, whether any improvements had been made."

"Race is not the issue in England like it is in the US. Back at home, the race angle is applied to everything we do. It does seem more relaxed, but I have to say, I think you're in danger of failing the black community here.

You have to police them properly, but you don't. That was evident when we went out with the night duty from Brixton. The officers we were with were highly professional, but they are scared. Now they should be scared, very scared, because they don't carry guns but that isn't what's worrying them. They're petrified of the young black youth, the gun touting, drug dealing, disrespectful black youth. In New York, if a suspect kicked off like I repeatedly saw last week, he'd be put to the ground and handcuffed immediately. Christ, if he was that bad, he could risk being shot.
Your guys were scared when they got into any sort of confrontations and you could see that in their eyes. Not physically scared, but worried about being accused of racism, or assault or unprofessionalism."

"But if they did what you said, they'd get no support from the public, or their senior officers, or the press or the IPCC. They could kiss their careers good-bye."

"You don't get it, buddy. It's not about the officers' neurosis, it's about the black community. If this continues, they are the ones that will suffer. You will create a wild west, a lawless society where the gun rules, violence prevails, and drugs are sold without fear of arrest or imprisonment."

"You've got to realise my colleagues have no support; zero, nothing. If they do anything they are destroyed. Last year in London we had race riots because a black man was shot dead in Brixton. He had a handgun, but it was still in his pocket, and we'd had intelligence off a line ..."

"What's a line?"

"... a wire-tap, that he was on his way to supply that firearm to an associate so that the associate could go and kill a rival drug dealer. Now, a year later, all the officers involved are still suspended and under investigation and, the rumours are, the officer that shot the suspect will be charged with murder just to placate the black community. Of course, no one can refer to the wire-tap evidence."

"Why not?" Vince asked.

"Because under the Interception of Communications Act it's a criminal offence to do so."

"As a consequence, no one knows this suspect was on his way to assist with a murder?"

"No. Except everyone does." I said.

"What a mess." Vince concluded.

"I couldn't agree more." I replied.

Chapter 4

I was driving home when Mrs M rang. It was gone eight and it was very rare for her to call me while I was at work, so I assumed something must be wrong with Pippa, my twenty-two-year-old daughter, who lived with us.

"Hi darling. We need to talk. Can you meet me at the Bull Faced Stag?"

"Is it Pippa?" I asked.

"Don't speculate, just meet me there."

I checked the dashboard clock.

"About half an hour." I replied and terminated the call.

The call was disconcerting, but I decided not to worry until I had a clearer picture of what was going on. This tactic was sensible, and I eked it out for about five minutes before reaching for the phone and calling Pippa.

"Hi Dad."

"Hi, darling. Are you at home?"

"Yes, in my room. Why?"

"I've just had a strange call from Mrs M. She wants to meet up away from the house. Have you two had an argument or something?"

"No, not at all. We had dinner a couple of hours ago and I'm just getting ready to go round to Ben's for the night. She seemed fine."

"Oh okay. What's she been up to today?"

"She's spring cleaning, like it needed it, not." Pippa replied.

"Has she seen the boyfriend?" I asked.

"No. She spoke to him earlier."

"But she seemed okay?"

"Yes, Dad, she seemed fine, honestly. I've no idea why she wants to meet you. Where are you meeting, anyway?"

"The Bull Faced Stag, top of Queens Road. I haven't been in there for years."

"Well, I'm sure it's nothing. Maybe she's marrying John and she wants you to give her away."

"He'll have to get divorced first." I replied.

Pippa laughed and hung up with a *'see ya, Dad'*.

Pippa had lived with Mrs M and I since 2007 when her Mum, Jackie, and her younger sister, Trudy, emigrated to Australia. We all got on fabulously and I couldn't believe how well everything had worked out. I had to smile because at first Mrs M kept calling Pippa *'Dawn'*. It was lovely and terribly sad, both at the same time. I can honestly say that in the four years we'd been together, we'd never had a crossed word.

In September last year, I'd won the MPFS monthly lottery and shared the £2000 first prize with an officer from Heathrow. I put my half of the winnings into my rather meagre savings and came up with just about enough to buy two return tickets to Perth. When Mrs M found out, she asked if she could come, too. I would love to have paid for her after all she'd done for me, but I didn't have the money without dipping into my precious savings. I did toy with the idea of putting it all on a credit card but a long time ago I'd got heavily in debt, a situation that had got me in a pile of shit, and I was determined not to go down that route again.

Mrs M paid her own way, I don't think she expected to do anything else. Then Ben, Pippa's boyfriend, asked if he could come too, which was absolutely fine. Ben was a nice lad, the same age as Pippa, and a chartered surveyor by trade. I liked him a lot.

And so, in just six weeks' time, the four of us were flying to Australia for a three-week holiday of a lifetime. I simply couldn't wait.

***

Mrs M arrived before me and had already bought my pint of Guinness and herself her usual vodka and tonic.

"Okay, what's going on?" I asked, as soon as I'd sat down.

Mrs M got out her mobile phone and touched the screen several times. She then handed the phone to me.

I was looking at a photograph of a small blue square with two wires going left and a small third, shorter wire, going right. The photograph was a close up, and very slightly out of focus and the backdrop was a cloth or material of some kind.

I frowned.

Mrs M took her phone back and flipped the screen across to reveal a second photograph of the same object but even less in focus, but this time the background was white.

"Where was this taken?" I asked.

"The first photograph was in the lounge, the second in the kitchen".

"Today?"

"This afternoon."

"How did you find them?"

I was cleaning above the kitchen cupboards, you know, wiping the layer of grease that always forms just below the ceiling on the coving."

"I'll take your word about that." I replied.

"It was wired into the lighting cabling at a small electrical connection box. I thought, 'that's funny' and turned on the torch on my phone for a closer look. You can't see it on the photographs but there's a small microphone like cover on the side. You know, it's got tiny holes in it."

"It's called a probe."

"That's what I thought. It's a listening device, isn't it?"

I nodded.

"See, I knew living with you would pay off. You've told me about them before. Didn't you use them to get evidence on that guy that shot the police officer in Stepney?"

I nodded again.

"You left it in situ?" I asked.

"I did."

"And then you searched the rest of the house to see if there were anymore?"

"I did. But I haven't done your bedroom or Pippa's."

"Well done, Mrs M." I replied.

"I wonder how long they've been there?" Mrs M asked.

"I'm more interested to know why they're there." I said.

Mrs M looked around to check we couldn't be overheard.

"It can only be that *other* matter. The one we never talk about."

"But that's been all quiet for like, ever. The Real IRA claimed responsibility; the inquest went off with the Head of Counter Terrorism informing the Coroner that he thought they were the only suspects. It hasn't been in the papers, or the news, or anything. Has John mentioned anything at all to you about it?" I asked.

"Not a word." She replied.

"But that's all it can be."

"Unless you've recently despatched anyone else to meet their maker?" Mrs M said, in a barely audible whisper.

"Well not this week." I replied.

My light-hearted humour however was just a mask. I was quite terrified by this turn of events.

"What do you make of it?"

"It's weird, it really is. I mean, I have to assume that's the reason, there is no other possible cause. But I've absolutely no idea what could have suddenly come to light to put me in the frame. I mean, it's good this is over four years old; the passage of time always makes investigations more difficult. But why put a probe in? We're hardly likely to be discussing it over dinner, are we? *'Pass the ketchup, Mrs M, and did I tell you about the time I shot Barry Skinner?'* There's something missing here, a big piece of the jigsaw. My head tells me this must be about Skinner, but my heart doesn't quite buy it."

"We need to do another search, your bedroom and the garage, too. I want to make sure I know where every one of these are?" Mrs M said.

Then I had a thought.

"Hang on a second, Mrs M. We're assuming these were placed by law enforcement but what if they were put there by a private investigator or even a journalist."

"Or a private investigator hired by a journalist? But why?" Mrs M said.

"Okay, don't freak out but, you are having an affair with a married man who's one of the most senior police officers in the country. That's probably a newsworthy story."

"Oh gosh, Christopher, that's really frightening. Do you really think so?"

"Okay, it's one explanation. Being honest, I hope it is. I don't really fancy going to prison for the rest of my life. Mind you, at least I'd get some sex."

"Don't be ridiculous, even in prison, who's going to fancy you?" Mrs M replied.

* * *

That evening, and after Pippa had gone around to Ben's, Mrs M and I conducted a silent but very thorough search of the whole house. We found no more probes. That worried me even more. Someone trying to expose Mrs M's affair would certainly have probed her bedroom, and an unscrupulous private investigator trying to dish any dirt on me, would have dropped a probe in my bedroom. The fact that neither rooms had been attacked left me with the distinct impression that this was the work of officialdom, not some two-bob P.I. outfit. I kept my thoughts about this specific point to myself.

We spent the last hour of the evening watching TV in an eerie, unnatural silence. It's not conducive to good conversation to know your every word is being listened to.

It felt like an unnaturally long day when at midnight I eventually crawled into bed.

Like the infantryman who, the night before battle, writes his last letter home, I had an ominous feeling. I was certain I had an unavoidable appointment with an unfortunate destiny.

Chapter 5

I didn't have long to wait.

The next day the letter arrived.

Police & Fire Headquarters
Valley Road
Portishead
Bristol
BS20 8JJ

Dear Mr Christopher Pritchard,

I have been appointed to investigate an historic murder in connection with which I wish to interview you.

The interview will take place under caution and you are advised to arrange to be legally represented.

We understand you are a serving police officer with the Metropolitan Police and have informed the Commissioner of this request. In terms of notifying your employer, at this stage you do not have to take any further action.

Please contact the above number to make the arrangements.

Jacob J Gregory
Detective Superintendent
Avon and Somerset Police

Avon & Somerset Police? What were they doing involved in an Essex murder? That didn't make a lot of sense but then I was aware that occasionally one force would call in another to review a particular case, especially if the first force's investigation had been unsuccessful.

The letter did explain the probes. They were no doubt listening for my response to the letter, to see and hear, for example, any immediate calls I might make. They would also want to know if I did anything unusual, like going to the middle of Epping Forest and digging something up. The letter was what we call in the trade, a trigger; that is to say, a planned event designed to solicit a response from the suspect. The thing was, there was absolutely nothing for me to do. The evidence was long gone and with it, I hoped, any chance of Detective Superintendent Gregory achieving a successful conviction.

I was also a little bit relieved that they thought it necessary to deploy this tactic, as it would suggest they didn't already have enough evidence.

I didn't show the letter to Mrs M. I figured that she'd only worry. Instead, I folded it carefully and popped it into my back pocket.

***

I collected Vince from his Belgravia apartment and drove him to this morning's *'Metropolitan Police Adventure'*, as we'd come to refer to his daily whirlwind tour of my organisation.

We were visiting the Central Criminal Court, better known as the Old Bailey, where an Inspector from the City of London Police was going to give us a personal tour of the most famous criminal court in the world.

As we were driving slowly through heavy traffic in the West End, I took a call from Detective Superintendent Steve Bryan. Steve had replaced Erling Kristiansen as A.C. John King's staff officer and was now, technically, my boss. Steve was a genuinely nice chap but only about sixteen years old, or so it seemed to this craggy, aging Detective Inspector.

"Nostrils, are you free to talk?" Steve asked, an urgency in his voice.

"Well, I'm driving Vince to the Old Bailey, so not really." I replied.

"Have you had a letter from Avon & Somerset?" He asked.

"It's really hard to say, at the moment." I replied, slightly annoyed that he hadn't listened to my previous reply.

"They want to interview you about a murder."

Before I could reply, a uniform officer stepped into the road just in front of me and indicated that I should pull over.

I dropped the phone on my lap and did as I was told.

"This should be interesting." Vince said.

"Let's see what happens." I said.

"What do you want me to do?" He asked.

"Absolutely nothing." I replied, quite firmly.

There is no reason the uniform officer would have known this was a police car, nor that its occupants included a Detective Inspector and a visiting very senior officer from across the pond.

As I stopped, I put the hazard warning lights on and undid my window.

The officer was white, in his early thirties and in other ways pretty nondescript. I'd been a detective for so long, all uniform officers had started to look the same to me. He walked around to the front offside door and bent down.

I knew what to do. He'd ask me why he'd stopped me, and I'd reply by saying because I was on my mobile phone, which would immediately take the wind out of his sails, and then we'd see how the conversation went from there. If need be, I'd apologise profusely and assure the officer that I'd never do it again. I wouldn't be arrogant, or rude, or stroppy. I wouldn't seek to improve my chances of prosecution by reminding him that I paid his wages, or that I was in the same Masonic Lodge as his Chief Superintendent, or that he should be using his time to catch murderers and robbers. I would swallow a large slice of humble pie.

"Are you some sort of cunt?"

I was completely speechless.

"Are you deaf, too? I asked you a question."

"Hey" Vince said loudly.

"You can shut the fuck up."

I put my left arm up with an open palm to indicate to Vince that, no matter how well-intentioned he was, I really needed him to 'shut the fuck up'.

"Would you like me to get out?" I asked, politely.

"I.D." The officer replied.

Just for the briefest of moments, I went to reach into my back trouser pocket and produce my warrant card, but I didn't.

"I've got my driving licence in my wallet which is in my inside jacket pocket, hanging up but I'll need to get out to get it."

I waved my thumb towards the back seat.

"Get it, meet me on the pavement."

He stepped away from the vehicle and, ignoring Vince's protestations, I got out, retrieved my wallet and joined the officer on the pavement. As I handed my driving licence over, I clocked his shoulder number.

"Is this your vehicle?"

"It's my employer's." I replied.

"Insurance?" He demanded.

"Actually, don't think the vehicle is technically required to have any."

In my experience only three types of vehicle didn't require insurance: those belonging to either Her Majesty Queen Elizabeth the Second, London Transport or the Metropolitan Police. The uniform officer should have sensed something from my reply, but he didn't.

"Six points. I might as well take this licence now."

The officer stepped away from me so that he could see the front registration mark. I looked over towards Vince and realised he had put his window down, presumably to hear the conversation.

"Echo Oscar, Echo Oscar, three one one; vehicle check please, stop, High Holborn."

"Go ahead, three one one."

He rattled off the index and waited.

I nodded, meekly. I was slightly enjoying how this was playing out but there was still every possibility I could end up being stuck on for being on my phone.

"Three one one, Echo Oscar, over."

"Go ahead."

"No reports; the registered keeper is the Metropolitan Police."

In that moment, the officer's face drained of colour.

"You in the job?"

I nodded.

"Why didn't you show out?" He asked, looking genuinely perplexed.

"Because you called me a *'cunt'*. And then you told the Deputy Chief of the New York Police Department, who incidentally three one one, is seconded to the Metropolitan Police at the personal invitation of the Commissioner, to *'shut the fuck up'*."

"Three one one, Echo Oscar one, over"

Echo Oscar one was the call sign for the Duty Officer, the Inspector currently in charge of all the officers at Holborn police station.

"Go ahead, Sir." The officer replied.

"What's going on? Do you require my assistance?"

The Duty Officer obviously wanted to know what was happening. The pressure was mounting on three one one."

"No, Sir, I'm fine. I can handle it, thank you."

No sooner had the words left his mouth, than a marked police car pulled up immediately behind my car. Before the officers alighted, they put on the blue lights to warn on-coming vehicles and divert them around what was rapidly becoming a traffic pinch point.

Vince took that as his signal to get out and he came to stand by my side.

The two new officers were both Sergeants and I was pleased to see, walked with an air of authority. I didn't recognise either but that was hardly surprising these days. It had been over ten years since I'd worked at a police station; in fact, it was almost as long since I'd been in one, which was shameful.

"You two in the job?" The female Sergeant asked.

I nodded.

"Just wait here, please."

The two officers took three one one a few yards down the street and just out of earshot. They spoke to him for what seemed like an eternity, although in reality it was probably about three minutes.

"What the hell, Chris?" Vince said.

"What can I say, I'm embarrassed." I replied.

"What would happen in New York? If this exact scenario had played out there?" I asked.

"That officer would have put his uniform on for the last time." He replied.

I didn't say anything. I was embarrassed; the way he spoke to us was appalling but I really didn't want three points on my licence, so I was somewhat conflicted. I was experienced enough to know I couldn't have it both ways. I could complain and take the ticket or, to coin the officer's terminology, *'shut the fuck up'* and keep a clean licence.

Eventually, the two Sergeants walked over. I thought it was intriguing that they clearly indicated to three one one that he should go on his way. The female Sergeant spoke.

"The officer says you were on your mobile phone while driving."

"I was." I replied.

"Who are you?"

I handed over my warrant card.

She glanced at it quickly and handed it back, saying:

"Thank you, Sir."

"The officer intends to take no further action but would like to politely point out that calling him a *'cunt'* was distasteful."

"What!" Vince exclaimed, a little too loudly.

"Vince, please." I said, the epitome of calm.

"I didn't say that to him, and I have a witness."

"That word is extremely offensive and, even if you used it jovially, it is a word no police officer should ever utter when on duty." The Sergeant said.

"I didn't say that word." I replied, but quietly and with a decent amount of dignity.

"We're going to leave that there, then. Please keep off your phone and have a good day, Sir." The Sergeant said, politely.

"I'm afraid that's not going to be possible." I replied.

"Would you like to make a formal complaint? His name's Darren Stiller." She asked.

"No, and anyway, I don't think I can because I'm not a member of the public. But I just can't leave it there." I reiterated.

"Why not?" The Sergeant asked.

"Because three one one has still got my driving licence."

"Oh, what a cunt." She replied.

* * *

On the way home that day, and after I had dropped off my American buddy, I pulled off the A11 and into a quiet spot in the forest. It was well gone five, so I thought I'd be leaving a voice message for the Avon & Somerset guy, Detective Superintendent Gregory. I was nervous. This was very much like the starting of a nightmare and I knew this could be the beginning of the end for me. After just two rings, a female answered my call.

"DS Sally Crane, can I help you?"

"Oh, hi there; my name is Christopher Pritchard, I've just had a letter from Detective Superintendent Gregory about coming for an interview."

"Oh hi, Mr Pritchard, yes, we do need to speak to you. When would you be able to come for an interview?"

"Tomorrow?" I said, thinking that I would appear helpful and unconcerned if I agreed to meet as soon as possible, as they'd requested.

"Oh, excellent. Can you be at the address on the envelope tomorrow at two?" DS Crane asked.

"Of course." I replied.

"We'll need to do a DNA test first thing. Are you okay with that?"

Of course I wasn't. They must think they've got my DNA at the scene and if they have, I was fucked. But I was certain I'd been so careful when I shot Barry Skinner. I'd worn double gloves, got rid of all my clothes and shoes. So how, oh how, could I have left anything there?

"No problem." I replied, lying.

"And you've got a solicitor?" DS Crane asked.

"No, I don't need one. I've not been involved in any murders, Sally, and an innocent man has nothing to worry about."

It was a bluff. I wasn't innocent, but I was determined that the impression I gave was of complete but polite indifference to the threat posed by their enquiries. I was using all my experience. Over the years I'd investigated hundreds of serious crimes and whenever I did, and the suspect declined to have a brief because *'I ain't done it',* I was inclined to believe them.

"Very well, Mr Pritchard, but of course if at any time you want one, you just say so and we'll stop the interview until one arrives. We just assumed you'd want to bring one because of the seriousness of the charge."

"Honestly, Sally, I haven't committed murder. I think I would remember."

"See you tomorrow, Mr Pritchard. Come to reception at two. We'll meet you there."

It all sounded friendly enough, but I was still gravely concerned. I turned the conversation with Sally over and over in my mind in an effort to identify anything she might have said that gave some clue to what was going on. The DNA request scared me terribly, but I had no choice, I'd have to provide it. Undisputable DNA evidence, plus the obvious revenge motive I had for killing Barry Skinner, would be enough to send me down for life.

I was starting to get mega stressed but at least I didn't have long to wait until I found out what was really going on.

Chapter 6

I drove down to the West Country the next morning, setting off at nine.

I left such a lovely house. Over their breakfast, Mrs M and my daughter, Pippa, were chatting, gossiping and laughing so much it was simply delightful. Radio Two was on, and they would occasionally burst into song and dance around. It was like watching some corny TV advert for a wonderful cereal product. It was my house, my home and my family and, if it wasn't all about to change, I would have been the happiest I'd ever been in my life.

The drive was easy; the M4, stopping at Membury Services for a coffee, then onto the Headquarters which were just off the motorway on the other side of Bristol. I was early, over an hour early, but it didn't matter because I'd rather be there early than one minute late.

Detective Superintendent Jacob Gregory was a white male in his mid-forties, unspectacular but not in a negative way. He was, sort of, like me. After a short interaction, during which time his DS took a DNA sample from the inside of my mouth, he came across as professional and unemotional, which was just fine. The DS, Sally Crane, was drop dead gorgeous. In her late twenties, long red hair, tied up in a knot, and the sort of face and figure that would make men stare. If I'd been twenty years younger, if I'd not been a murder suspect in a case she was dealing with, I might have chanced my arm.

I followed the two officers up several flights of stairs and along two corridors to a small interview room with all the necessary equipment to conduct a tape-recorded interview. There were also several buff files already on the desk which no doubt contained documents and photographs appertaining to the case.

I was nervous but absolutely determined to come across as if this was of no concern to me at all, an act which was more difficult to pull off than I thought. I was chatty, using every opportunity to engage these officers in casual conversation, but by the time we arrived at the office I thought I was probably coming across as someone who was nervous. I decided to tone it down.

"Would you like pre-interview disclosure? We have a page of A4." The Superintendent asked.

Of course, I should have said yes, but I declined, saying confidently.

"It won't mean anything to me, just ask your questions. I'm entirely comfortable that I have done nothing wrong."

They switched on the tape machine and after the long, single, monotonous tone, the Detective Superintendent read the preamble from a sheet of laminated paper. I had said it so often, it was a diatribe I could have recited with my eyes closed.

Once I had agreed on tape that I didn't want to be represented, the first real question was asked.

"Have you ever been to no. 36 The Royal Crescent, Bath?" The Detective Superintendent asked.

I was completely taken aback, what the fuck was going on? This was meant to be about an address in Essex not Bath.

I must have looked so baffled that the DS asked.

"Are you alright? You've gone completely white."

"No, I'm fine."

I suddenly realised that my reaction was making me look guilty but as I didn't know anything about an address in Bath, I realised they had the wrong person completely and I almost jumped for joy.

"No. I don't know anything about an address in the Royal Crescent. Isn't that the really expensive bit, where that posh hotel is? I've never been there, well not since I lived in Bradford-on-Avon, as a kid." I replied.

"Yes, it is. It's the most exclusive address in the city. So, you have been there?"

"Yes, maybe half a dozen times but not for, look I'm forty-seven, I left Wiltshire in January 1983, before then I was at school in Bradford-on-Avon. As sixth formers we would occasionally go into Bath, I remember having a couple of picnics, well parties, in the summer of '82 on the lawn in front of the Royal Crescent."

"Did you ever enter an address there?" The Detective Superintendent asked.

I thought hard, just in case.

"Most definitely not. No one I would know would live anywhere as nice as that. We were council estate kids. Anyway, what exactly are you investigating? Perhaps I should have asked to read your disclosure."

The DS handed a piece of A4 paper to the Detective Superintendent which he read out loud.

"On 12th March 1982, Mrs Eileen Armstrong, an eighty-two-year-old spinster who lived alone, was murdered by a person who broke into her house at 36 The Royal Crescent, Bath, and stabbed her seventeen times. She was also raped, probably post-mortem. Hearing the commotion, a couple who were walking by the address, stopped immediately outside. They were certain they had heard screams and were contemplating calling the police. A few moments later, a young white male emerged from the front, ran down the steps, and barged past them before turning right and running off at speed. They were able to provide a very accurate description of the suspect and also to assist police to create a photofit image. The murder investigation was unsuccessful, despite an appeal on the BBC TV programme Crime Watch and the offer of a twenty-five-thousand-pound reward. No one was ever arrested for or charged with the offence. As I am sure you are aware, there have been recent advances in DNA technology and as a result, this murder investigation was re-opened as a cold case review. We resubmitted vaginal swabs for forensic examination. The results of those swabs identified one match to the current profiles database. That match is with your DNA profile, Mr Pritchard."

Perhaps I should have been worried, but as I knew I had absolutely nothing to do with this dreadful crime, I really wasn't.

"There must be some mistake, guys. I have no idea what you're talking about. I have never murdered and raped anyone. Certainly, not some old lady living in the Royal Crescent. Somebody's got the wrong DNA match."

"But it's a huge coincidence that you lived locally, isn't it?" The Detective Superintendent asked.

"What can I say? I either did this terrible thing, or I didn't, and I didn't."

"Tell me what you were doing in March 1982, Mr Pritchard?" The Detective Superintendent asked.

"I was seventeen, I was living with my Mum in a small town called South Wraxhall, which is a few miles east of Bradford-on-Avon. I was doing my A Levels at the local comprehensive, Maths, English and Economics. My Mum wasn't very well, so I spent a lot of my time looking after her. She died in May. I fell apart. It was a bad year. My neighbour, Gerald, a retired police officer, took me under his wing. He helped me arrange Mum's funeral and sort out everything. He got me to apply to join the Met and the rest is history."

"Any father, or brothers or sisters?"

"No. My Dad died before I was born. He fell down the stairs at home and broke his neck. Obviously, I don't remember it, but my Mum told me. She wasn't very strong and never came to terms with his death. She started to drink too much; I don't know whether she had a drink problem before he died, she said she didn't but who knows? Anyway, over the next seventeen years she drank herself to death. By the time I was at senior school, Mum was drinking from when she got up until she fell into a stupor late in the evening. It was very sad. She tried so hard to be a good mum, but she just couldn't cope. I loved her very much."

"Definitely no siblings?"

"No, I was an only child."

"And you've never been inside any address in the Royal Crescent?"

"No, never. Besides, you said the DNA which matches mine came from a vaginal swab; so it's irrelevant whether I've been inside the victim's address, the only question is did I rape and murder her, and I didn't, obviously." I replied.

"The victim's name was an Eileen Armstrong and the case attracted quite a lot of media attention at the time. Do you remember it?"

I paused and thought hard.

"I'm really sorry but I can't remember. It was such a long time ago and I've spent a career dealing with murder and other serious crimes." I replied.

"Also found at the scene was evidence that the suspect had taken heroin. Have you ever taken heroin, Mr Pritchard?"

Jesus Christ! That was a development I didn't need!

"Yes, but not then, not when I was seventeen. I got addicted in my twenties, it's a long story and irrelevant here. In 1982 I'd never even heard of heroin, let alone taken it."

"Can I ask you to cast your mind back to 1982? Can you please describe your appearance?"

I exhaled in exasperation.

"Really?" I asked.

"Really, Mr Pritchard. I know it might be a lot to ask, but please do your best."

"White ..." I said, slightly sarcastically.

"Seventeen, although I probably looked slightly older, I'd been able to get served in pubs since I was fourteen."

"Same height, five ten and a half. Short brown hair, in those days in a side parting on the left. I had a thirty-two waist when I joined the job the following January, so slim, almost thin, build. I was fit, playing rugby a couple of times a week. Clean shaven, or did I have a moustache? I can't remember. I didn't wear glasses. No scars or broken nose in those days. Will that do?" I asked.

The Detective Superintendent produced a small passport size photograph which he slid across the desk. I picked it up. It was my training school photograph, which they took when they were getting your warrant card ready. I knew from experience that they took two, one went on your warrant card and the second was attached to your personal file. I stared at a fresh-faced young man, so innocent, just a child, really. I smiled to myself, momentarily forgetting where I was.

"Can you just confirm that that is a photograph taken of you in January 1983?"

I nodded.

"For the purpose of the tape, please articulate your reply." The DS said.

"Yes, it is a photograph of me."

The Detective Superintendent dipped his right hand into a large brown envelope and produced a piece of A4 paper which I immediately noticed was a hand-drawn photofit picture. He handed it to me.

"Please look carefully at that picture. It was drawn a week after the murder by a specialist artist and based on descriptions given by the two witnesses I mentioned earlier. The people who saw the suspect run out of the address, down the stairs and off down the street."

I picked it up and stared at it. It was almost identical to the police photograph. The hair was a lot longer but my god it was an amazing resemblance.

"Do you think the photofit picture looks similar to you?" The Detective Superintendent asked.

"It does, but I didn't do this, guys. Please, please believe me."

There was an awkward atmosphere in the room. I didn't say a word, I knew better than to speak into such a silence.

"I have to tell you, Mr Pritchard, the DNA is an exact match; I mean the chances of it not being you is like one in fifteen million. Of course, we need to recheck with the new sample which you provided today, but when you bear in mind that not only is it a one in fifteen million chance it's not you, and you add in the fact that you lived locally, knew the area, indeed had visited to within a couple of hundred yards of the address. Then there's the photofit – even you admit, it's you. Finally, if you'd seen the look on your face when we first mentioned the address of the offence, it was so obvious that you were in shock. I have to say, I believe this offence was committed by you."

"Mr Gregory, with due respect, it really doesn't matter what you think. I didn't do this, and the new sample from me will not match that recovered from the victim. I am completely innocent."

I looked at the two police officers sitting opposite me, and it suddenly dawned on me that they thought I had done this. I don't think I'd ever experienced a feeling quite like I felt at that moment, even though I knew I was innocent. I felt shame.

Chapter 7

I hadn't been arrested for the offence so there was no necessity for me to be released on bail, which made things easier. After the interview, I drove back to Buckhurst Hill. A big part of me wanted to detour and pay a visit to my old house in South Wraxhall, but I thought it best, under the circumstances, to give the place a wide birth.

I was in a bit of a daze. I know I had nothing to do with the murder, but it was pretty scary to think my DNA could be a match. I wondered, for the first time ever, whether anyone else had been similarly mistakenly accused. I also decided, I did need a decent legal representative, primarily to get me through this sticky situation but also, to help me sue the arse off who ever had made this monumental fuck up.

After the events, I was even more confused by the deployment of the probes. The tactic didn't make any sense. Did they honestly expect me to go home and then start admitting to Mrs M and Pippa that I'd raped and murdered an old lady in Bath when I was only seventeen. The more I thought about it, the more concerned I became that the probes were in fact nothing to do with this murder but rather the Barry Skinner matter. Could it be possible that I was being investigated for two murders? Then I turned my thoughts as to whether I could use the probes to my advantage. If the probes recorded me saying that I was innocent, it would be very difficult to exclude those conversations from any subsequent court case. The prosecution would have to make a public interest application on the grounds of protecting the tactic, and I'm not sure that would be successful.

Besides, I couldn't hide what was going on from Mrs M and Pippa, so I decided I would tell them what had happened and what I was suspected of doing. After all, the allegation was so incredible, I felt no reason to be embarrassed.

I did have one small dilemma. My instincts were to go home and Google the old murder to see whether there were any facts that would exclude me as a suspect. If I did that however, I might lose my ignorance which perverse though it sounds, may put me at a disadvantage.

When I got in, I was tired but determined. I sat both Mrs M and Pippa down in the kitchen and told them exactly what had happened that day, what I said during the interview and how I thought the police investigating the offence were convinced I was guilty.

Mrs M was furious; Pippa was alright at first but, when Mrs M's indignation went into orbit, she started to get upset, too. It ended with everyone in tears.

Chapter 8

Ten months later – October 2011

I suppose in one sense I was lucky. Being a serving police officer, and Mrs M's surety of £20,000, meant that I was never remanded in custody before my trial at the Central Criminal Court. So, even though the CPS made a strong case to oppose my bail, the Judge decided I wasn't a flight risk. The only real annoyance was that I couldn't go on the big family holiday to Australia. Pippa and Ben went, but Mrs M and I stayed behind and, of course, lost the cost of our flights which we'd already paid in full. In the grand scheme of things, that didn't really matter. All that was important was that I was able to convince a jury that I wasn't a monster and hadn't done such terrible things when still little more than a child.

As soon as I was charged with the murder and rape, a Detective Superintendent was present to formally suspend me. I'd guessed that was going to happen, so it didn't come as a surprise.

The fact that it was such an old matter, the basic facts established without doubt and for such a long time, the case for the defence was straightforward, and there were no living witnesses, meant the time from committal to trial was extraordinarily short. This was a good thing, as living with such a frightening event hanging over your head, is enough to drive anyone insane.

At the beginning, I never thought I'd be convicted but the longer the matter went on, the less confident I became. The DNA evidence was as damning as it was inexplicable. The fact that it was discovered at the scene of a crime about ten miles from where I lived was even more puzzling. I considered every option from *'had I actually done this?'* to *'had someone got hold of my semen and framed me?'*, but nothing made any sense.

One key piece of evidence was the presence of a class A drug at the scene. At some stage during the crime, the suspect had taken heroin. For me, this was a double-edged sword. In 1982, at the age of seventeen, I'd never taken any illegal drugs, not even a bit of cannabis, let alone heroin. If my defence team could establish that, it would greatly help my case. Establishing something from thirty years ago, however, is almost impossible. On the other side, I had, of course, got a history of heroin addiction. This didn't start until the early 1990s, but if the prosecution made a big thing of it, the jury might get confused or, at the very least, think I might have also been addicted previously.

I wanted us to call the prosecution forensic expert, because I knew he was wrong, but my legal team were dead against that course of action. They were of the view that the impact of his evidence would be reduced, if it was read into the evidence straight from his statement. They made it clear, of course, that the final decision was mine. It was a difficult one, but I took their advice in the end. As it transpired, prosecution counsel mentioned the *'damning DNA evidence'* at absolutely every opportunity, so we might as well have called the bloody scientist anyway.

As the trial date neared, I started to feel a growing anxiety about the outcome. I became obsessed with going over and over the evidence I would give, upon which my future freedom would rest or fall. I was, after all, the only defence witness. As such, therefore, the jury would hear day after day of reasons why they should convict me and then I'd have one shot to save my soul. The pressure was almost overwhelming, and surely too much for one, very ordinary, person to bear.

By the morning of the first day, I was absolutely exhausted. I hadn't slept more than six hours in the last three days. I put on one of my suits and wore a shirt and tie for the first time in months. In one of the pockets of my jacket, I found a calling card. The name on the card *'Louise Lusher'* meant nothing to me. I was curious but also immediately suspicious. I'd become quite paranoid, finding listening devices in your house and being charged with a murder you know nothing about, kind of does that to you!

Even though it was the morning of my trial, I picked up my mobile phone and dialled the number. After just the one ring, and so quickly it almost caught me by surprise, a pleasant female voice said.

"Louise, who's this?"

"I'm sorry to trouble you, my name's Christopher, I know that sounds daft, but I've just found your calling card in my jacket pocket, but I can't recall meeting you. Do you work for Baines, Barnes and Stockton solicitors?"

"No, I most certainly don't."

"Well, I'm sorry to trouble you. I'm just trying to solve this mystery. It doesn't matter, I'm sorry to trouble you." I said.

"Hang on, don't go. I don't give my cards out to many people, so I must have done so for a reason. What do you do for a living?" She asked.

"I'm a police officer." I replied.

There was a moment's silence.

"Were you at Heathrow airport, a few months ago? In Arrivals at Terminal three?"

The penny dropped. She was the really attractive woman with the lovely hair and the two boys.

"I remember now. Oh god, sorry." I said, suddenly feeling a bit nervous.

"Why didn't you call?" She asked.

I didn't know what to say, so decided I'd tell the truth, well partially, at least.

"I'm sorry, I forgot. I've been so ridiculously tied up with work stuff."

"Oh, not to worry, at least you've called now. How are you?" She asked.

She spoke with a tone which indicated we'd only met a few days previously.

"I've been better, got a few things on my plate at the moment. How about you?" I asked.

I checked my watch. I'd have to go soon but this ridiculous and random conversation was a welcome, albeit momentary, distraction from the inevitable impending doom of my day ahead.

"I'm good, thank you. I gave you my card in the hope that you'd call. I don't do this very often, well once or twice a year, but I'd like to invite you for dinner." She said.

I didn't know what to say. I could hardly say *'Oh I'd love to come, Louise, but first I've got to be acquitted of the murder and rape of an 82-year-old woman. Does Tuesday work for you?'*

"Is your husband back in the States?" I asked, deliberately avoiding her question.

"No, he'd be joining us, too." She replied.

"Louise, gotta be honest, I'm a little confused." I said.

I checked my watch, again. I had run out of time.

"Come out with us, have dinner, see what the chemistry's like and, if it's good, and honestly I think it would be great, then Mike and I would put a proposition to you."

I knew she wasn't talking about a business proposition.

"Just so we're clear, you're proposing a menage a trois?" I asked.

"Oh god, yes, mister police officer." She replied.

Wasn't that just fucking typical! I hadn't had sex for years and, somehow, I'd managed to miss this wonderful opportunity to have some harmless fun with a married woman. Was I put off by the fact her husband would be there? Absolutely not. In some ways, it meant, the whole scenario was safer and considerably less likely to explode in my face.

To be honest, in recent months I'd even considered just going out and paying for sex, I was that desperate. Not with some crackhead street girl, but with some five hundred a night escort. I'd even started searching the internet for suitable girls, but every time and at the last moment, I chickened out.

I told Louise I'd call her in a few weeks when my diary was clearer. At least, if I did get acquitted, I'd have something to look forward to.

Chapter 9

Of course, Kitty Young's statement had been disclosed so I knew the complete untruths the Deputy Commissioner was about to give evidence against me under oath. I just hoped my counsel was able to prove her to be a lying, deceitful, spiteful bitch.

Kitty wore full uniform and entered the courtroom with an air of confidence bordering on arrogance; she even had the audacity to smile warmly at the Judge. I gave him a small tick for not acknowledging the gesture.

Prosecution Counsel
"Would the witness inform the court of her name and rank?"

Kitty Young
"My name is Dame Kitty Young. I am the Deputy Commissioner of the Metropolitan Police, your Honour."

Prosecution Counsel
"Would you give the court a synopsis of your career to date, please."

Kitty Young
"I joined the Metropolitan Police in 1984 and was posted to Stoke Newington police station. I resigned about a year later because I wasn't sure the job was right for me, but I re-joined in 1987 after the organisation contacted me and begged me to return."

Prosecution Counsel
"And why, in 1984, did you think the job wasn't right for you?"

Kitty Young
"Two words, racism and sexism. My colleagues were appallingly prejudiced against women and black officers. I was both. I wasn't wanted."

Prosecution Counsel
"And yet you came back?"

Kitty Young
"In 1987 the Met launched a huge recruitment campaign targeting black and minority ethnic officers. They persuaded me that I should re-join."

Prosecution Counsel
"Where were you posted?"

Kitty Young
"I went to work at the Yard. I was promoted to Sergeant very quickly because of my exceptional potential. Then a few years later I transferred to Surrey Police as an Inspector. I worked in Guildford. In 1997 I came back to the Met as a Detective Inspector and was posted to Tottenham police station. In 1999 I was promoted to Detective Chief Inspector and in 2003 to Superintendent. I made my way up through the ranks and last year was promoted to Deputy Commissioner."

Prosecution Counsel
"And have you always held operational positions?"

Kitty Young
"Oh yes, fully operational at all times; front line and front end, as we used to say."

Prosecution Counsel
"Thank you, Deputy Commissioner. Now will you please tell us how you know the defendant?"

Kitty Young
"I first met the defendant in 1984 at Stoke Newington police station; we were on the same team. Then I worked with him again in 1997 at Tottenham police station. I was his line manager."

Prosecution Counsel
"And am I right in saying that you recall a conversation you had with the defendant in 1997?"

Kitty Young
"I do."

Prosecution Counsel
"And where did that conversation take place?"

Kitty Young

"In my office, the DI's office, on the first floor."

Prosecution Counsel
"And what can you recall about that conversation?"

Kitty Young
"I had just started at Tottenham. I was the Detective Inspector and the defendant's manager. He was a Detective Sergeant and I asked him to outline his team to me, you know, their strengths and weaknesses, things like that. Anyway, towards the end of the meeting I asked him to outline his own strengths and weaknesses. The question seemed to annoy him. He said that he was someone who shouldn't be messed about with. I didn't like his attitude and asked him what he meant and whether that was a threat. He replied that he'd killed before and he'd do it again, if I crossed him. Before I could say another word, he stood up and walked out."

Prosecution Counsel
"Did he say who he'd killed?"

Kitty Young
"No. That was the whole conversation."

Kitty's evidence married with her statement, which I'd already read. It was, of course, absolute rubbish. Well, like the best lies, it wasn't all false. Yes, we had had that conversation about my team and yes, she had asked me about my own strengths and weaknesses, but I'd never said I'd killed anyone. Why, oh why, would I be stupid enough to do that? Besides, it wasn't true."

Prosecution Counsel
"Did you question him further?"

Kitty Young
"I didn't get a chance. He stood up and walked out. I was absolutely shocked. I didn't know what to do. It was my first day at the new station, in fact, it was my first day back in the Metropolitan Police. I was nervous, and a little afraid. I was confused, and ..."

She paused, clearly for dramatic effect.

... in shock."

I slowly shook my head from side to side and glanced across at the jury, who were lapping up the evidence of this exalted police officer.

Prosecution Counsel
"Did you ever speak to the defendant again about this matter?"

Kitty Young
"No. I went sick very shortly afterwards. I never got the opportunity. I did speak to several people who'd also heard the rumour that he killed an old lady."

My counsel, Alison, was on her feet but it was too late. That statement was outrageous and so clearly hearsay that I found myself standing up, too.

The Judge instructed the jury to retire and then asked the witness to wait outside. Then prosecution counsel started their verbose diatribe.

Prosecution Counsel
"My Lord, I am most dreadfully sorry. The court has my humblest apologies, I never anticipated the witness would make such a basic error; she is, after all, a professional and as such should have known better."

The Judge looked furious and turned to my counsel.

"If you request a retrial, I will order one. If you decline, you will not be able to use this incident as grounds for appeal. The choice is yours; would you like to take instructions?"

Defence Counsel
"My Lord, yes."

***

While a retrial would guarantee my freedom for another six months, I just couldn't take it anymore. I was living on the proverbial knife edge and thought I was starting to have a mental breakdown. I was anxious all the time. It was as if someone had just walked up behind me and gone 'boo' to make me jump, but I had that feeling in my chest all the time – even in the middle of the night. It was absolutely terrible, and I didn't know how much longer I could cope with it. Therefore, while the prospect of taking the offer of the retrial was the sensible course of action, I instructed counsel that I wanted to proceed.

"I'm glad you said that, Christopher. I'll need to clear it with the Judge first, but I would welcome the opportunity to cross examine the witness on that comment." My defence counsel, Alison, said.

"I agree." I replied.

As the words left my mouth, I suddenly understood what was going on. Of course, I'd never had a conversation with Kitty about killing an old lady, that was just her spiteful lie, but I did suspect I knew where the rumours had come from.

Back in 1983 when I was a probationer at Stoke Newington, during a foot chase I'd accidentally knocked an old lady over. She broke her hip in the fall and died a few days later from complications. I was lucky because nothing ever came of it. The old lady's husband had been a Met police officer, so the family never made a fuss and besides, there was some confusion at the subsequent inquest as to who exactly had knocked her over, me or the suspect I was chasing. I suspected that the story had sort of followed me through my career and that those were the 'rumours' Kitty had picked up, probably when she went to Stokey the following year, and then presented as fact. I couldn't be absolutely sure, but I'd wager a great deal of money that was in fact the scenario that was playing out here.

My small dilemma was whether to share my thoughts with my defence counsel, but I decided against doing so – it was just too complicated and convoluted.

"Kitty Young is one vicious cunt." I said.

In the last six months I 'd been dealing with my defence counsel on an almost daily basis, but I'd never used that word before.

"You two do, as they say, have history." Defence Counsel observed, without flinching at my use of the 'C' bomb.

"Why in god's name would I ever tell her I killed someone? Even if I had! What would be in it for me?"

"I'm glad she's here. Quite frankly, Christopher, it's the only chink in the prosecution armour, and we need to open it up until it becomes a gaping wound. We really can't odds the DNA evidence, and the photofit is, I am afraid, a dead ringer for you. Those two pieces of evidence I can't undermine, but the Deputy Commissioner, she is a sitting duck and I intend to take her apart, piece by piece."

"Now that, I shall enjoy." I said.

Chapter 10

Defence Counsel
"I'd like to hand the witness a document, your Honour."

Alison handed over a couple of pages of typed A4 which had been stapled together at the top corner.

The usher took the document and handed it to Kitty, who, having glanced at it for only a few seconds, handed it back but she did so in a manner which was dismissive and rude, as if to say, *'why are you wasting my time with this?'*. I glanced across at the jury, a few raised their eyebrows disapprovingly.

Defence Counsel
"Do you recognise that document? And if you do, please tell the court what it is?"

Kitty Young
"My CV. I think it's published on the MPS website, along with the CVs of other members of the Senior Management Team."

Defence Counsel
"You joined and left the Met in 1984, after only a few weeks at Stoke Newington, is that right?"

Kitty Young
"Yes"

Defence Counsel
"When you re-joined in 1987, am I right in saying you didn't have to re-train? I mean, you didn't have to attend Hendon Police Training college again, did you?"

Kitty Young
"I did not. When they made me the offer to re-join, they agreed that I didn't have to go to Hendon again, nor did I have to complete my probation."

Defence Counsel
"Gosh, very favourable terms, no wonder you came back. Where were you posted?"

Kitty Young
"I joined a recruitment project within HR. It was called Operation Balance. My role was to advise the Met on how to increase the recruitment of Black and Minority Ethnic officers. I would go into schools and colleges and speak to young people and try to persuade them to join. I would run stalls at employment events. I would mentor new BME recruits as they went through training school.'

Defence Counsel
"Important work, no doubt, Deputy Commissioner, but hardly 'fully operational; front line and front end' as you claimed during your evidence-in-chief. Would you agree?"

Kitty Young nodded and murmured.
"Yes"

Defence Counsel
"From your CV I see you were promoted only two years later. When you were promoted, were you still working at Operation Balance?"

Kitty Young
"I was."

Defence Counsel
"And to what role were you promoted?"

Kitty Young
"For the first year or so, I remained at Operation Balance. It was a really vital piece of work and my role there was really important. In early 1990, I was posted to the CRIS implementation team."

Defence Counsel
"CRIS implementation team?"

Kitty Young
"CRIS was the new computer system which replaced paper-based crime reports. I was a crucial part of the team that rolled out the training of the new system to twenty-eight thousand police officers. It was a fascinating project and an important one, too. Having crimes recorded on a central computer enabled better analysis, which in turn, enabled a more accurate and effective deployment of resources to counter risk and threats."

Defence Counsel
"Important yes, vital perhaps, but, Deputy Commissioner, not exactly fully operational; front line and front end. Would you agree?"

Kitty Young
"No. I was dealing with serious crime every day; murders were recorded on CRIS; as were kidnappings, rape and racist assaults."

Defence Counsel
"But you were recording these crimes, not investigating them, or speaking to victims. Or identifying and arresting suspects: or were you?"

Kitty Young
"Well, no, but ..."

Defence Counsel
"Moving on to your next role ..."

It was a perfectly timed interruption, but Kitty didn't complain.

Defence Counsel
"You transferred, on promotion to Inspector, to Surrey Police in 1993."

Kitty Young
"I did."

Defence Counsel
"And what fully operational, front line, front end role did you perform there?"

Kitty Young
"I was in charge of the Special Constabulary."

Alison looked down at the CV and read out loud.

Defence Counsel
"I was responsible for the recruitment, training and deployment of members of the public who volunteered to work as Special Constables. Where were you based, at a police station?"

Kitty Young
"No, at Headquarters in Guildford."

Defence Counsel
"Did you ever take these Specials out on patrol?"

Kitty Young
"No, it wasn't that sort of role; it was more strategic."

Defence Counsel
"Moving on. In 1997 you transferred back to the Met and to Tottenham police station as a Detective Inspector. Perhaps I missed it, but had you ever been a detective before?"

Kitty Young
"No"

Defence Counsel
"And had you ever had any specialist CID training?"

Kitty Young
"No"

Defence Counsel
"Any training or courses that could be considered investigative in nature? Had you, for example, completed the Exhibits Officer course?"

Kitty Young
"No"

Defence Counsel
"So how, may I ask, did you land such an important and impressive role? I mean a Scotland Yard Detective Inspector. That's extremely impressive for an officer with absolutely no relevant training or experience. And at last, a fully operational, front line, front end role. How long did you remain in this role at Tottenham?"

Kitty Young
"Two months."

Defence Counsel
"Why so short a time? Did you get another promotion?"

Kitty Young
"I was unwell. I had work related stress."

Defence Counsel
"I'm sorry. Anyway, moving on. The next entry on your CV says you were a Detective Inspector at Operation Otter and that you were responsible for reviewing cold storage facilities within custody suites. Is that where evidence such as DNA and blood samples would be kept before going for analysis at the Laboratory?"

Kitty Young
"Yes"

Defence Counsel
"Interesting I'm sure ..."

Alison said with more than a little sarcasm.

"... but hardly fully operational, front line and front end. I mean, you were looking at fridges for a living!"

Kitty Young just nodded. She was starting to look punch drunk.

Defence Counsel
"Just a year later you're promoted to Chief Inspector. Please tell the court what your responsibilities were?"

Kitty Young
"I was part of a team reviewing stop and search, specifically why more black and ethnic minority members of the public were being stopped and searched than their white counterparts."

Defence Counsel
"Another strategic role? Not really fully operational, front line and front end."

Kitty Young
"When you get to Chief Inspector rank, there are very few frontline roles."

Defence Counsel
"Can I assume then, that after this role you always held similar non-operational jobs?"

Kitty Young nodded.

Defence Counsel
"Glancing at your CV, thereafter you were a Superintendent staff officer?"

Kitty Young
"Yes"

Defence Counsel
"A Chief Superintendent in the Diversity Command?"

Kitty Young
"Yes"

Defence Counsel

"A Commander in the same Diversity Command, and then finally, well before your current role, a Deputy Assistant Commissioner in Human Resources."

Kitty Young

"Yes"

Defence Counsel

"Deputy Commissioner, I put it to you that when, in your evidence-in-chief, you claimed to have always been …"

Alison looked down at her notes; I was sure it was more for dramatic effect than to refresh her memory.

"… fully operational at all times; front line and front end, that statement was simply untrue."

Kitty Young

"Well, no that's not right. I mean, operational and front line can mean different things to different people. The work I did was vital. I shaped the way the Metropolitan Police is today. I have fought inequality and injustice at every turn of my career. I completely revamped the Special Constabulary in Surrey where we recruited our very first non-white volunteers. Operation Otter was the only really non-operational role I had and notwithstanding that fact, the work was vitally important."

Alison "Hmmmed" like only a barrister can. It meant *'I think you're talking bollocks'* but was a much politer way of saying it.

Defence Counsel

"Shall we leave it to the jury to decide whether that was a lie?"

Kitty Young

"Quite happy to."

Kitty sounded really cocky and I don't think it went down well. Several members of the jury glanced at one another and I knew she'd made a mistake.

Defence Counsel

"Oh, I'll tell you what, this may assist us all. Perhaps you can tell the court, in your long and distinguished *'front line'* career, how many people you have arrested?"

Kitty looked aghast.

"Ummm, well I can't remember exactly." She replied.

Defence Counsel

"A thousand?"

Kitty Young

"No"

Defence Counsel

"At least a hundred, I mean, that would only be, what? One a month?"

Kitty Young

"As a senior officer, which I've been for most of my service, you just don't arrest suspects."

Defence Counsel

"Oh, I see, I see. Have you arrested ten people?"

Kitty Young

"I would think so."

I had a really good idea. I coughed loudly and distinctly. Alison turned round and I indicated that I wanted to speak to her.

Defence Counsel

"If it pleased your Lordship, I would like to take instructions."

Alison walked over to me and I stood up in the dock and whispered a dozen words quickly into her ear. She returned almost majestically to her previous position in the court.

Defence Counsel

"I'm obliged, your Lordship. Deputy Commissioner, I believe that every police officer remembers their first arrest. Please tell the court, under oath, about your first arrest."

Kitty Young
"I can't remember." She said, but her voice was almost inaudible.

Defence Counsel
"You can't remember?" Alison said, incredulously.

Defence Counsel
"Was it a robber, or a burglar, or perhaps someone for drink drive, was it an arrest for possession of drugs?"

Kitty Young
"I can't remember?"

Defence Counsel
"Where was it? Were you at Stoke Newington? Or Tottenham?"

Prosecution Counsel rose to their feet and, as court etiquette demands, my counsel sat down.

Prosecution Counsel
"My Lord. My learned friend is clearly badgering the witness. She had answered the question on several occasions."

Judge
"I agree. Defence Counsel will move on."

Defence Counsel
"Am obliged, your Lordship. Deputy Commissioner? Have you ever given evidence before?"

Kitty Young
"Of course."

Defence Counsel
"Perhaps you could provide the court with more details?"

Kitty Young
"I gave evidence at the Aachi Enquiry and the Lord Morrison Enquiry."

Defence Counsel
"Both of those were public enquiries, were they not?"

Kitty Young
"Yes"

Defence Counsel
"My sincere apologies, Deputy Commissioner. Please put public enquiries aside. Have you ever given evidence in a criminal court? Either at a magistrates court or a crown court?"

Kitty Young
"No"

Defence Counsel
"Let me get this straight. In your evidence-in-chief you claimed to have served a police career that was *fully operational at all times; front line and front end*, yet we have now established, have we not, that you have never held a proper operational police role, can't remember whether you've ever arrested anyone for anything, and this is the first time in twenty-eight years that you've given evidence at court. Not the most impressive police officer, are you?"

Kitty Young didn't reply.

Defence Counsel
"Let's try from another angle. Any awards for bravery?"

Kitty Young
"No"

Defence Counsel
"Any Commissioner's Commendations?"

Kitty Young
"No"

Defence Counsel
"Any other awards or commendations?"

Kitty Young
"I have the Queen's Police Medal."

Defence Counsel
"So does every officer of your rank, isn't that right? They just give them out, don't they?"

Kitty Young
"I wouldn't describe it like that. They are awarded for a lifetime's commitment to policing. Mine was presented to me by the Queen."

Defence Counsel
"Well, they're clearly not awarded for fighting crime. Otherwise, one would have to ask why you got one, would one not?"

Prosecution Counsel almost jumped to his feet.

Defence Counsel
"I withdraw the question."

Prosecution counsel sat down, and the Judge looked down over his glasses at my barrister and said.

"Behave, Mrs Pascal."

My Barrister smiled, apologetically, but she knew exactly what she was doing.

Defence Counsel
"Deputy Commissioner, I put it to you that when you said you'd been operational and front end, you lied to this court."

Kitty Young
"I disagree. My interpretation of 'operational' is different to yours. It's simply a matter of subjective semantics."

Defence Counsel

"Let's discuss the alleged conversation you had with the defendant when, according to you, he said ..."
Again, Alison paused while she studied her notes.

"... he'd killed before and he'd do it again. Were those his exact words?"

Kitty Young
"Yes"

Defence Counsel
"Interesting. Deputy Commissioner, I know it's a long time ago now, but can you recall any of your police training?"

Kitty Young
"I can."

Defence Counsel
"You went to Hendon Police Training School, did you not?"

Kitty Young
"I did, back in 1984."

Defence Counsel
"How long were you there for?"

Kitty Young
"It was a twenty-week course, but I was ill, so I think I was there about twenty-six weeks, although many of those were spent in the medical centre."

Defence Counsel
"From your training, can you explain to the court about 'original notes'?"

Kitty Young
"What would you like to know?"

Defence Counsel
"What are they?"

Kitty Young

"When a police officer makes an arrest, or attends an incident, she should make a written record of the event. Those written records are called original notes."

Defence Counsel
"And when should they be made?"

Kitty Young
"At the time."

This was a really poor answer and clearly demonstrated to anyone with any knowledge that she had never given evidence at court because there is a stock answer to that question which every police officer knows by heart.

Defence Counsel
"At the time? What if you're too busy dealing with an incident to get your pen out and start writing?"

Kitty clearly had a brain wave and, from the mists of her memory, produced the right answer.

Kitty Young
"They should be made at the time or as soon as practicable after the incident and while it is still fresh in your mind."

She almost smiled but her facial expression changed when Alison asked her next question.

Defence Counsel
"Please can you show me the original notes you made of this 'alleged' conversation with the defendant? The one where he admitted to murder."

Kitty Young
"I didn't make a note of that conversation."

Defence Counsel
"I beg your pardon?"

Kitty didn't say anything.

Defence Counsel
"Why not?"

Kitty Young
"Well, I thought, perhaps he was joking. I wasn't sure. I was confused. It wasn't like an incident where you'd make notes."

Defence Counsel
"Okay. When you gave your evidence earlier, you didn't say anything about the fact that he might have been joking. Yet that's really important. A man is on trial here for murder. Why didn't you mention that Deputy Commissioner?"

Kitty Young
"I wasn't, I mean, I didn't know for certain. It all happened so quickly; and it was a long time ago, over ten years. I mean how can anyone remember something that old with any degree of certainty?"

Defence Counsel
"Isn't that why you're taught to make original notes, so that you have a written record of exactly what was said?"

Kitty Young
"Yes. But I didn't realise how important his comments would become. I mean, you don't go around writing everything down, do you? That's not how life works."

Defence Counsel
"A man, one of your own staff, apparently admits to having killed someone and you, at the time a senior detective, didn't think it merited writing down? You can't honestly expect the court to believe that, do you?"

Kitty Young
"Yes I do. I am a very senior police officer and I don't lie. What I have told the court is the truth, to the best of my recollection."

I was disappointed, just when I thought Alison had Kitty on the ropes, my old adversary got out of it.

Defence Counsel
"How would you describe your relationship with the defendant?"

Kitty Young
"We were colleagues whose paths crossed on several occasions."

Alison nodded, like only a barrister can.

Defence Counsel
"Were you friends?"

Kitty Young
"No"

Defence Counsel
"Were you enemies?"

Kitty Young
"No"

Alison put on a most shocked expression.

Defence Counsel
"You weren't enemies?"

Kitty Young
"No."

Defence Counsel
"Did you like the defendant?"

Kitty Young
"I don't think that's relevant."

Defence Counsel
"Not relevant, you say? I consider it to be extremely relevant. I'll explain why. I believe you have lied to the court. I believe you have committed

the most grievous perjury. I put it to you that not only do you not like the defendant, you dislike him so much you came to this court determined to see him sentenced to life imprisonment."

Kitty Young
"That's not the case."

Defence Counsel
"Is it right that in 1984 the defendant gave evidence against you in a claim you brought against the Metropolitan Police?"

Kitty Young
"Yes, but that was twenty-five years ago. I've long forgotten that."

Defence Counsel
"Is it right that in 1997, when you worked together at Tottenham police station, the defendant accused you of planting racist material in his desk?"

Kitty Young
"Yes, he did. But I completely deny doing that and nothing was ever substantiated."

Defence Counsel
"So, would you agree, you are enemies rather than friends?"

Kitty Young
"I have no enemies."

Defence Counsel
"How would you describe the defendant? I mean his character, Deputy Commissioner?"

Kitty Young
"He's a typical, white, male, 1980s police officer."

Defence Counsel
"What do you mean by that?"

Kitty Young

"He's over-confident, he's probably racist, albeit unconsciously, he's typical of the macho breed of dominant males. He's good at his job, not as good as he thinks he is, but he knows his stuff. He knows the criminal law well; he's good at talking to people. He's hard, you wouldn't want to cross him on a dark night."

Defence Counsel
"You're not painting a pretty picture, you really don't like him, or his sort, do you?"

Kitty Young
"When the service has less of them, it will be a better place."

Defence Counsel
"You're determined to make sure the service has at least one less, aren't you?

Kitty Young didn't answer.

Defence Counsel
"I have no further questions for this witness."

Chapter 11

Prosecution Counsel
"Mr Pritchard, after your evidence so far to the court, I don't think anyone can have any doubt about your distinguished police career."

"Thank you." I replied, humbly.

Prosecution Counsel
"You have been nothing short of a hero, and I would like to add my gratitude for the twenty-seven years' of impeccable service you have provided to the people of London."

I didn't say anything; after all, it wasn't a question and besides, I knew the purpose of this flattery was not in any way to my benefit.

Prosecution Counsel

"But I want to take you back to a time before you became a police officer. I want to question you about your childhood and adolescence. Perhaps you could start by telling the court everything you know about your father."

"Sir, that won't take very long. My father died before I was born. My mother told me he fell down the stairs at our home and broke his neck. He was, apparently, dead before his body came to rest by the front door. Although I would point out that is hearsay, obviously."

Prosecution Counsel
"How pregnant was your mother?"

I'd never really thought about that before and when I did, I realised, somewhat to my surprise, that I didn't know the answer.

"I don't know." I replied.

"Oh" Prosecution Counsel replied, almost sarcastically.

"That event happened before I was born and it wasn't something my mother liked to talk about." I replied, even though 'oh' wasn't a question.

Prosecution Counsel
"Are you aware your mother was arrested on suspicion of murdering your father?"

"No" I replied.

Jesus Christ! That was news to me.

Alison, my defence counsel got to her feet and Prosecution Counsel sat down.

Defence Counsel
"My Lord, it is grossly unfair to question my client about events that happened before he was born. Especially matters that might be dreadfully prejudicial."

The Judge looked at Prosecution Counsel in such a way that requested an explanation. Prosecution Counsel got to his feet and Alison sat down.

Prosecution Counsel
"I completely understand my learned colleague's concerns. But I do believe this line of questioning is relevant as I wish to establish the defendants state of mind at the time of the offence."

"You will proceed with extreme caution, Sir Ian, or I will terminate this line of questioning."

Prosecution Counsel
"I'm obliged, your Lordship."

Prosecution Counsel
"Just to clarify, Mr Pritchard, you were not aware that the police were concerned your mother had pushed your father down the stairs?"

"No" I replied.

Prosecution Counsel
"Did you have a happy childhood, Mr Pritchard?"

"Not especially. But you don't realise that at the time. What you have is all you know, so I think, at the time, I was quite happy. My mother loved me, she showed it and I loved her. We didn't have any money, but we got by."

Prosecution Counsel
"What did your mother do for a living?"

"She didn't work." I replied.

Prosecution Counsel
"No? Not at all? No part time cleaning job? Not a dinner lady or a lollipop lady?"

"No. She wasn't very well; she was an alcoholic. She would drink from morning to night."

I thought I might as well get it all out in one go.

Prosecution Counsel
"That must have been very difficult for you." He said, with fake sympathy.

"It was all I knew." I replied.

Prosecution Counsel
"What did you do for money? I mean, if your mother wasn't working but she was buying enough alcohol to 'drink from morning to night' then there can't have been anything for food or other essentials."

"I don't know but we always had food on the table." Was my honest reply.

Prosecution Counsel
"Had she inherited any money? Did she have some other source of income?"

"I don't think so. I don't know." I replied, once again, completely honestly.

Prosecution Counsel
"Were her parents, your grandparents about?"

"No, I never knew my grandparents."

Prosecution Counsel
"Older siblings? Cousins? Uncles, Aunties?"

"No, just the two of us." I replied.

Prosecution Counsel
"It must have been extremely hard for you?"

"It was not an unhappy childhood. We had love."

Prosecution Counsel
"When did your mother die?"

"The 4th May 1982. Before you ask, the cause of death was alcoholism."

Prosecution Counsel
"Just under two months after the matters for which you stand trial?"

"Yes" I replied.

Prosecution Counsel
"Was it getting difficult for you at home in the last months of your mother's life?"

"No" I replied.

Prosecution Counsel
"You were at school, weren't you?"

"I was. I was doing three A levels."

Prosecution Counsel
"Studying for A levels, your mother an unemployed alcoholic, no money, little food. Life must have been a genuine struggle, Mr Pritchard?"

"I suspect my upbringing differs completely to your own, Sir Ian. In fact, I suspect to most people in this court room, it sounds terrible. But I am telling you now, I loved my mother as much as any son ever did. My mum loved me and told me every day. I wouldn't change my mum. She was and continues to be one if the bravest people I have ever known. She wanted to die when my dad did. She never got over his death. She couldn't cope. But despite this, she hung on for another seventeen years to make sure that I got through my childhood and adolescence. Bravery is comparative. Soldiers going over the top to certain death are brave, yes, but so was my mum, in her own way. You've no idea, none of you have got any idea. And here you all are, thirty years later ..."

I stopped talking. I couldn't say another word. Tears were rolling unreservedly down both cheeks. Emotionally, I had fallen to pieces.

"I think we'll take a fifteen-minute break" The Judge said.

When we got going again, defence counsel had wisely decided to change his tack.

Prosecution Counsel

"Mr Pritchard, can you explain how your DNA came to be at 36 The Crescent, Bath on 12th March 1982?"

"I cannot. In fact, I'll go further than that. My DNA wasn't and never has been at that address. There has been a mistake. I cannot explain how this has happened, I'm not a scientist. I just know it has. I have spent my whole life protecting people, helping them, arresting those that hurt or murder them, helping them through their grief and sorrow in the hardest of times. I would never, have never, hurt an old lady who should have felt safe in her home. It is simply not possible that I've done this, not possible."

Prosecution Counsel

"Mr Pritchard, the court has heard the forensic evidence. It is overwhelming. The chances of the suspect not being you is one in fifteen million."

"No, Sir Ian, the chances of the suspect not being me is one hundred percent. I don't care what your forensic evidence says, I did not do this horrendous thing. Not an atom in my body has ever been capable of such a dreadful thing."

Prosecution Counsel

"And yet the court has seen the photofit. You have to admit, there is a remarkable resemblance?"

"I do."

Prosecution Counsel

"And you admit that you lived locally and often visited the Royal Crescent with friends for …"

He deliberately hesitated for effect.

"… picnics."

"I did not do this. I am innocent."

I turned to the jury.

"I am innocent." I said, but my voice had lost its strength and my words were barely audible. I felt physically sick.

Chapter 12

I know I should be grateful for small mercies; like being on bail before and during the trial. I wasn't even remanded in custody when the jury were sent out, which is almost unprecedented. The only downside was that having been found guilty, I was totally unprepared, both mentally and in every other way, for going to prison.

Of course, I had visited prisons before, every experienced Detective had. I'd interviewed prisoners in legal visits and collected them when they were released on temporary licence to assist with enquiries. I'd even investigated a male rape in one establishment, which involved sealing off the cell and treating it as a crime scene, taking the sixty-year-old serial sex offender victim to a rape suite, where, incidentally and ironically, most of his own victims had previously been treated.

So physically I knew what to expect, but nothing can prepare a forty-seven-year-old man of previous good character for incarceration. I tried to take some solace in the fact that similar people had gone through this experience. Jeffrey Archer, Jonathan King and Boy George sprung immediately to mind, but there must have been plenty more. The big difference for me was that I was, or rather had been, a police officer and while I didn't expect to meet anyone who I'd personally sent down, it was a pretty established fact that police officers had an even worse time in jail than rapists and sex offenders.

There were other differences, too. Not only was I ex old bill, I was also, according to the jury at the Old Bailey, a sex offender who'd raped and murdered an eighty-two year-old lady. In terms of prisoners, I would be the lowest of the low and everybody, even people convicted of the most terrible sex offences, would treat me with contempt and violence. I could expect no protection from the prison officers. Why would they feel obligated to help a monster who had done such a terrible thing to such a lovely old lady?

I was also sentenced to life, with a minimum tariff of twenty-two years. If I ever got out, I'd be seventy. So basically, I could give up any romantic idea of counting the days and years down to my release.

After the judge passed my sentence, I went into shock and the next couple of hours, being taken down to the holding cells beneath the court and booked in, were just a blur.

Ridiculous though it seems with hindsight, I never thought I'd be convicted simply because I was innocent.

When Alison told me my performance in the witness box was the best she'd ever seen, I thought my acquittal was only a matter of time. What a fool I had been. The forensic, circumstantial and identification evidence was just too overwhelming, and it took them just less than six hours to return their verdict. It may have been a staggering miscarriage of justice but the more I turned it over and over, the more I understood. And the more I understood, the deeper I fell in to absolute and total despair.

As I travelled in the SERCO van from the Old Bailey to wherever they were taking me, I experienced what I can only describe as a complete mental breakdown. My brain refused to accept my predicament and I started to hyperventilate. Within seconds I could feel my heart beating so hard it was sure to break out of my chest and I started to shake uncontrollably. I was trapped in the smallest space, a cell in fact, and my legs collapsed beneath me so that I fell at an unnatural angle and found myself wedged between the seat and a toilet. I knew I wasn't, but I felt a sinking feeling like I was falling uncontrollably down and there was a feeling in my chest, a nervous gripping fear, that was crushing. It was just like someone had gone 'boo' and made me jump but the sensation just didn't subside.

I lost all sense of time as every second seemed to take an hour to pass.

Gradually, slowly, my breathing started to settle down. I took my pulse – it was one hundred and five! No wonder I was breathless and dizzy.

After what felt like a lifetime, the van stopped and from the conversation I could overhear from the prisoners in other cells, we had arrived at our destination, which, they agreed, was HMP Waterloo. I'd been to HMP Waterloo a few years ago when I was investigating a murder. We'd got a prisoner out for interview. The murder weapon had been found in his car when he'd been arrested in respect of an unrelated matter.

HMP Waterloo was what's called a 'Cat B Local'. 'Cat B' means it was one down from a 'Cat A High Security' prison and 'Local' meant it accepted those remanded in custody from nearby courts. As a consequence, there was a high turnover of prisoners and the establishment had a busy, unsettled atmosphere. Cat B Locals had a reputation for being volatile and violent and because of the high turnover of prisoners, they were invariably full of contraband, most notably drugs and illegal mobile phones.

I had managed to get back to my feet, which wasn't easy because I was handcuffed. The SERCO guard unlocked my cell and led me out of the van and through a gate into a large metal cage. There was a bench in the corner where he sat me down.

I had been the first off the van and three more prisoners followed my path so that within a few minutes there were four of us on the bench. The other three, one white, one Asian and one black, were all younger than me by at least twenty years. I tried not to catch their eyes and hung my head almost between my knees. The white guy sat immediately to my left.

"Sentence or remand?" He asked.

"Sentenced" I replied.

"What d'ya get?"

"The lot." I replied.

"Life, eh. You'll be on suicide watch for a while, Geez."

If took a gargantuan effort but I asked.

"You?"

"Remand, geez, just half a fucking kay, they're taking the piss."

That didn't sound right. Remanded in custody for just half a kilo of class 'A' and from the Old Bailey, too? Most cases at the Old Bailey were really serious. I wasn't inclined to ask him any further questions.

"This your first time, geez?"

I nodded.

"Who did you kill? The missus?"

I shook my head.

"Fuck me, you're not that rozzer who raped and killed that old lady, like in 1970?"

I turned my head so that I was looking my new best friend straight in the eye. He was a fairly typical scally and in my previous life, I'd have given him a tug every time.

"No, I'm not. But I am the rozzer who's been fitted up for that fucking terrible crime."

"Fucking hell, geez, you're fucking dead. They'll fucking kill you in here."

Although the words he spoke were both aggressive and painful to hear, he wasn't actually being threatening, merely factual.

"Any advice?" I asked.

"Get on the VP's wing as soon as you can. Once you're there, stay in your cell twenty-four seven, geez. Don't think for even a second you can go on, like, exercise, or get your scoff. Don't leave that fucking cell, ever. In fact, see if the screws will put you in the Seg, probably safer there, but watch the red bands, they're all cunts."

"Thanks, my names Chris." I said.

"Good for you, geez; but we won't be speaking again. I'm not having a go mate, but if anyone in there sees me talking to you, fucking dead, geez. Anyone you nicked when you were a rozzer in here?"

He laughed; the thought obviously amused him.

I put my head back down between my legs and shook my head.

"Geez, listen, you need to get tooled up. You're gonna need a shank, mate. I hope you're fucking hard; you're gonna need to be, geez."

I knew a shank was prison slang for a home-made knife. I'd seen many different versions over the years, but the most common was a sharp piece of metal melted into the end of a plastic toothbrush handle.

"You got any money, geez?"

I shook my head again. I mean, I did have eighty odd grand in a savings account but I really didn't want to admit that to anyone.

"Fucking shame 'cos you could have bought some protection. You know, pay a monthly fee to the main man and he puts the word out that you're to be left alone. Might work, but not without any money, geez. You are fucked man."

I didn't say a word or otherwise react.

I discretely took my pulse again – it was ninety-two, which was better.

We sat on that bench for what seemed like an hour and then a guard emerged and called a name. The Asian guy stood up and followed the guard inside the main building. I was the last one to be called, not that it mattered. I was led into what I was soon to learn to be Reception. There I was booked in. The process was almost identical to a Met custody suite, although obviously you weren't given your rights or informed that you could call a solicitor and there was a lot more emphasis on your mental and physical health, your addictions and any ailments you might be suffering from.

Instead of a custody officer, there was a uniformed guard sitting behind a desk, who was asking me questions and writing copiously into what, I can only assume, was my file. He was a white man in his forties, overweight, with a completely bald head and a detached attitude.

The three prisoners who had entered before me were sat on another bench and it appeared that whatever event was to take place next, was waiting for the completion of my process. The way they were all looking at me, watching my every move, I suspect my 'friend' had told them which infamous prisoner I was.

I had to fill in a prop card and list everything I had. I didn't have much, so that didn't take long.

Then someone who I assumed to be a prisoner, gave me a pile of clothes and I had to go into a little cubicle and change. I had to add my old clothes, my suit, shirt and tie, which I'd worn at court, to the items on my prop card. I was given a pair of white plimsolls but without any laces. They were a size twelve; I was a ten.

I was taken into a small adjoining interview room where a nurse called Susan asked me questions about my health, many of which I'd only just been asked by the bald man. I got the feeling she was making some sort of assessment about me.

"Have you ever considered suicide?" She asked.

I knew this was an important question and the answer was 'yes'. I mean if any person on this planet found themselves in the dreadful predicament I was in, they would at least consider that option, but I knew if I was honest, I'd probably have someone watching me twenty-four hours a day for the next month or two. I wouldn't even be able to have a shit in private.

"No, never." I replied, definitively.

When I emerged from my interview with the nurse, I looked around and immediately noticed that the three stooges had gone and I was the only prisoner in Reception.

"Sit on the bench." The bald man said.

So I did.

I didn't wait for long. A new officer came in and he had two stripes on his epaulette, which I knew from previous experience, meant he was a Principal Officer, equivalent to an Inspector in the Met.

"Hi Bill." He said.

Apparently, the bald guard's name was Bill.

"Hi Andy. Susan's just finishing off the ACCT, do you want a cup of tea while you wait?"

"No, I'm fine."

Andy picked up some paperwork off Bill's desk and started reading through it.

"Where's the warrant?" He asked.

"It should be in there, probably at the back."

Apparently it was. The warrant authorising my detention was a document produced by the court and signed by the sentencing judge. It directed Her Majesty's Prison Service to detain me for the period stated and was giving them the authority to do so.

Susan emerged from her office.

"Hi Andy." She said.

"Your recommendation?"

"Fifteen-minute watches for two weeks. Seg?"

"VP"

"At least." Susan replied.

"Can I ask? VP?" I spoke quietly, so as not to piss them off, if they wanted to ignore me.

"Vulnerable Prisoner Wing." Andy replied, not unpleasantly.

"Because of your former trade or calling, we will need to put you with other Vulnerable Prisoners for your safety. It means you won't associate with mainstream prisoners, you'll be kept apart at all times. It's the best we can do. Well, you could go to the Segregation Unit, but that's a punishment block and you can't spend the rest of your sentence there."

I nodded to acknowledge the information.

"First night centre?" Asked Bill.

"No, straight to the VP wing. Too dangerous in the Induction Wing, I'll take him over." Andy replied.

"Thank you." I said, to no one in particular.

All three, Susan, Bill and Andy, stopped what they were doing and momentarily stared at me. I got the impression no prisoner had ever thanked them before.

Chapter 13

I followed the guard called Andy through many corridors and landings and then back outside again. When I say 'outside' I mean a caged walkway in the open air but obviously still within the prison. My plimsolls kept falling off, they were way too big for me, but I kept walking and didn't make a fuss. Eventually, we entered what I immediately recognised as a wing – a big square building with cells on four levels around the outside. On the ground floor was the association area, as indicated by the presence of several pool and table tennis tables. At the same level of each floor, or landing as they're known, is a net to make sure that anyone jumping or being thrown from an upper landing comes to no harm.

It was early evening and everyone was in their cell, but the place still buzzed with activity. From several cells came ridiculously loud music; from others there was just meaningless banging; many prisoners were having shouted conversations with one another from one cell to another. The smell of cannabis was overpowering.

We went up to the third level or 'the threes', as I later discovered they were called, and I was led to my cell.

"After you" Andy said.

I went in.

I was standing in a room eight foot long and four foot wide. On the left was the bed, unmade, with a mattress no more than three inches thick. Immediately on the right was a metal toilet and a metal sink, then opposite the bed was a desk with drawers beneath; a broken three-legged chair was propped up in the far corner. And that was it. There was nothing else in the room. The wall desperately needed plastering and painting and someone had made a hole in the plastic window which they'd then pushed toilet paper into.

"You've missed scoff, I'm afraid."

I nodded my head in acknowledgement.

"A member of staff will check you every fifteen minutes to check you've not done anything stupid."

I nodded again.

"Is this wing all VPs?" I asked.

"No, just the threes and fours. You have separate association and exercise. You don't, you shouldn't, mix with the other prisoners at all."

"Any advice?"

"Keep your mouth shut and your head down. You'll transfer out of here in a few months; make that your goal, getting to the next establishment. Nowhere else will be as bad as here, so you've always got the next place to look forward to. Are you appealing?"

"Counsel says they'll have to wait and see if they can find any grounds. I know they all say this, but I didn't do it."

Andy smiled but not nastily.

"They don't all say it. That's a bit of a fallacy. Most of them don't give their offence a second thought once they get convicted."

Andy sat down on the bed next to me.

"I've followed your trial with interest. I grew up in Trowbridge, just down the road. I'm too young to remember the original crime …"

"Ironically, so am I." I replied.

Andy laughed.

"Fifteen billion to one, can't beat those odds." Andy said.

"I didn't." I replied.

"I've got a brother. He married a Scottish lady called Fionna, they're both in the Prison Service, too."

I had no idea where this conversation was going but I was interested, nonetheless.

"They had a prisoner, a female police officer, who was convicted when her fingerprints were found at the scene of a murder."

"Of murder?" I asked.

"No, no. Listen. She attended the scene of the murder but said she never went into the address. But they found her prints inside. She still denied going in, even under oath, and was convicted of perjury. Then, years later, it turns out the experts got it wrong and it wasn't her fingerprints after all, just someone with similar fingerprints. She did like eighteen months. Like you, she always said she hadn't lied. She was released and paid like a million pounds."

I was absolutely gobsmacked! I'd never heard of that case. It was so similar to my own story. I could barely believe it. At last, was there a chink of light somewhere in the darkness?

Chapter 14

That first night, I didn't sleep for one minute.

I had an anxious sensation in my chest that made relaxation impossible. On at least six occasions I convinced myself I was having a heart attack. My pulse was racing, as high as one hundred and ten, at one point. I tried walking up and down my tiny cell. I tried doing press-ups and various stretches. I tried controlling my breathing. Nothing I did worked. By dawn, I'd decided I was really going clinically insane.

Every fifteen minutes I heard the wicket twitch and felt an eye observing me. It happened so often, I started to not notice it.

Early in the morning, someone unlocked my cell and pushed the door open a few inches. Within seconds I heard other cells open and movement and conversations amongst my fellow prisoners. I had no inclination to join them. Despite not having eaten for at least twenty-four hours, I had absolutely no appetite. I could drink from the tap on my sink, but I wasn't interested in food.
I thought perhaps I might be able to get a few hours kip. The routine, familiar noises outside now were much more reassuring and settling than the strange sounds of the night and I suddenly felt tired.

Just as I was drifting off however, I heard my door open wider and I opened my eyes to see who had come in. I was looking at a white man in his seventies, with a few strands of grey hair, yet he had more hair than teeth. He looked dirty, unkempt and just fucking horrible.

"May I politely enquire, who are you?" He said, with an impeccable upper class English accent.

"Chris" I replied.

"Would you like me to get you some breakfast? It's cereal, two slices of bread and butter, an apple and a carton of orange juice."

Even though I wasn't hungry, I thought I should accept his offer.

"Please" I replied.

"Ten minutes." He turned on his heel.

A few minutes later a uniformed female guard entered my cell carrying a file and a clipboard. I wasn't sure whether I was expected to stand up, so I compromised and sat up, swinging my legs around so that I sat on the edge of the bed.

"Good morning." The guard said.

She was white, in her late twenties; with jet black hair neatly tied up in a bun, a little overweight but in a voluptuous, curvy way and she had an attractive face, with just a subtle hint of make-up.

"I am Kate Bradley, your personal officer. I see you arrived late yesterday. You'll need to get some breakfast; you must be starving."

"Some old guy has offered to get me some, I think he's in the cell next door."

She frowned.

"Check it before you eat it." She suggested.

I nodded.

"How was your first night?"

"Alright, I suppose." I replied.

"Any thoughts of suicide or self-harm?"

"In my circumstances, if I said 'no' you would think I was seriously mad, wouldn't you?"

My reply seemed to confuse her. She was obviously expecting a simple yes or no.

"No" I said, quickly.

"Good" She replied.

"You haven't got any personal effects. Not even a radio. I'll see what I can get you. Do you read? Would you like some books and magazines?"

"Please" I replied.

She wrote on what, I can only assume, were my notes.

"Any questions?"

"Any advice?"

She looked at me properly, probably for the first time since she'd entered the cell.

"Bit late for that now, isn't it?"

There was a cut in her voice, an edge, which suggested she had zero sympathy for me. I knew she was right, and I understood her attitude, I really did. But it still hurt. There was a bit, deep down inside me, a child, who, more than anything, wanted his mother to cuddle him and reassure him that everything was going to be all right. But no such person existed, and this was a lonely, frightening place.

When I looked up again, Kate had left.

I lay back down and took my pulse – only eighty-five.

Suddenly there was an explosion of music from a nearby cell. It was some awful modern pop song with a ridiculously loud 'boom boom boom' beat and very little melody. I wondered why it was allowed. I cupped my lifeless pillow and wrapped it around my ears and shut my eyes.

Right, was suicide a realistic option? And if it was, how was I going to do it? I knew from experience that it wasn't uncommon for prisoners to hang themselves, and as there was no way I could get my hands on sufficient medication to do any harm, that seemed the best option. I really didn't know if I could open a vein, I just didn't think I was capable of driving a knife that deeply into my body. So, hanging it was. I'd need three things: a ligature, a pivot point and sufficient height. I figured, even if I was unlucky, it would take more than a couple of minutes to die. I also needed to make sure that once I was hanging, there was no way back. That is to say that I couldn't reach out with my legs and find some support somewhere, because I knew I was such a coward that is exactly what I'd try to do.

I felt a gentle tap on my arm, it was the old grey man. I released the pillow.

"Gangster rap not your thing then?"

He had to almost shout to make himself heard over the music.

"Not really."

"Your food is on your table."

"Thank you."

He looked around the cell.

"Where's all your prop?"

I shook my head.

"Nothing? You've got nothing?"

"I'll see what I can find. There's a tele in the storeroom, it's broken, you can only get BBC1 so no one wants it but it'll be better than nothing."

I mustered a grateful smile and he left.

Now, where was I? Oh, yes, how to end my life by hanging.

Chapter 15

The first few days in prison passed very slowly. Each minute felt like an hour. The old grey man, Albert, did get me a TV set as he'd promised and while the picture was dreadful, it was great to have a low noise on in the background. My personal officer, Kate, was good to her word, too, and got me a small FM/AM radio and some headphones, so every night I went to sleep listening to one of London's numerous talk radio stations.

I thought more about the suicide option, but I'd have to park that idea until the guards stopped doing fifteen-minute checks on me. I also thought, what if I kill myself and then they discovered they'd made a mistake with the DNA and it wasn't me after all? How stupid would I feel? Or not, as the case would be, as I'd be dead.

I rarely left my cell, only to get my food, or scoff, as it was known in here. The other prisoners left me alone; all except Albert, who occasionally popped his head round the door to ask if I was alright. Undoubtedly, putting me on the Vulnerable Prisoners' wing was a shrewd call. I gathered all other prisoners on this wing were paedophiles or worse, child rapists and murderers, so there was at least a little safety here for the time being.

There was no doubt, I was going slowly mad. I was so anxious and screwed up that it was only a matter of time before I had a complete system failure, although in exactly what guise that breakdown would be, I wasn't sure.

The irony of my situation was perhaps the only thing that prevented that ultimate collapse. I knew that I was in fact a murderer. I had despatched Barry Skinner to the afterlife without a second thought. Well, that's not completely true, but it wasn't too far away either. I'd completely got away with that crime, only to be convicted of a murder I knew absolutely nothing about.

On my first night inside, when the guard had told me about the Scottish plonk wrongly convicted of perjury on faulty fingerprint evidence, my hopes had been briefly raised, but when I thought about it in more detail, I remembered that one of the first things my legal team had done was to hire our own forensic scientist to review a new sample from me against the one from the murder. Our scientist had found one or two areas of inconsistency, but it only brought the chances of it not being me down from one in fifteen million, to one in eight million, so we'd decided to disregard our own scientist's findings, as it hardly aided our defence.

It was at lunchtime on my sixth day of incarceration that I received my correspondence – three letters in all.

The first was from the Metropolitan Police and had been opened. The top of the letter had been stamped 'HMP Waterloo' and the envelope stapled carelessly to the back of the letter.

Dear Detective Inspector Christopher Pritchard,

Following your conviction for murder and rape at the Central Criminal Court on 29th October 2010, on the 1st November 2010 a Misconduct Board was held in your absence. This was chaired by Commander Anna Bloomfield.

The Board found you guilty of being the subject of a criminal conviction which is a breach of Section 8 of the Metropolitan Police Code of Conduct. The Board dismissed you with immediate effect.

Your pay will terminate at the end of this calendar month.

Yours sincerely

Michael J Parker
Head of Human Resources.

The second, in a typed envelope which was marked 'On Her Majesty's Service – Private and Confidential', was unopened.

Dear Mr Pritchard,

Her Majesty has asked me to write to inform you that, following your conviction at the Central Criminal Court on 29th October 2010, a decision has been made to annul the award of the Queen's Police Medal for Gallantry conferred on you on 26th June 1986.

Please be advised that following this annulment you are no longer entitled to the rights, privileges and prerogatives granted to the recipient.

Yours sincerely

Izzard Sampson - Grange
Deputy Private Secretary to HM Queen Elizabeth

The third letter had been opened and was also stapled to the envelope. I immediately recognised Mrs M's handwriting. I sat on my bed and read every word slowly and carefully.

My dearest Christopher,

I cannot put into words my feelings when I heard the verdict. I looked down to try to make eye contact and to tell you everything would be all right, but you didn't look up to the public gallery and they led you away only seconds later.

I know you could not have done the terrible things they described during the trial. That poor old lady, and in her own home too. I have known you longer than I knew my daughter. I know you too well. There is not a bone in your body or a hair on your head that could do such terrible things. Not in 1982, not today, not ever.

I will spend the rest of my life championing your innocence and campaigning for your release. I will do it every minute of every day until I join Dawn in heaven. Nothing will stop me.

I did briefly flirt with the idea of setting myself alight outside the Old Bailey to draw attention to this appalling miscarriage of justice. You'd be too young to remember, but several monks did this to protest against the Vietnam War, and their sacrifices did make a difference. I would willingly do that for you, but then there'd be no one left to fight your cause.

Pippa and Trudy are writing to you separately, but both send their love. Like me, and anyone else close to you, they know you have been wrongfully convicted.

I will visit you whenever it is allowed. I don't care where they put you, I will be there. I will not miss even one visit.

I have had a meeting with your barrister and solicitor. They are looking at grounds to appeal. I have told them that I will never give up and they have suggested several other things we could do, like hire a team of private detectives and try to get the BBC or someone else in the media on board. I don't care what it costs so I have put my house up for sale.

I have delivered a large package of stuff for you - but they said it would take several days for them to go through it before you get it.

Try to be strong, Christopher. Remember that you are loved more than you will ever know.

Remember Dawn is looking down on you. She sees everything. She will come to your rescue, I promise.

You are the bravest person I have ever known. Now you must be brave again, brave beyond belief, brave beyond brave. Do not give in to evil thoughts. I mean that, Christopher, I would never forgive you, if you did that.

You are and always will be, my hero.

Love

Jennifer (Mrs M. Mum)

That effectively ended my immediate thoughts of suicide. Mrs M had suffered such terrible losses in her life; I couldn't possibly be responsible for adding to that list.

Chapter 16

The following week Mrs M's delivery arrived. It included a decent DAB radio, underwear, loads of toiletries, a dozen books and countless magazines.

The decent DAB radio didn't last long. Four of my fellow prisoners came in and asked for me to donate the radio to a charity auction. It was one of those moments. Whatever I did I was going to lose the radio. The only choice was do I fight them, get injured, perhaps seriously, and lose the radio, or just surrender it without protest? The problem was, if I just gave it up, that was going to be it going forward. They would just come in and take whatever they wanted.

I told them to 'go fuck themselves' but that didn't work.

When the spokesman of the four took several steps towards the item, I jumped to my feet and planted a haymaker from behind him on the left side of his face with considerable force. He clearly hadn't expected that, and he briefly staggered under the weight of the blow. But my glory was only momentary as the other three, who were now behind me, attacked me all at once. I was pulled to the ground and kicked in the head and body until I went unconscious.

I woke up in the medical wing where I spent the next week recovering from several cracked ribs and what I was convinced was a broken jaw. Fortunately, it wasn't but I couldn't chew anything for a month. When, eventually, I got back to my cell, everything Mrs M had sent in had been stolen, with the exception of the books. The FM AM radio that the guard Kate had given me was there, but it had been stamped on several times and was now completely useless.

When I was in the medical wing a guard from Security visited me several times to ask me what had happened. I refused to tell him. He said that he'd studied the CCTV and identified the four prisoners who had entered my cell and all he needed was a short statement from me confirming that they'd assaulted me. I declined. I knew he was trying his best to do the right thing, but I also knew if I said nothing, there was just slightly less chance of it happening again. Next time, I thought, I might not be so lucky. I'd investigated too many murders caused by kicks to the head, I didn't want to be the victim of another.

I'd only been back in the cell a few minutes when Albert came in. As I saw the door open, I nearly had a heart attack. I thought it was all going to happen again and I was mightily relieved to see it was only my ageing neighbour.

"You alright, son?"

"Been better." I replied.

"Bastards"

I nodded.

"Not worth having anything nice, not in here anyway. Wait until you get to a nice Cat C Trainer, then you might stand a chance of keeping it."

"It was sent in." I replied.

"I know it was. That's what I need to talk to you about. The chaps want you to get some more."

I looked at Albert, he seemed embarrassed.

"Are you part of this?" I asked.

"No. But they know I talk to you. They want me to get you to get more stuff sent in."

"They really can go fuck themselves." I replied.

As I was talking, I could feel my anxiety reaching an all time high. My racing heart was pounding and the feeling of dreadful nervousness, which these days lived permanently in my chest, grew in size and threat.

"If you don't do this, they'll pay you another visit."

"Then they'll pay me another visit." I said.

"They'll really hurt you this time, last week was only a warning."

"I ain't going to do it." I replied.

"Listen Chris, you're here for a while. You've got to do what they want. They do it to everyone, not just you. The worst thing you did was get that parcel. Now they know that someone on the outside cares for you and will spend their money to help you. They'll exploit that ruthlessly."

"If you're really not in cahoots with them, tell me what else I can do?"

"Barricade yourself in and demand a move to the Seg or use this."

He reached in his pocket and handed me a small thin implement. I had a quick glance. It was just a thin piece of metal, but it had been sharpened to a really sharp point. The other end had been wrapped in masking tape to fashion a make-shift handle.

"For fuck's sake, Albert, that would kill someone."

"What do you care? You're in for life anyway? You couldn't get any more time."

"Yeah, that's all I need, another conviction for murder."

I went to hand the implement back, but he wouldn't take it.

"Great, now if I'm found with this, I'll get done for that too."

"Who are these people, anyway?" I asked.

"The main lad is Eric Halfhide; he's in for possession with intent, GBH and firearms. He wouldn't normally be on this wing, he's not VP material, but he's made some major enemies, the Bryans, who are also in here. He allegedly shot their cousin or something. Anyway, now he's got his little groupies. He's the one you slugged. Apparently, you caught him really good."

"Didn't do me a lot of good though, did it?"

"You kept your mouth shut, though. That was smart. If you'd said anything to Security, you wouldn't even be safe down the Seg."

"Do the guards know what's going on?"

"Guards?" Albert laughed.

"Screws, Chris, they're called screws. Yeah, they know but there's not a lot they can do. Most of them are okay, especially on this wing. Miss Bradley's okay, she's your P.O. isn't she? She's mine, too."

It was the longest conversation I'd had with anyone since I'd arrived and it felt almost normal. Did Albert have an ulterior motive for being nice to me? I couldn't see one, but I was also conscious of the advice I'd had not to trust anyone.

"What are you in for?" I asked.

The question felt out of the blue, but he obviously knew who I was and what I was said to have done.

"The usual, kiddie porn. Half the VP wing's in for it. Ridiculous isn't it? Being sent to jail for having a wank over a few pictures on your computer."

"How long?" I asked.

"Well, I got two years and was out on parole after fifteen months, but I was breached for getting access to the internet and got recalled, so I've got to finish my sentence. Only eight weeks now."

"Good for you." I replied, a little sarcastically.

"You don't admit your offence, do you?" He asked.

"Nope"

"That'll really fuck you up. You won't get anything, you won't get parole, you'll fuck up your rehabilitation programme, so you won't get to better nicks. You'll never get to a Cat D. I'd reconsider your stance if I was you."

"I ain't going to do that, Albert, but thanks for the advice."

"So, what do you want me to tell Eric? That you'll order another parcel?"

"No, tell them to fuck off. I'll take the consequences. And you can have your thing back …"

"It's called a shank."

"Then you can have your shank back."

I pushed the item towards him, but he held his hands up in an *'I'm not touching it'* gesture, backed off, turned and left.

I held the shank in my right hand and waited for my next visit from Eric and his crew.

Chapter 17

I lay on my bed trying to control my breathing in an attempt to calm my anxiety. I was starting to lose my sanity and I knew it. I calculated that it would take an hour for the news to get from Albert to Eric that I didn't want to play ball. I figured they'd take their next opportunity, which would probably be just before lock down, at seven. Was I going to use the shank? I really didn't think so. If I did, I didn't see any good would come of it. I'd either kill someone or they would get control of it and kill me. Either way, I was fucked.

Sooner than I thought I heard several footsteps coming along the landing. I pushed the weapon down the side of the mattress and stood up. This was it, I decided to fight until I went unconscious, again.

Chapter 18

The cell in the Seg was much nicer than the one on the VP Wing. It was much newer for a start; slightly bigger; the furniture was in better shape; the mattress thicker; but above all else, it had a fully functioning Freeview TV.

When I thought it through, old Albert had done me a huge favour. He'd given me the shank and then told the guards, sorry screws, that I had a weapon in my cell. I was subject to a cell search and put on report. Apparently, I'd have to go to something called an adjudication, which was like a prison court. When they asked me why I had the weapon, I said I was going to defend myself against Eric and his cronies. They had to move me to the Seg, so I got away from Eric and avoided the inevitable beating, but perhaps more importantly, everyone, including Eric, would learn that I was prepared to stab him, if he tried any shit again. What's more, in the whole sorry tale, it was established that I wasn't a grass. In fact, I'd been the victim of a grass, as someone had clearly told the authorities about the weapon.

In every way, I came out on top. It felt good, for the first time in a long time.

With that said, my anxiety didn't subside. Would I just have to get used to feeling like this? It was absolutely horrible and 'getting used to it' was the last thing I wanted, but what alternative did I have? It wasn't like I could wish it away.

In the Seg I was locked in my cell twenty-three and a half hours a day. The remaining thirty minutes was for a shower and we were let out separately, so you never saw, let alone met, any other prisoners. I got the feeling that only about half the cells were occupied. There was an additional blessing, no one was playing ridiculously loud music.

Every day a governor came round to speak to us individually and asked if everything was all right. I told her, an attractive middle-aged woman called Dawn Flynn, with a cracking figure, I'd like to serve the rest of my service in the cell. She laughed.

"We call it a sentence, Pritchard."

"Oh yeah." I replied.

"Are you well? Would you like to see the doctor?"

Her question surprised me. I'd never really thought about it and didn't realise just 'seeing a doctor' was an option.

"I think I'm having a mental breakdown. Yes, please, I'd like to see a doctor."

Governor Flynn turned to a uniformed colleague and asked him to make an appointment for me.

"Thank you." I said.

I felt a sudden rush of emotion and started to well up. Seconds later, tears were rolling down my cheeks. I wiped them away with my sleeve. I really don't know why it hit me at that moment, I think I'd detected a touch of kindness, and it just set me off.

"Sorry, I'm getting upset." I said.

Governor Flynn looked me up and down.

"You're the police officer convicted of that historic murder because of DNA evidence, aren't you?"

I nodded, pulling myself together.

"This place must be quite a shock."

"Just a bit." I replied.

"When I come and see you each day, one of my responsibilities is to decide whether your continued detention in the Segregation Unit is required. Take it from me, I shall not be returning you to a standard or VP wing, you will be kept here for your own safety and well-being until you transfer on. Here, you will be safer than anywhere else. I shall endorse your file accordingly."

"Thank you." I said.

My voice was quiet, barely audible.

***

I saw the doctor the next day.

It meant going back into the main jail to get to the medical wing which made me really nervous but, in the end, the journey to and from was uneventful.

The doctor diagnosed General Anxiety Disorder and prescribed an antidepressant medication with an unpronounceable name. He explained that, as I was in the Seg, the tablets would be brought to my cell every morning and I'd have to take them in the presence of the dispensing nurse. He warned me that they would probably make me drowsy.

The following day I took my first dose. I fell asleep for the next sixteen hours but at least, while I was asleep, I didn't feel anxious, so I suppose they worked. Perhaps, I thought, my strategy should be to try to sleep for the next twenty years.

***

The following week, it was just before Christmas, I had another appointment with the doctor which meant another trip to and from the medical wing. I realised I was becoming more than a little agoraphobic as the thought of leaving the Seg brought me out in a cold sweat. But last week's journey had been event free and besides, the following day I had my first visit from Mrs M so I'd have to leave the Seg again. I needed to grow a pair of balls.

I was collected from my cell just before ten and made my way with someone else from the Seg, a white guy in his early twenties, and of course the escorting screw, a really young white guy who could only have been about nineteen. We made our way through the maze of corridors and walkways towards our destination, the medical wing. Once there, we sat down in a pristine white waiting area with half a dozen other prisoners, who were all waiting to see the doctor. The last time I'd come, I was the only one and I felt nervous being near so many other prisoners. I kept my head down and my mouth shut. I didn't even look up when I heard a commotion to my right in the corridor outside the waiting area.

"Fucking hell, mate. Watch where you're fucking going with that." A loud voice said, with a strong Yorkshire accent.

"Get out of my fucking way, you cunt." Another voice responded.

"Nothing to do with me, bro. Don't you fucking talk to me like that."

The door to the waiting room flew open and someone came running in.

'Keep your head down', I reminded myself.

Then I felt a searing, unbelievable pain down the top of my back and realised with unreserved horror that someone had just poured boiling water down my back. I screamed and screamed, falling to the floor in unbearable pain. I could hear several other prisoners laughing. I passed out.

When I came to, I was on a stretcher being carried urgently through the prison by several ambulance crew. I didn't scream anymore, the pain was too much, but I was shaking uncontrollably. I was aware of several conversations going on around me.

"How much morphine did you give him?"

"They're third degree burns on twenty percent of the body."

"We need to call ahead as soon as we get going."

"He was lucky it missed his head and face."

"Have we got details of a next of kin, just in case?"

Even after the bombing, I hadn't been in this much pain. I wanted to die; I didn't care about upsetting Mrs M. I wished my heart to stop beating because the pain would be gone forever. I couldn't cope with this. Not the pain, not the wrongful conviction, not the dreadful, soul destroying, constant, unremitting anxiety.

"Please kill me." I whispered, as they lifted me into the ambulance.

They ignored me, of course. We drove off but then waited at least twenty minutes, it felt like a year, to get back out through the gate. The ambulance crew were getting really agitated with the screws.

"This man could die. Just get us out of here, for Christ's sake."

The ambulance man sitting next to me had been busy hooking me up to a variety of devices; he'd put a cannular in my arm; taken my blood pressure and pulse; given me another shot of what I assumed was morphine, but when he stopped he did something unbelievable – he held my hand.

"You're going to be all right, Christopher. I've seen worse."

He had a southern Irish accent and he sounded like a saint.

"It hurts so much. I want to die." I said.

"We don't let people die; our bosses don't like it." He replied and squeezed my hand.

"I cannot bear the pain. What has happened?"

"Someone has poured boiling water from a kettle down your back. I think they mixed sugar with the boiling water, so your skin has peeled off your back. It is a bad burn, Christopher, but I have seen and dealt with a lot worse. Last week, we had a four-year-old girl who'd pulled a boiling pot off the stove and managed to pour the contents over her head. She was worse than you. She managed to get through it and so will you. I'll be here for you until we hand you over."

"Thank you." I whispered.

I started to moan. I couldn't help it. The pain was indescribable.

The ambulance man held my hand and kept telling me everything would be okay. His actions and compassion will live with me forever.

Chapter 19

Strangely enough, whilst I was at the peak of my suffering, my anxiety had gone. Not that I noticed its absence, I was in too much pain to think straight. After nine days in hospital, the pain began to ease and when it did, the anxiety demons returned. All I had to look forward to in my life was going back to HMP Waterloo where, almost certainly, I'd get jugged again. I learnt that the act of throwing boiling water mixed with sugar over someone was colloquially known as 'a jugging'. There was absolutely no way out of my tortuous situation except suicide. After Mrs M's letter, I had decided against that course of action, but the jugging placed it firmly back on the agenda.

It was perhaps curious that just as I was once again working out how I could end my life, Mrs M managed somehow to visit me in hospital. Clearly, fate wasn't going to let me escape that way.

I had drifted off to sleep after my midday meds and was just rolling over when someone held my hand. I opened my eyes to see Mrs M standing immediately beside me and leaning forward. She kissed me on the forehead, like every parent does to their child. I smiled for the first time in months.

"Hello, Mrs M."

She didn't say a word but just smiled. The gesture melted my heart. That one smile contained more love, affection and compassion than I had ever received. Quite literally, I gasped.

"I'm so sorry." I said.

She gripped my hand and I drifted off to sleep again.

When I woke up Mrs M was still there and still holding my hand. I glanced past her at the clock on the wall. It was two-thirty.

"Sorry, I fell asleep." I said.

"I have to go in a minute, Chris. The guards said I could only have an hour and a half."

"And I've been asleep all the time? Sorry."

"I need to tell you something, try to remember it's important." Mrs M said, but her tone had changed.

I frowned, trying to focus on what she was about to say.

"Yesterday, they announced Kitty Young's been suspended. All the Met are saying is that, following a communication from the Recorder of London, they have made a self-referral to the Independent Police Complaints Authority. The Home Affairs correspondent on the BBC Breakfast programme was saying their sources suggest it's to do with the evidence she gave at your trial. They're saying she either perjured herself by lying, or, if she was telling the truth, then by failing to record and properly deal with your admission to her back in '97, she was guilty of a gross dereliction of duty. This is great news Chris. It might help the appeal."

"That is good news." I said.

"I've got a meeting with the legal team tomorrow to discuss this and lots of other things we're doing. I've hired a private investigation firm, two ex-Met officers, to re-investigate the original murder. I did a TV interview on Tuesday with London Tonight. I told them this was a grave miscarriage of justice. They were fantastic and the reporter guy gave me his mobile phone number and asked me to keep in contact. I'm going to approach the victim's family. If I can convince them you're innocent, then we could really get some traction."

"Thank you, Mrs M." I said.

The problem with Mrs M championing my innocence was that she actually didn't know whether I'd done this crime or not because it happened a year before I'd met her. I was fully aware that her repeated protestations that I was innocent were purely an emotional argument. Had she been my mother and able to testify that on the night of the murder I'd been with her at some family function, or that I'd never come back home with blood-stained clothing, then she might have more credibility. So, while in terms of dedication and loyalty, she was the most fantastic advocate an innocent person could have, she wasn't a witness in any shape or form.

"Are you still in dreadful pain?" She asked.

"It's getting better." I replied.

"I don't want you to go back there."

"I'll be fine, Mrs M." I lied.

"You've got to trust me, Chris, I will get you out of this."

I mustered the best smile I could find under the circumstances.

***

On the way back from hospital I found and seized about the rarest item a person can find in jail; a copy of the *Observer* newspaper.

As a general rule, I didn't read newspapers in prison. For one, it reminded you too much of what you were missing in the outside world, but probably more because all you could ever find was the *Sun* or the *Daily Mirror*, both of which I disliked with equal disdain. The *Observer*, however, I used to enjoy because, traditionally, like it's sister publication the *Guardian*, it's views on everything were so diametrically opposed to my own they got me thinking.

Back in my cell, I thumbed through the pages, carefully reading each article, when I came across a long read on the latest situation in Northern Ireland and, in particular, the history of, and the on-going battles between, what was, the Provisional IRA and the Real IRA. The article also discussed the Good Friday Agreement and the on-going tensions with Unionists and their pseudo- paramilitaries.

As I read, I kept scanning ahead for any mention of Barry Skinner. Halfway down the article and my eyes raced forward to read that section.

Barry Skinner was killed by the Real IRA in June 2007 in a revenge style assassination. Skinner, aged 72, who was in the Metropolitan Police's Witness Protection programme had been given a new identity and was living in Essex, when he was kneecapped and then executed. It is believed Skinner had agreed to give evidence against former associates. The Real IRA claimed responsibility for the killing. The incident is another example of on-going tensions between the various factions and their inability to put the past behind and move on.

Sources suggest the killing of Skinner adversely impacted upon continuing back door peace negotiations between all parties and that these have now stalled. A spokesman for the Office of Secretary of State for Northern Ireland declined to comment upon this speculation, nor did they confirm that any negotiations had taken place, but the representative did say "We will always explore every opportunity for peace in Northern Ireland.

Skinner had pleaded guilty to two bombings on the mainland UK which led to the deaths of three children and one police officer. Security Services, however, suspected his involvement in a tranche of terrorist related atrocities in the province, going back over several decades.

If negotiations were taking place under some self-imposed, informal ceasefire, then Skinner's murder would probably have been enough to derail them.

I didn't read anymore. I put the paper down, lay back and shut my eyes. I could feel my heart pounding.

Had my actions in killing Barry Skinner actually terminated Northern Ireland peace negotiations? Then why did the Real IRA claim responsibility? The last question was fairly easy to answer - I suppose they had to. Otherwise, they'd have looked weak and ineffective. My actions had in fact, put them in an impossible situation.

Strange really, how far the ripples reach out.

Chapter 20

The next few months rolled by between continued bouts of uncontrollable anxiety and slumber. There was nothing in between. In mid-February I was transferred from HMP Waterloo, one hundred and fifty miles north, to HMP Bankside, another Cat B, but in a much more rural location.

On arrival, I went straight into the Seg. My cell was nowhere near as nice as the one at HMP Waterloo, being both smaller and damp, but by now I'd gathered a small collection of personal effects which made life a little bit more pleasant. I'd learnt only to have things that other prisoners wouldn't want. So, no DAB radio, just a cheap, ten-year-old set with poor reception. No Nike trainers, just Primark cheapies. Only store branded toiletries and cheap Bic razors. The only exception to this rule was books. Of these, you could have and keep whatever you like. You could leave Charles Dickens' first edition of Oliver Twist, worth millions, on your bed with your cell door open all day and it would still be there in the evening.

I had become an ardent reader; I devoured so many of the classics, Orwell's '1984', Tolkien's 'Lord of the Rings' and the complete works of Jane Austen and Arthur Conan Doyle. My favourite book of all time was F Scott Fitzgerald's *'The Great Gatsby'*. The way the prose danced and sang was mesmerising.

I had another escape. Perhaps not quite as healthy and pure, but a great source of happiness to me, nonetheless. It was inspired by Robert Graves 'I Claudius'. I imagined myself as the Emperor of Rome and that I lived in a palace on Capri with all my favourite friends. Now, as it happened most of these friends were attractive females that I'd met at some stage of my life. Dawn was there, as was the lovely Sarah, and, of course, Wendy. But there were other young ladies of my erstwhile acquaintance, too. The strange thing was, although this sounds terrible seedy, it really wasn't. We would talk, and perhaps go for a swim in the Mediterranean Sea, eat fantastic exotic food and have slaves to serve us but this wasn't a sexual fantasy, it was much, much more than that. It was my escape. No one could take it away and every time I went to sleep, it was the place I went to before I drifted off.

I had a couple of advantages over other prisoners, too. I didn't smoke. I didn't take drugs and I didn't want or need a mobile phone. As a result, I was never in debt to anyone. I did miss alcohol and would have given my right arm to have a bottle of Scotch a week but that was merely a pipe dream. Before I went to prison, I was, like a decent proportion of the country, drinking way too much, so I figured my body must be appreciating the forced abstinence.

My mental health was my biggest concern. I was still suffering from the most overpowering anxiety and how I hadn't gone mad was a mystery. But as the weeks rolled into months, I realised I had hit rock bottom. That is to say, I had got to a point where it wasn't getting any worse. The terrible feeling in my chest only disappeared when I went to sleep. Even a quick visit to the toilet at three in the morning would be enough for it to return.

I'd worked out that most of the guards were as good as gold. As long as you treated them with a bit of respect and courtesy, they would do the same. I overheard other prisoners talking about their mate on another wing who had a corrupt guard in their pocket, and he'd bring anything in for the right price. It was similar to my old police life when everyone knew someone else who'd been beaten up in a police cell, but you never got to speak or to meet the victim himself.

I knew the place was awash with drugs and phones but because I wasn't in the market for either, it was of no concern to me.

Shortly after my arrival, Mrs M came to visit.

The contrast between Mrs M and the other visitors was striking. Most of them were women and they were dressed up like they were going out on Saturday night to some tacky, classless night club. In fact, I'd seen hookers plying their street trade dressed more discreetly. Someone once told me, that a lady should never flaunt both her breasts or her legs. These women simultaneously attempted to display their hair, face, breasts, shoulders, hands, beer belly, arse, legs and toes. If that wasn't enough, they were covered in cheap, uncoordinated and really quite hideous tattoos, some from head to foot. Then they all teetered about in the highest heeled platform shoes I had ever seen. Finally, they all needed to lose some serious weight, on average, about three stone. I had never seen such a collection of ghouls.

For the record, Mrs M was dressed in a discreet dark blue trouser suit with flat patent leather black shoes and her hair tied neatly up. I was proud that she was *my* visitor.

"How's your back?" She asked, as she sat down.

"It's a bit sore now and again, and they have to keep checking for infection, but its ok." I replied.

"Is this any better than Waterloo?" She asked.

"Yes, definitely. The atmosphere isn't as full on. It's not the first jail you get sent to, so everybody here has already done a little bit of time. I am in the Seg and that's ok. Thanks for sending in the parcels, but remember, there's a real art in making sure you don't send in anything anyone else would want."

"I know, I'm getting quite good at that. Anyway, let's get down to business. The private investigators are doing an excellent job. They've found a school photograph of your class taken a week before the murder."

I frowned, as I wasn't quite sure how that was going to help.

"In the photograph, you have short hair."

The penny dropped.

"In the photofit, remember, you had quite long hair, around neck length. Well, the detectives have taken a statement from a professor at London University who's an expert in human hair. His professional opinion is that your hair couldn't have grown that fast in only four weeks. We're starting to undermine the photofit evidence that was so damning at the trial."

"But I suppose they could argue I was wearing a wig? Mind you, that would be a bit desperate. They'd have to find someone who remembers me owning or having access to a wig, at the time."

It was an exciting development. I always thought at my trial the photofit was the nail in my coffin. The old black and white charcoal drawing looked so remarkably like my first warrant card photograph that it was uncanny. My defence counsel made a compelling argument during her closing speech that in the early eighties living within twenty-five miles of Bath were about five thousand white males, aged between sixteen and twenty, who were about 6' tall, slim, with dark brown hair but even I knew the person in the drawing looked like me.

"I don't suppose there's any news on Kitty? I mean these disciplinary actions can take years, so I don't anticipate anything's happened". I asked.

"Look, entirely off the record, John's been feeding me the gossip he's picking up …"

John was John King, an Assistant Commissioner, and Mrs M's boyfriend.

"… apparently, the silence from Emu has been deafening. The Job was expecting some huge backlash, you know, a wave of publicity about how the decision was racially motivated and all that rubbish, but they're saying nothing."

Emu was in fact the 'Association of Minority and Ethnic police officers' but everyone in the Job just called it Emu.

"I agree, that is strange."

"He also reckons Kitty is bang to rights. The original complaint came from the judge at your trial. He referred the matter to the Commissioner, who went to see the Home Secretary. Now loads of other stuff is coming out. Like, she always claimed to be a graduate but she's not, she hasn't even got an A level."

"Didn't she start claiming to be a doctor a few years ago?" I asked.

"Yes, she did, but that was because some University gave her an Honorary degree for being like the first black woman Deputy Commissioner. She wasn't meant to use the award and title professionally."

"Any other gossip?"

"She's also in trouble about some Emu expenses scandal. She signed off some false accounts to cover up some theft. She didn't formally tell the job the full extent of the matter, saying she was just a witness but apparently whoever's investigating the whole thing is about to issue a summons."

"I know a bit about that, well half the Met knows about that. It was a jolly to San Francisco or something and she was the treasurer or trustee."

"John says she's offered her resignation, but the Commissioner and Police Authority have refused to accept it. Or they can't accept it, or something like that. John was speculating and he said if she does go down for perjury, she can expect between three and five years' imprisonment."

It was the best news I'd heard in a long time.

Over on the far side of the Visits Hall, a fight broke out between two prisoners on adjoining tables. The guards went rushing over and, almost in unison, every visitor on a table on our side of the hall, passed something to their incarcerated loved one.

"How's it going with John?" I asked.

"It's great. We see each other once a week, occasionally twice, and the time we spend together is really special. I don't know why I didn't start dating married men years ago. It's all a lot simpler and there's no dirty underwear to wash."

I smiled.

"You don't really approve, do you?" Mrs M asked.

"No, that's not true. Honestly, if it makes you happy then I'm fine with it. Remember though, it didn't work out for Dawn and her Barry. He ended up emigrating to Australia."

"That was completely different because of where Dawn was in her life compared to me. She was young, her whole life was ahead of her, marriage, children, buying a house. But with John and me, it's different. I don't want to get married, nor do I need to buy a house, and I certainly don't want kids, even if that was biologically possible. An affair was a bad situation for Dawn, but it's a great one for me. What's more, if it doesn't work out, no divorce pains, no legal costs. Honestly Christopher, it's one of the best things that's ever happened to me and the situation is almost risk free. I like John, I enjoy being with him, but more than anything else, and I mean this way …

Mrs M lowered her voice to an audible but light whisper that was more air than speech.

"… it means I get an inside line of what's happening with you."

I laughed.

"You're a CHIS." I declared.

"What does that mean?" Mrs M asked.

I shook my head.

"It doesn't matter, it's a sort of police joke." I replied.

Chapter 21

A couple of weeks later, we had a minor breakthrough.

A letter arrived from Mrs M. It had of course been opened, read and stamped but everything was essentially still intact.

Mrs M explained that the reporter from London Tonight also wrote, under a pseudonym, for an online news entity called the Wellington News. It was, she said, the UK version of the Huffington Post, but as I'd never heard of that, the comparison was lost on me. The article was enclosed and had clearly been printed off a computer screen because the font was too small to read easily and some of the ink had faded making the words only legible with care and a squint. I read the article first.

Has the British Justice System just delivered its worse miscarriage of justice since the conviction of Timothy Evans?

There are growing concerns about last year's conviction of former senior police officer Christopher Pritchard for the murder of Eileen Armstrong back in 1982.

Pritchard, a 47-year-old Scotland Yard Detective Inspector with an unblemished career and awards for bravery, was convicted after a trial at the Old Bailey which only lasted three weeks.

The evidence against him was threefold. First, DNA matching Pritchard's was found at the scene. The matching sample was taken from the victim's vagina. Secondly, at the time of the crime, eyewitnesses created a photofit which bore a striking resemblance to the then young Pritchard. Thirdly, the Metropolitan Police Deputy Commissioner, Kitty Young, gave evidence that in 1997 Pritchard had admitted to her that he had murdered an old lady.

On the surface, the evidence appears overwhelming. What has changed to persuade the Wellington News that the conviction was not safe?

Two essential parts of the case against Pritchard have now been eliminated.

The Wellington News has seen scientific evidence disproving that Pritchard could have been the person the eyewitnesses drew in their photofit because only weeks before and in a school photograph, Pritchard had short hair. The photofit was of a man with shoulder length hair. "It is impossible to grow hair that quickly" says a leading academic in the biology of human hair.

The Washington Post has learnt that the trial Judge was so concerned with the evidence given by the Deputy Commissioner, that he demanded an investigation commence into whether the senior officer committed perjury. Perjury is the offence of lying under oath and can attract a seven-year prison sentence. A second pillar has fallen.

All that remains is the DNA evidence. DNA evidence that sat for twenty-eight years, goodness knows where and under what conditions, perhaps in some long-forgotten cupboard; all the time decaying and possibly corrupting.

Most of the witnesses in the case had died. All those that remained admitted in court that the passage of time had deteriorated their memories.

Pritchard received a sentence of life, with a minimum tariff of twenty-two years. He will be an old man when he is released.

The Wellington News had doubts about the safety of the conviction but apparently the criminal justice system has none because they have just turned down his leave to appeal. Remember Timothy Evans and ask yourself, will we ever learn?

I didn't know my leave to appeal had been turned down so that was a kick in the teeth, but the article was brilliant, so I had mixed emotions after reading it. I read it again; then I read the letter from Mrs M which was really short. She was obviously keen to get the article to me as soon as possible, but she also acknowledged that the appeal decision was a 'minor setback'.

I had to be honest with myself. There was one 'pillar' of evidence against me that the Wellington News had ignored. I know it was only circumstantial, but if I was assessing the case, I'd find it hard to ignore the fact that the defendant, me, resided only ten miles from the crime and had never denied knowing and frequenting the location where the offence took place. Painful though it was, if I were independently deciding this case, that would be compelling.

I suddenly felt really down. Even with the photofit and Kitty's evidence discounted, I still thought there was enough to convict me. There was no way out of here for me. I knew that deep down, that's why I was still suffering from the most horrendous and permanent anxiety.

I sat on the bed and put my head in my hands.

I was so used to it that I hadn't even heard the wicket drop down. I heard the key in my cell door and a guard walked in. It was Chloe Nuffield, a white prison officer, in her late thirties. Like all the female staff in any prison, her attractiveness to male prisoners was completely exaggerated. It was only natural, and I'd noticed that some of the female officers played up to it, by wearing lots of make-up and doing their hair really nicely. Chloe wasn't one of those. She wore only a touch of make-up and kept her long blonde hair neat and functional rather than attractive.

She came and sat down next to me on my bed.

"You alright, Christopher? You look so down." She asked.

I handed her the news article and she read it slowly.

"No appeal then?"

I shook my head.

"Sorry. It must be very hard."

I nodded and laughed.

"You seem to have settled in well here. It's a bit quieter than Waterloo, isn't it? I did some detached duty there a couple of years ago. Didn't like it much but the extra money was great."

"Where did you stay?" I asked.

"In a B&B in Putney."

"I know Putney well."

"How do you think you're getting on here?" Chloe asked.

"Well, no one's jugged me yet, which is a bonus. Will I spend the next twenty-two years in the Seg?"
I asked.

"That's up to you, but I would suggest you do, at least until you get to a Cat C trainer. Then you might be able to go on the VP Wing."

I nodded. I was ambivalent. In the Seg I felt safer. It also meant I didn't have to do any work so I could read for hours on end. I had learnt to sleep for up to twelve hours a day. This was great because it meant I could dream and escape my confinement. But obviously my standard of life was about as low as it could get because to all intents and purposes, I was a caged animal in a zoo.

"Are you married? You don't wear a ring?" I asked.

Chloe smiled.

"Sorry, Chris, I don't discuss my private life at work. We're not allowed to."

I nodded.

"Fair enough." I said.

"I was just interested. Believe it or not, I used to be quite a people person. Now ..."

I let the sentence hang.

"It must be hard." Chloe said, after a few moments.

"No idea." I replied, quietly.

"But you must think we're all guilty, anyway. So, we're just getting what we deserve. And if I'd raped and murdered the old lady, like they say I did, I'd deserve to be here."

"You are different, Chris. Over the last fifteen years, I've worked with lots of prisoners who were ex-coppers and more than a few ex-prison officers. We get politicians, the occasional bent lawyer. We even had an ex-judge in here when I first arrived. We had a famous footballer, the one that played for Leeds who killed that young girl when he was three times over the limit. He got seven years, I think. Yes, we've had them all."

"In what way am I different? Surely, it was just the same for all the people you've just talked about?"

"Honestly?"

"Of course." I replied.

"I don't think any of them tried to argue they were innocent. It's a bit of a fallacy that prisoners always do that. They don't. Some are proud of their crime, it gives them credibility and status. Like the big money launderers, or those in for fifty kilos of class A, even the odd armed blagger is proud that he had the balls to go across the pavement, is that what they call it?"

I nodded.

"Then others, the nonces, they keep very quiet about what they've done but they don't deny it. No, you're not unique, but you are a bit different. My colleagues know it. You're always very polite and they appreciate that, mainly because they don't think you have an ulterior motive. The only surprise is that at your last jail you were caught with a shank, which seems completely out of character."

I wanted to say, 'it wasn't mine' but I thought that might undermine my credibility.

"I've been told that unless I admit my offence, I won't make any progress rehabilitation wise, and therefore I won't get to a nice, quiet Cat D somewhere – nor will I ever get parole. Is that right, Chloe?"

"Yes, I'm afraid it is. I'd forget about a Cat D anyway; you only go to those a couple of years before you're due for release. No, whoever told you that was essentially right. You need to admit what you've done, or you will lessen your opportunities and chances in here."

Chloe turned to look me square in the face.

"Oh, you poor thing, you look so desperate."

She leaned towards me and put her arm around me. I hadn't expected that and felt my whole body going tense. She squeezed me briefly, like a mother would a child before their first day at school and let go. Just for a second, I smelt her. Not her perfume, I don't think she was wearing any, but her. I hadn't been that close to a woman in years and I suddenly felt a rush of sexual arousal. I couldn't help it, but I started to get an erection which was clearly visible in my prison issue grey tracksuit trousers.

I think Chloe sensed my unease and stood up.

"Thank you." I said, referring to her kindness and sympathy.

I looked up but she wasn't looking back into my eyes but about two feet lower.

***

It was a long time since I'd just got an erection. When I was fourteen, it used to happen all the time, on the bus, during a swimming lesson, watching TV, walking the dog, eating dinner, but as the years rolled by, a spontaneous erection became extremely rare.

When I turned the sequence of events over in my mind, it didn't need a genius to work out why it had happened. I wasn't especially drawn to

Chloe, but she wasn't unattractive and when she put her arm around me, my subconscious obviously interpreted the gesture as an intimate act. The thing that triggered my very visible response, however, was the smell, her odour. It was extremely evocative.

Let me make it clear, I didn't think for one second Chloe was being in any way provocative. She was just being nice. I didn't misinterpret her gesture as anything other than what it was, a show of sympathy and a touch of support. I was embarrassed about what had happened, but I wasn't going to attempt to apologise or even mention it again. As my Mum used to say, *'least said, soonest mended.'* I guessed I wouldn't be getting another friendly hug off Officer Chloe any day soon, which was a shame because it was really comforting.

I didn't see Chloe for a couple of days. She must have been on leave, or perhaps she was working on another wing, but when I did, I was pleasantly surprised that our short interaction, which was about whether I required a medical appointment that week, was without awkwardness.

I was still taking medication for my anxiety which was absolutely crippling on some days, but fortunately, less so on others.

Only a few minutes after Chloe had walked off, my door was unlocked again but this time by a male officer I didn't recognise. I looked up.

"Sorry, mate, should have told you yesterday but for some reason no one appears to have mentioned it. You've got a visit at two today. You'll be taken down about one-thirty."

"Is it a Mrs Jenny Matthews?" I asked, already knowing the answer.

"No, I don't think so. Sorry, the list's in the office. Oh well, it'll be a nice surprise, wont it?" He replied.

His attitude was a bit annoying. I did want to know who it was so that, if it was someone I didn't want to see, I could decline. But it was no good asking him to check because he'd say yes, and then not bother. I knew how things worked in here. With that said, he'd almost certainly got it wrong, and it would in fact be Mrs M after all.

Going to and from visits is not a pleasant experience. Firstly, being out of my cell had become something of a mental health issue for me because I feared being jugged or stabbed. Secondly, because there was a justified assumption amongst staff that every visitor was going to traffic contraband to every prisoner. As a consequence, there were no end of searches and other security measures to endure. Thirdly, everything happened so painfully slowly. From leaving your cell to sitting opposite your visitor should only take about ten minutes, but it could take anything from forty-five minutes to an hour, which is really frustrating when you're as stressed as I am outside the safety and protection of my pad in the Seg.

The final part of the process involved being given a table number on a little card and then sitting in a large soulless room until you're called out to enter the Visits Hall.

I was the very last of all forty prisoners to be called out. I had almost given up, thinking the whole thing had been an administrative fuck up.

"Pritchard, table forty."

I looked at my card to check the number which was a ridiculous thing to do because I'd been staring at it intermittently for the last thirty minutes.

I walked into the Visits Hall. A large, single open space with about sixty small round tables, around which were set usually about four chairs, all hideously orange in colour. To one end of the room, set behind a small white picket fence, was a childrens play area with toys, a Wendy house and coloured murals painted on the wall. In the wall opposite the play area was a serving hatch and many prisoners were queuing to purchase hot drinks and snacks for their loved ones.

I had no idea where table forty was, so I just looked for any visitors still obviously on their own. My eyes came to settle on the table furthest away from where I'd come in. Sitting with her back to me was a lone female with long black hair. Surely, it couldn't be?

Chapter 22

Wendy was the true love of my life. I'd had an affair with her for four years and, when my marriage crashed and burned, I'd moved in with her for about six months but then she'd left me for her best friend's brother because she wanted to have children. I'd had the snip and made it abundantly clear I didn't want any more kids. Since we'd parted, we bumped into each other once or twice at the Yard, but we'd never said more than a polite 'hello'. I occasionally heard from friends about what she was up to and what was happening in her life, and yes, for several years I did, usually after a few large scotches, check out her Facebook page.

Over the last year however, I'd started to get over her and to move on. It had been a long time coming but when it did, the freedom of at last falling out of love, was really very refreshing.

The thing was, and terribly sad and desperate as it may sound, Wendy was the last person I'd slept with. When Wendy and I had split up, I was in my early forties, I'd put on some weight, lost some hair and got completely out of the habit of either dating or chatting women up. A few years later, I had a disastrous blind date with a friend of a friend, who ended up stalking me. It wasn't that I wasn't interested in having sex again or indeed having a serious relationship, it was just that neither happened.

As I approached my visitor, I checked the number on the table to make sure I wasn't making a mistake. No, this was table forty and now I was only a few yards behind her, I knew for certain I was looking at my old girlfriend.

"Hello stranger. What the fuck are you doing here?" I said, as I swept past her and sat down.

"Hello, Chris." She said, without getting up.

Unlike all the other women in the room, Wendy looked really classy. She was wearing a black and white check suit and although the skirt rode above her knees, she was wearing discreet thick black tights and smart leopard print shoes with kitten heels. Wendy was now in her mid-to late thirties, tall, nearly six foot, with the longest hair of the deepest black and an olive, Mediterranean skin tone. I can honestly say, I'd never seen a more attractive woman anywhere or anytime in my life than at that precise moment.

I started to shake, so I clasped my hands tightly together on my lap.

We sat for a few moments not saying a word; I, for one, was too overwhelmed with emotion to speak. Just when it was beginning to get awkward, I muttered four words that were barely audible.

"Why are you here?"

Wendy looked down at the table, to such an extent that I couldn't see her face, but she didn't reply. She started to rock gently forward and backward. I looked around self-consciously to see whether anyone else was looking at this rather bizarre scene, but no one was taking a blind bit of notice.

Then I noticed tears were falling on the table. Wendy was crying.

Wendy stayed like that for several minutes. I really didn't know what to do. Then, after what felt like an hour, she put her head back and looked me straight in the face. Her face was a mess of mascara trails, but her eyes sparkled. They were the most beautiful eyes I'd ever seen. In that second, I knew a part of me would always be in love with her.

"I had to see you." She said.

"Does the Job know you're here?" I asked.

She nodded.

Serving police officers don't usually make social visits to prisoners convicted of murder and rape but from her reply, it was clear Wendy had obtained the appropriate authorities.

"Everyone who knows you, knows you're innocent, my darling." She said.

Her statement hit me like a train. I breathed out heavily. What she said next was even more amazing.

"I love you, Chris. Utterly and completely. I always have, from the first time I saw you at Chigwell police club, up to and including this very second."

"But you left me." I said.

"I had to have children, Chris. You knew that. But I never stopped loving you."

I smiled.

"You used to ignore me; well, practically ignore me whenever we met. That used to kill me."

"I had to, Chris. If I'd have done anything else, in no time at all, we'd have arranged to meet up, all the feelings would have been released and before we'd have realised, we'd have been back in a relationship. I couldn't let that happen. Not when I had such a young family. I had to put them, my child, my children, before myself and before you."

"I do understand." I said.

"I know you do. You always understood. That's one of the reasons I loved you so much. You even understood over the Matthew …"

Wendy paused briefly while she found the right word.

" … incident. You were a star. You are a star. And now you're here …"

She looked around the visit's hall.

" … and it's all so very wrong, my darling. I just had to come and see you. I had to tell you I love you. I had to tell you that I know you're innocent."

"Christ, you are last the last person I thought would come and visit me, Wendy. I couldn't believe it when I saw you. I'm still shaking."

I held my right hand out. Typically, it remained completely still.

"I had to come. I couldn't sleep. I've started to suffer from, like stress. I've had to see a counsellor. It's like, I feel responsible for what's happened to you. I mean, I know I'm not, but somewhere deep inside, I feel so guilty."

I laughed but kindly.

"This is nothing to do with you. Christ, the offence happened in 1982. You weren't even born!"

"I was." She replied.

"But this is nothing to do with you, is it. Why, how can you be feeling guilty?"

"I don't know. I don't understand it either. My counsellor says it's something called 'Guilt Transference Syndrome' or something like that."

"Did your counsellor tell you to come and see me?"

"No, not at all."

"Are you seeking some form of absolution?" I asked.

"No, Chris. It's not like that. I just had to come and see you."

"Does your husband know you're here?"

She shook her head.

"Why didn't you tell him?"

"He's a bit insecure. He's been divorced before, his first wife went off with an old boyfriend she met on Friends Reunited. She said he was too boring to spend the rest of her life with. He spends his life worrying about me leaving him. I don't need to add to his stress by telling him I'm seeing an ex-boyfriend."

"Even if that ex is serving life imprisonment?" I asked, sarcastically.

"Even then." She replied.

The conversation stopped naturally and we both sat in silence once again.

"Do you still love me?" Wendy asked.

"I did. Well, I thought I did, until about a year ago when it felt like, at last, I was moving on."

"Is there anyone else?" She asked.

"No"

I hesitated. I wanted to expand my answer and tell her there hadn't been anyone else since she dumped me, but that sounded way too desperate. Damn it, what did I have to lose?

"You're the last person I slept with. You're the last woman I've been out with. I haven't even kissed another woman. And now ..."

I looked around, tragically.

"That may remain the case until I die. Well, if I stay incarcerated, I really hope it does!"

Wendy laughed.

"I never realised there wasn't anyone else. Did you never get together with that Julie? Your partner on the murder squad."

"No, she was in a relationship with a guy from the Flying Squad, she married him. There was never anything between us."

"I used to hate it when you two went OMPD overnight. I was convinced you were shagging."

"We never were." I replied.

"I have to confess I've sort of followed your life, you know, asked mutual friends what you've been up to. I knew you were living on a boat for a few years, then I heard you'd moved to Buckhurst Hill and someone said you were living with Dawn's mum. Then I heard you might be going to Australia."

"That was Jackie, not me." I interjected.

"I know. I nearly went into meltdown when I heard but then someone else told me it was wifey and the girls and not you. I was so relieved."

She paused.

I'm sorry, Chris. I'm sorry for everything."

"You don't have to be sorry for anything. When you left me so that you could have a baby, you did absolutely the right thing. We would never have been happy together in the long run because of the baby thing." I replied.

"Okay. I need to ask you something." Wendy said.

She took a deep breath and looked me straight in the eye. I realised Wendy was about to reveal the real reason for her visit.

"And just so you know, I have rehearsed this a thousand times, so here goes. If you ever get out of here, if your appeal is successful …"

I decided not to tell her at that precise moment that my leave to appeal had been declined.

" … I'd love to spend the rest of my life with you. Of course, you'll have to have the kids as well, I am a package, not an individual. I've completely realised that you are the one for me. You are my soulmate. Everyone has one person, and for me you are that person. I don't expect an answer, but I want you to know, if you get out of this hell hole, and if it is what your heart wants, we can spend the rest of our lives together."

"But what about putting your family first?" I asked, incredulously.

"I still will, but you coming to prison like this, really made me realise how I feel about you. I'm living a lie; I'm pretending I'm happy but I'm not and only you can change that."

I went to speak but Wendy interrupted me.

"Don't ask me about my husband, I'll deal with that. I'll hate myself for doing it but I will end our relationship so we can be together."

"If I don't get out, or if I say *'no, I don't want to be with you'*, will you still end your marriage?" I asked.

Wendy was clearly thinking. I guessed from the time it took her, she hadn't even considered that variant."

"I don't know. Honestly? Probably, oh I don't know." She replied.

"Do you not love him?" I asked.

She shook her head.

"Have you ever loved him?" I asked.

"Yes, but not anything like I loved you. And besides, when I did love him, it was just my hormones desperately wanting a baby. He's a nice guy, he is, but he's boring. He doesn't like socialising, or going out, or holidaying abroad; my god, the man doesn't even drink."

I laughed.

"Gosh" I replied.

"Don't ask me any details of my plan, there are none. Just know that if you ever get out and you want to spend the rest of your life with me, you can. I will make it happen, whatever it takes."

Chapter 23

To say I was absolutely and totally blown away is an understatement. I was in shock and walked back to my pad in a daze. In fact, I had to ask myself on more than one occasion, if that had actually just happened or whether I was dreaming.

After we'd split up, Wendy had gone off to start a new life with a new man and have a family. I never thought I'd ever crossed her thoughts again. I was, I assumed, just a distant memory that would be jogged by the occasional event, but who, other than that, would be largely forgotten. With that said, I do remember one conversation I had with Wendy, in the early days of our relationship. She told me once and can even remember where we were both standing in her house at the time, that one day she would have to leave me to have children with somebody else, but that, when she did, I shouldn't worry because after a few years, she would come back to me.

Later that day, I was lying on my bed, turning and dissecting every word we had said during the visit, when my door was unlocked and Chloe, my now favourite guard, came in. She must have been on a late because that was the first time I'd seen her that day.

"How are you doing today, Chris?" She asked.

"I'm okay, had a rather surprising visitor today." I replied.

"I heard. Some Amazon Greek goddess, my sources tell me."

"Your sources are good, Miss. She is Greek, well half-Greek, to be exact."

"Very hairy, though. Greek women, very hairy."

I laughed.

"There's something different about you today." I observed, with more of a statement than a question.

"I don't think so." She replied.

"I went online yesterday when I got home and read all about your case. There's loads on there about this being a massive miscarriage of justice. And who's that woman? Jenny something, is that your mum?"

"That's Jenny Matthews, she's a friend. I used to live with her."

"Not the Greek goddess?"

"No, hang on. The Greek girl, Wendy, she was my girlfriend and Jenny Matthews is a family friend who I moved in with when I got divorced."

I know it wasn't exactly accurate, but it was the simplest way to explain it.

"Oh, I see. But the DNA evidence? You're screwed. Can you explain that?"

I shook my head.

"All I know is that I didn't do it." I replied.

"Is it possible you did it, you know, and have blocked all memories of it out of your mind? A few years ago, I had a really bad accident on the M40. I was in a coma for about ten days and the passenger in the car with me, another prison officer, died. I don't remember anything about that accident. I don't even remember anything about that day. My mind has completely erased it. Is it possible that's happened to you?"

"I didn't do it. There's no way I would rape and murder an eighty-two-year-old woman, I was only seventeen. If I did, which I didn't, I would most certainly remember. I did not rape and murder that poor old lady, which means, not only am I wrongfully in prison, but the bastard also that did it, is still out there."

"He's probably dead by now." She pointed out.

I immediately realised the significance of that comment; it, well, sort of, meant she believed me. That was nice.

"Do you see why I can't admit to the offence just so I can improve my situation in here?"

She nodded. She'd been standing by the door up until that point in the conversation, but she then came over and sat next to me. I immediately smelt a subtle hint of perfume. I also started to feel sexually aroused, which was completely ridiculous, but prison does something very strange to a man. There was nothing in her manner to suggest this was anything other than a casual conversation between a prison officer and one of her prisoners. I exhaled slowly in an attempt to get the situation into perspective.

"Yes, you're in a pickle, Mr Pritchard. Let's hope your friends on the outside can convince the system that you're innocent."

"What about you? What do you honestly think? Don't worry about offending me, just tell me what you think."

She rubbed both her hands along the tops of her legs. I recognised the avoidance gesture.

"Don't worry, you don't have to answer that."

"The problem is, if I tell you I think you've been wrongly convicted then where does that leave me and my colleagues? I mean, we lock you up twenty-four hours a day, we deprive you of your liberty, we tell you when to eat, sleep and shit. If you know that I know, if you follow me, that you've been wrongly convicted, then where does that leave our authority?"

"Oh, fair enough. I get it, I understand." I replied.

"I am conscious that in the six months you've been in prison, you've spent just about every day in a Seg. That's not healthy, Chris."

"It's better than having boiling water and sugar poured over your head." I replied.

I had a rush of anxiety as I thought she might be about to tell me I had to go back onto a normal wing.

"I know, I do. But if you stay locked in a cell for the next however many years, even if you do get out, you won't be able to cope with people and the world. I just want you to think about that."

"Thanks, Miss." I said, with a rye, cheeky smile.

Chloe stood up.

"Anything else I can get you?" She asked.

"Books, all books, any books, books, please, Miss." I said.

"I'll see what I can do."

She walked to the door but as she got there, she turned round abruptly and caught me staring at her arse.

"Oh. About the hairy Greek girl …

I frowned.

" … unlike her, below my eyebrows, there's not a hair on my body. Not anywhere, Chris."

She winked, almost comically.

She slammed my cell door shut behind her.

In my whole life I had never been more sexually aroused.

Chapter 24

Chloe had read all the information about my case and possibly, although she wouldn't admit as much to me for professional reasons, come to the conclusion that I was in fact innocent. As a result, Chloe's attitude towards me had shifted which allowed her, perhaps even subconsciously, to drop her guard a bit.

I knew her comment about being hairless was just a bit of banter, but it really did something to me. Sad and desperate though it sounds. Only the previous week I'd got turned on when she put her arm around me. Her latest comment was enough to stir every last ounce of testosterone in my body. I really needed to get a grip.

Then I had the Wendy situation to mull over. While I was kind of delighted, I did realise it was all a bit meaningless unless I did in fact get out. It was now six months since my conviction and the primary avenue to justice, the Court of Appeal, had refused to give my lawyers the requisite authority to initiate the process. I'd always assumed that anyone could appeal either sentence or conviction, or both. Now I'd learnt that you had to have grounds to appeal, and the list of potential grounds was quite specific and really limited. You had, for example, to prove the legal process had been correctly followed. We had appealed the decision not to allow me to appeal and were still awaiting a result. My lawyer explained to me that cases involving life sentences were at the back of the queue because they had to deal with shorter sentences first, lest a wrongly convicted defendant ends up completing their six-month sentence before the Court of Appeal had time to find them innocent.

Anyway, back to the Wendy dilemma. Assuming for a second I did get out, did I want to start over again with Wendy and somebody else's two young sons? I had in fact started to get over her and now I felt like I was being thrown back in at the deep end. Did I still love her? Yes. Would I be saying that if she hadn't, only yesterday, been sitting in front of me looking absolutely gorgeous? Probably not. Was I even capable of thinking straight while locked up inside a jail? Definitely not. It was nice to know that she had still been thinking about me for all these years. That did make me feel better.

I mulled these various matters over for hours. It made a nice change to have something to think about. For once, I didn't pick up a book and escape. Before I realised, it was getting dark. I walked over to my window, which was not made of glass but rather thick clear plastic. The window was immediately above the two heating pipes that ran along the outside wall and, as a result, on cold winter days, the plastic was covered with a thick layer of condensation. I wiped the condensation away with the back of my hand and looked out. I couldn't see much. Eighty percent of my view was taken up with the inner brick wall but above that I could just make out a clear sky of the deepest blue. I felt a sudden alignment. In that dark hue, the universe and my life had come together in synergy.

I cupped my face to block out the light from the cell and let my eyes adjust to the darkness. After a few minutes, I could make out a few stars. They were the first stars I had seen since my incarceration and I was momentarily fascinated. For the first time I realised that all the people I knew were somewhere under those stars, that life in the real world was still going on with an abject disregard for what had happened to me. I felt very small and unimportant but for a few moments that somehow didn't matter. In fact, there was some solace in such insignificance.

Chapter 25

Two months later

Every day in prison, whether you're on a standard wing, a vulnerable prisoners wing or in the Seg, is the same as the last.

By the way, the full title for the Seg is the Segregation Unit. In the old days, this would have been called the punishment block and its primary purpose was to be a prison within a prison. It was where prisoners were sent for punishment because, while there, you were kept in your cell twenty-three and a half hours a day, only being let out to shower and walk around the exercise yard. I was originally sent to the Seg in HMP Waterloo when they found the shank (a homemade knife) in my pad, but I'd been kept in the Seg because I was an ex-police officer and quite simply it was the saftest place for me to be.

The only thing that slightly disturbs the routine, are those days on which you have visitors, and they are few and far between. There are two types of visits, social, where your friends and family come to see you; and legal, which as you'd expect from the title, is when your solicitor or another representative from your legal team pay you a visit. After your conviction and appeal are over legal visits might not occur from one year to the next.

Sometimes a prisoner might get a legal visit from the police. For one of two reasons, these are greatly feared. First, the police might want to discuss your old crimes, those you thought you'd got away with; and secondly, they might be trying to get information out of you about illegal activity of your associates. In other words, trying to *'turn'* you. While the former, the unsolved crimes visit, was unwelcome, you really feared the latter because, even if you remained completely uncooperative, you may be accused of grassing up your mates. This would put you in a very dangerous position and possibly next in line for a jugging.

My day in the Seg started when the staff on earlies replaced those on nights. This was just before seven in the morning. I would put my television on and snooze for an hour, listening to the BBC Breakfast Show quietly in the background, and try to drop off again. My plan rarely worked because over the next hour or two, the Seg cleaners, other prisoners, would start clanging and crashing about doing their work. They would chat and shout to one another with breaking news and I'd end up trying to listen to what they were saying for some morsel of exciting gossip.

At eight I'd have my breakfast, which had been delivered the evening before, along with my dinner. Breakfast was always the same; a small packet of cereal, usually cornflakes, a pint of long-life milk in a carton, an apple and two pieces of bread with never enough butter and jam, which came in tiny pots. Oh, and two teabags. I was lucky because I was in the Seg for my own protection, I was allowed a kettle.

Another advantage of being in the Seg for your own protection, as opposed to a punishment, was that they didn't come around in the morning and take out your mattress, which they did to everyone else.

After my breakfast, I would tidy my pad. I know that sounds a bit weird, but when you live in a space only 8' by 4'6", and you have quite a lot of stuff, it gets really cluttered, really quickly.

At some stage between nine and twelve, it varied greatly, I'd be taken out for a shower and offered twenty minutes exercise on my own in the Seg outside cage. As I never knew when this was going to happen, I would get myself ready, with towel and toiletries, and listen to Radio Two, often failing abysmally at Pop Master but nonetheless keeping a score every day and trying to beat my best.

When I returned to my pad after shower and exercise, the orderlies, prisoners who are trusted with small menial tasks, would have been in my cell and left my lunch, which was just a sandwich and a packet of crisps. Perhaps twice a week, they would also have left my post. Like buses, this never came one letter at a time, but in batches. I hated the fact that this system gave other prisoners an opportunity to read my personal correspondence before I did, but what could I do about it?

I would normally keep my sandwich and have it much later in the evening.

At twelve I would read for an hour and then listen to Radio 4's World at One. I did this religiously and then followed that with the Archers and whatever was on until Play for the Day at three.

At four, I did an hour's hard exercise. Never easy in a tiny cell but still possible. I stretched every muscle I had; waved my arms about like those blonde girls in the films you used to watch at school on the Hitler Youth; did star jumps; sit-ups; core strengthening leg raises and press ups. At the end, I was sweaty, breathing hard and always ready for another shower. Of course, I'd already had my one shower for the day, so it didn't matter, I was hardly meeting anyone.

From four, I read until dinner was delivered, usually about five. I ate the dinner, usually pretty dire, a pie and cold chips or someone's attempt at a curry.

I then read again, unless I had any letters to write and then at about eight, I watched the TV until I went to sleep about midnight.

That was my day, every day, until I died or got released. It was monotonous, boring, tiresome and uninspiring. Nothing of any importance, excitement or interest ever happened. That was why the most trivial thing, like for example, a new female guard appearing for a tour of duty, could generate such a ridiculously high level of excitement. It was why 'he said, she said' events became something people lost their lives over. I kept my mouth shut, always, and kept my head lower than a burrowing mole.

I had realised however, that if I lived in prison like this for any more than a few years, I'd never mentally recover enough to have anything like a normal life in the outside world. My head would be too firmly rewired to cope with an existence outside.

Before I went to prison, I used to listen to uninformed people rant about how easy prisoners had it. How they got a nice, warm cell and a comfortable bed, and three healthy meals a day. And how this was all free, and they didn't have to pay council tax. About how they got a colour TV for which they didn't have to pay a licence. Even how some of them had a computer games console. If you listened to these ill-informed people, you might nod and agree. After all, everything they say is fundamentally true.

Here's what they don't tell you. Unless you are the hardest man in the prison, you will live forever in fear. Unless you lock yourself in your cell, you will be threatened, intimidated and assaulted every day of your life. You will be forced into making your friends and relatives traffic drugs to you during visits. If they do not, you will be beaten. Not just a TV Western style few punches, but broken limbs, fractured ribs, teeth knocked out and head stamped on. Everything you possess of any value will be stolen, well just taken, from you. Your cell will be tiny, and you will often have to share it with another prisoner. He will probably not be very nice. You will defecate and urine only a few yards from one another. Even on the best regime, where you are meaningfully employed in a prison-based job, you will be locked in your cell for at least fourteen hours Monday through Thursday. On Friday, Saturday and Sunday, you can count the hours out of your cell on these three days on just two hands. By the way, that prison-based job will pay you about £5 a day.

Access to the gym, if you are lucky, will be for two hours a week.

You will never be allowed to smoke tobacco or to drink alcohol, but you will be offered illegal drugs every day of your life; you will be tempted to take them – if only to escape the monotony of your existence.

No one in authority will listen to you or care about you. How can they? There are so few of them. Why should they? You are a criminal and will forever be regarded as such. No one will show you respect, not ever. If you are seriously ill, it will take probably months to get any meaningful medical intervention.

When you have a visit from a friend or family member, you will feel more shame and degradation than you thought possible.

You will be overwhelmed by the despair of your situation. I have known young men tragically take their own lives even when they had received comparatively short sentences. That demonstrates just how tough jail time is. You will consider suicide often and in great detail. So much so that you will find yourself fantasizing about the end that death would bring to your torment.

The only true escape you will have is your memories, dreams and imaginings. Of these three, the dreams are the best because they can truly take you away on adventures to unexplored places. But eventually, they will start to become based on your life in the prison. At that point, many inmates crack.

Finally, you will suffer mental illness. Doesn't matter how tough and resilient you think you are, you won't be strong enough.

So next time someone in your local starts spouting off about how easy life is in prison, turn your back on them and walk away.

Chapter 26

As the weeks rolled by, it became clear that I wasn't going to get out. My appeal for leave to appeal failed. My lawyers told me the DNA evidence was just too powerful. They also thought the criminal justice system was worried that, should I get my conviction overturned, it would irrevocably undermine the thousands of genuine DNA based convictions. Such an outcome, they calculated, would throw the whole system into turmoil. It appeared, they opined, I was to be sacrificed for a bigger cause. Stupidly unjust as this was, as a former police officer, I sort of understood, but my comprehension didn't make me happy about it. This was my life and I only got the one chance at it. The only sense I could make of the whole thing was that I was actually being punished for the Barry Skinner murder. In that sense, there was a kind of justice being delivered. I had murdered a man in cold blood and now I was paying my dues.

I was still suffering from the most acute anxiety, but I had learned to live with it. When it kicked in, and that was almost every day for at least an hour, I would say to myself, *'okay, you know what this is, just let it be'*. I had steadfastly refused to increase my medication and remained on the lowest prescribed dosage of tranquilliser. I thought I was slowly winning that battle.

Mrs M worked tirelessly to prove my innocence but there were few options left. The private investigators completed their work, but the offence was so old, there really was little they could do. Establishing that the photofit evidence was unreliable had been their greatest achievement but it just wasn't enough. After two months, they closed their enquiries. When they presented Mrs M with their bill, it became evident they had given their time *pro gratis* and only charged for their actual out of pocket expenses. I wrote to them to express my gratitude, saying that although it was a somewhat empty gesture, given the circumstances, I owed them a favour.

I wish I could say the same about my legal team, but you know what they say a duck and a swan regularly do, a solicitor never does? Although some of their charges were covered by legal aid, they still presented Mrs M with an invoice for fifteen thousand pounds. That reminded me, I'd had several messages that morning that they wanted me to book a legal visit for them.

I am pleased to report however, that Mrs M managed to find the money without selling her house.

As time passed, Wendy must have known that I wasn't going to be released, but to my surprise she told her husband that she didn't love him and wanted a divorce. I felt sorry for him, I really did. I knew what it was like to dumped by Wendy, who kept visiting despite the vanishing hope that we would one day be back together.

When you're a convicted prisoner you are allowed one two-hour visit every four weeks. It's not a lot and it also means you have to choose who you really want to see, which is difficult, because you don't want to upset anyone.

During my first year, Mrs M, Wendy and Jackie came to see me. Jackie only came the once because she was living in Australia. She wanted to bring the girls, but I firmly declined. My beautiful daughters were not stepping foot in a place like this, even if it meant we would never see each other again. Usually, Wendy and Mrs M came on alternate months, which was fine.

When you're serving a life sentence for an horrendous crime, you certainly find out who your true friends are – they are the ones that keep in touch. It's hard to explain the delight in receiving a letter, especially when the writer tells you that they don't believe for a second you did the terrible crime. Sergeant Bellamy wrote every couple of months, as did

Dave Walby, the guy who came to Thailand to save me all those years ago. Julie wrote a couple of times with news, gossip and scandal from my old murder squad team. Brucie, the guy I'd worked with on the Marcella Parker case, was also a regular correspondent. Although I'd only known him a couple of years, we'd become really good friends.

My daughters, Pippa and Trudy, were complete stars and wrote every week, which was lovely.

Whenever I received a letter, I wrote back within a day. In a year, I never failed to do so, not once.

I was due to move cells today. They did that occasionally. It didn't bother me, as long as they kept me in the Seg. I think the concept behind the regular moves was to make sure we weren't all busy tunnelling our way to freedom like the guy in the Shawshank Redemption.

Not only was I moving, but I also had a visit from Mrs M in the afternoon. In my routine life, days rarely got as exciting as this one. Even my anxiety had temporarily rescinded, which was such a relief.

I lay on my bed listening to several of my fellow prisoners move cells and anticipating my turn, when I heard a slight commotion and anticipated that an unplanned event was occurring. It was strange in prison in some respects your senses became hypersensitive and could detect the slightest change from the normal atmosphere.

Then I heard several prisoners saying 'number one' and I guessed the Governing Governor was on the Seg. This was a rare, but not unheard of, occurrence.

In any prison there are three types of staff; the ancillary, the uniformed and the suits. The ancillary were those not employed by the Prison Service, such as the doctors and nurses and the maintenance guys. The uniformed officers were either prison officers, who dealt with prisoners, or Operational Support Grades (OSGs), who manned the gate and conducted searches. The suits were all Governors but there were various grades of Governor, the most senior was called 'the Number One Governor' or the 'Governing Governor', both terms being interchangeable.

The Governing Governor was in charge of everybody - in a prison, they were god.

I had never met or even seen the Governing Governor at HMP Bankside, although I did know his name was Max Hastings, which always for obvious reasons, made me think of the military historian. I occasionally overheard the uniformed staff discussing him and their views differed widely, but from their conversation I knew two key facts; he was old school and seriously feared.

I guessed he was undertaking a spot inspection. As such, I anticipated the Governing Governor would probably speak on a one-to-one basis to each of us to ascertain whether we were being treated fairly, what the food was like and other things about our welfare. As my current cell was located right at the end of the bottom lower wing, I figured I'd either be the first or last prisoner he'd speak to. I waited in anticipation. What an exciting day this was turning out to be!

I was apparently, to be the first. As I heard the cell door lock turn, I stood up and turned to face the door. One of the uniformed Seg staff, a nice young officer who went by the very old-fashioned name of Edward, entered first, quickly followed by a suited white male in his early sixties, with a distinguished and striking full head of grey hair.

"This is Christopher Pritchard." Edward said.

"Chris, this is Governor Hastings."

The Governing Governor put out his hand and I shook it – I hadn't done that for a long time. Perhaps he did this with all prisoners. It was a nice gesture, I liked it.

"Christopher, please sit down." The Governing Governor said, indicating that I should plant my arse on the side of the bed.

I did as I was told. It was only then I noticed he was holding a letter.

"Please listen carefully to what I am about to say. This is a letter from the Minister for Justice, the Right Honourable Susan Todd MP. The letter is addressed to me."

He looked down at the letter and read.

"I write to you in respect of the prisoner Mr Christopher Pritchard, who is currently in your charge at HMP Bankside. On 29th October 2010 at the Central Criminal Court Mr Pritchard was convicted of the murder and rape of Mrs Eileen Armstrong.

Evidence has recently come to light which casts the gravest doubts upon the safety of Mr Pritchard's conviction, and as a consequence I have referred the matter to the Lord Chief Justice Denis Spearman. In the interim, the Lord Chief Justice had ordered Mr Pritchard's immediate release on unconditional bail pending the requisite judiciary review.

Please inform Mr Pritchard of my decision and release him from your custody on his own recognizance.

Kindly advise my office when these actions have been undertaken.

Your sincerely

The Secretary of State for Justice".

I didn't know what to say or do, I just sat there, motionless.

"Mr Pritchard, would you like me to read the letter again?" The Governing Governor asked.

I didn't respond, so he did. He read the whole letter out, slower this time, pausing between sentences and looking at me to make sure I'd heard and understood him. As he finished, I started to shake, very gently at first, but then my shaking became quite uncontrollable. My mind was a complete blank. Not a single thought crossed the empty space between my ears.

"Get someone from Healthcare." The Governing Governor barked.

I closed my eyes and took slow, deliberate breaths. Gradually, I started to calm down.

"Are you alright?"

I nodded and opened my eyes.

The Governing Governor and Edward were standing by my bed, looking down at me.

"You are free to go. We need to do some paperwork and dig out your property, but you can start packing."

The Governing Governor looked around the cell.

"But apparently you're already packed." He said.

"I'm moving cells, today." I replied.

"Not anymore you're not." He replied.

The Governing Governor turned to Edward.

"Can you give us two minutes, please."

Edward nodded and left. Sensing something important was about to be said, I sat up.

The Governing Governor looked serious.

"I'm sorry for what you've been through." He said.

"That's not your fault." I replied.

"How have my staff treated you?" He asked.

"They've been fine, they really have. They're okay. I've got no complaints. I find that if I treat them with respect, they always treat me the same way." I replied, honestly.

"I need to ask you about one specific member of staff?"

I looked confused, well I tried to.

"Officer Chloe Nuffield?" He said.

"She's my personal officer. What about her?" I asked, frowning.

"We have intelligence that she's in an inappropriate relationship with you? Is that true?" He asked.

"I don't know." I replied.

"How can you not know?" He asked, incredulously.

"I'm not sighted on your intelligence, am I? I don't know what you've got." I replied.

"No, Christopher, you misunderstand me. Have you been having any kind of relationship with Chloe Nuffield?" He asked.

"No, not at all. She's friendly but we're not friends." I replied.

"And that's the truth? Now you're going, it's really important you tell me the truth." He asked.

"She's never said or done anything with or to me that wasn't fully and utterly professional." I replied, with complete conviction.

He nodded.

"Good" He said and walked out.

I exhaled long and hard. After the shock of being informed I was being released, the question about Chloe had come out of left field and caught me completely off guard. I'd held it together and done my best to protect the woman with whom I'd been having the most fantastic sex for the last six months. She was the one reason I hadn't taken my own life.

Chapter 27

I had to smile. When they left me alone to prepare for my imminent release, they still locked my cell door. I mean, by their own admission, I had done nothing wrong and was free to leave, but I suspected old habits die hard. Mind you, over the last year that locked door had protected me as much as confined me.

I had nothing to do because I was already packed in anticipation of the cell move. I put the television on and turned to BBC2 which, at this time of day, ran the BBC News channel. I waited eagerly to see whether there was anything about me but there wasn't.

Although I was perplexed as to what might have happened *'to cast the gravest doubts upon my conviction'*, I had two guesses.

The most likely was that they realised the DNA was not a match to mine. This had happened years ago with a police officer's fingerprint in a Scottish murder case. Eventually, and using their third forensics expert, the analysis came back as not identical. This is what I'd maintained all along, but when our own forensic scientist analysed the samples and agreed with the prosecution, I was somewhat fucked, to use an old police term.

The second possibility was an outside one – was there a chance that whoever had committed these offences had confessed? Thus, exonerating me?

I was also rather relieved that Chloe was off today. Should I try to get a message to her about what the Governing Governor had said to me? Or should I just let sleeping dogs lie? I decided on the latter. Whilst the sex had been great, mainly because I was so desperate but also because it was against every rule, I didn't think for a second that either of us had developed an emotional attachment.

For the first month, after her comment about not having any hair below her eyebrows, Chloe spent the next month, whenever we were alone together, flirting outrageously with me. She would say the most provocative things and stand too close. It was like she was doing everything she could simply to wind me up. For ages, I pretended not to notice. I didn't join in the banter nor did I give even the merest hint that I was getting aroused when she sat on my bed so close to me that I could feel the edge of her right breast just touching my upper right arm.

Eventually however, I cracked.

One day, as she was leaving my cell, having spent the last ten minutes telling me how the previous day she had visited an Anne Summers shop to try on some new knickers, having selected two, she was going to wear one to work next week. I jokingly asked her whether she said such things to all the prisoners.

"Oh, flirting's great. It's only a bit of fun. But no, Christopher, I only flirt with people I fancy."

Her use of the word 'people' rather than 'prisoners' was interesting.

"You see, I'm wired a particular way."

"Tell me more?"

"I love to tease. I love the thought of men fantasizing about me. I love frustrating them; it turns me on. I go home and tell my husband about what I've said and done to you all. He loves it, I love it.

"A win, win. Well, except for the poor man you're winding up." I said.

"Don't worry, I won't keep you waiting forever." She replied and walked out.

Chloe was good to her word. After that, we snatched opportunities whenever we could, although in reality, this only amounted to once every week or two. It was a great distraction from my mundane life and, quite frankly, for me anyway, it was risk free.

Whilst I was turning these thoughts over in my mind, I suddenly realised that Mrs M was due to visit me that afternoon. That was just wonderful because it would mean I could see her face when I told her the news and, I'd be able to get a lift home.

My cell door unlocked – it was Edward, on his own this time.

"Fucking hell, Chris, that's unbelievable!" He said, the smile on his face beaming.

I laughed.

"I mean, fucking hell. You always said you didn't do it."

"I didn't." I replied.

"How long did you do? In the end." He asked.

"Coming up on seven months." I replied.

He put his hand out and I shook it. I mean, you don't shake anyone's hands for a year and then two come along in the same morning!

"I'm not taking the books; leave them for the next innocent sod that gets wrongly convicted."

"I'll make sure they get to the mobile library." Edward replied.

"You ready for the outside world?"

I nodded. The question had a slightly unsettling effect on me. I wasn't sure I was prepared. It had all happened so quickly. In one hour, I'd gone from nothing to everything.

"Will you still see Officer Nuffield? You know, when you're out?"

It would appear our clandestine affair wasn't quite as clandestine as I'd thought.

Chapter 28

By midday I was walking out of the gate; my property in a holdall and five carrier bags. I was a mess. My hair desperately needed cutting and I'd been released before I'd showered or shaved. I had, at least, managed to clean my teeth. I didn't think Mrs M would mind.

I was still wearing my prison issue grey tracksuit trousers and T shirt. I'd found my old suit jacket, the one I was wearing when I was sent down, and put that on, but I was hopelessly underdressed for a freezing April day in Yorkshire and was soon starting to shiver.

The thing was, Mrs M was on afternoon visits so she wouldn't arrive for at least another hour, so I huddled down in the corner of a bus stop which afforded me a long eye on the visitor's car park. I hoped she still drove the same car, a silver Citroen C4 which she'd had since new.

It started to snow.

I saw a large unliveried white van pull up about ten yards away. I assumed the driver was there to pick someone up who was also being released. After a few minutes, three people, two men and one woman, all white and in their late twenties, got out of the front seat and started busying themselves at the far end of the van. I changed my mind; this wasn't anything to do with meeting someone. One of the men emerged with a large object which he hoisted onto his shoulder. It was a large camera. The second man was carrying a silver case and the third occupant, the female, clearly the boss, was now giving directions as to where they should 'set up for the best shot.' The boss wanted the prison gates and sign in the background.

They clearly had no idea I was there, only a few feet away from them.

From their sporadic and at times very technical conversation, I gathered they were delighted to be the first news crew to arrive, keen to get their 'piece' done and back to some guy called 'Bernie', so they could lead with the story at the 'top of the hour'.

While they were still discussing everything, a Sky News van arrived, fully kitted up with two large roof satellite dishes, and this put a sense of real urgency into the activities of the first group.

It was snowing heavily now, and I was getting really cold, cold to that stage where you start to feel cold inside as opposed to just on your extremities. I opened my holdall and removed more items of clothing which I put on as best I could. I wrapped the arms of an old sweatshirt around my neck and from the back, lifted it up and over my head, to make a sort of hat that I then held in place at the sides with my hands. I put two socks on each hand and an old jumper added an extra layer between my top and suit jacket. I must have looked like a right old tramp. I settled down into my spot again, but I wasn't there long because the arrival of the third TV crew, in a large grey ITN commercial vehicle, blocked my line of sight to the visitor's car park. So I decided to relocate and just stand at the entrance to the visitor's centre, a red brick building outside the jail where all visitors went prior to being escorted inside.

Three film crew were setting up, all vying for the best position and there was some friendly banter between them to suggest that, despite the rivalry, they were all quite good friends. The thing was, these were news reporters, cameramen and sound engineers for some of the biggest news agencies in the world and yet they were so young. There wasn't one of them whom I couldn't have fathered. How long exactly had I been in prison? More to the point, when did I get so bloody old?

I sat on a small wall near the entrance and watched as the afternoon's visitors started to arrive. As ever, I was fascinated by them but this time my attitude had changed. I felt such sympathy. They had committed no crime, their young children who they brought to this terrible place, had done nothing wrong. Yet they always came to see their loved ones, through rain and shine, floods, gales and blizzards. I knew some had travelled for hundreds of miles, a few by public transport. And prisons were rarely located next to railway terminals or bus stations, they were in the middle of nowhere, where buses ran, if you were lucky, every hour or two. Not one of the people who passed by me was having an easy life. Most, I was sure, were struggling with financial worries with the family's main bread winner inside and unable to earn. I knew a few prisoners earned very good money controlling the trafficking of contraband, mainly drugs and mobile phones, but the vast majority of prisoners didn't, and they were the ones whose families I felt so sorry for.

I must have missed her car, but I saw her from a hundred yards. At first, just her head was visible above the carpet of car roofs, as she weaved, turning at constant right angles, to make her way from the far side to the entrance. I stood up and dropped my makeshift hood back. I just stared in silent awe as she grew nearer and nearer, and our moment of reconciliation approached. For so long, she didn't look up, but when she did, just ten yards away, she froze to the spot like one of Medusa's victims.

I didn't move, I just smiled.

For about thirty seconds, we were frozen in time. I wasn't even sure I was still breathing.

Chapter 29

The drive from Doncaster to Buckhurst Hill took five hours, largely due to an accident on the M1 just after Watford Gap services. I think it was the happiest five hours of my life. Nothing will ever come close to the feelings of joy and relief I experienced in that car on that freezing April afternoon. Everything was made even better by being with Mrs M. The one unerring constant in my life. In the twenty-five plus years we'd known one another we'd never argued, disagreed or raised a voice in anger. Over the last fourteen months, she had proved her unconditional love for me. I would never be able to repay her loyalty and support, and that thought humbled me.

"I knew the lawyers wanted to see me, but I just thought they were going to tell me we'd got to the end of the road." I said, as we passed a sign stating London 50 miles.

"I had a couple of missed calls from them this morning on the way up, but you know me, Chris, I won't answer the phone when I'm driving."

"Was it on the news?" I asked.

"Sorry, darling, but I was listening to an Audible book and didn't have the radio on. I've become a big fan of the talking books, much more convenient than the more traditional ones."

"When I left the prison, there were loads of news crews setting up. I presumed they were there to cover this story, didn't you see them?"

"No, my darling, I only saw you."

"You didn't have any idea I'd just been released?"

"No, not at all. What did they tell you, exactly?" Mrs M asked.

"Hardly anything, the Governor came to my cell and read a very short letter, he left me a copy, it said I was to be released immediately because 'recent information had come to light to cast the gravest doubts on the safety of my conviction'. All I can imagine Mrs M is that someone else has admitted it and they've managed to convince the police that they're telling the truth because they know stuff about the offence that only the killer could have known. Either that, or they've suddenly realised it's not my DNA but that seems unlikely as everyone, even our scientist, thought it was mine."

"No one said a word to me." Mrs M said.

I borrowed her phone and called the lawyers. I normally dealt with a guy called Nicholas Cousins. When I asked for him I was informed he was in a meeting, but I could leave a message with his secretaries. I agreed but as soon as the secretary found out who I was, she didn't take a message and asked me to hold. I put the phone on my right knee, and pressed speaker so that Mrs M would be able to listen to the conversation.

"Christopher? Nicholas here. You're on the spider phone in the conference room. Can you hear me all right?"

"Yes, you're on the speaker phone in the car, there's just Jennifer Matthews and myself here. I was released this morning and we're on our way home. Do we know what's going on? Why have I been released?"

"We were only informed of this development ourselves at nine o'clock this morning. We left messages for both you, at the prison, and Mrs Matthews to contact us urgently. I received a telephone call from the Principal Private Secretary to the Secretary of State for Justice. She read out an obviously prepared statement saying that recent information had emerged to cast doubts on your conviction and that you would be released on bail pending action by the Court of Appeal."

"That's exactly what they told me." I replied.

"The Private Secretary wouldn't answer any questions. That really was the end of the conversation."

"Does that sound right to you?" I asked, incredulously.

"No, we're instructing counsel. It'll all be covered by legal aid, so don't worry. We're trying to find the right barrister for you as Alison is not available and besides we require a really specialist one."

The line went silent momentarily as each of us thought the other was going to speak.

"Sounds like there's been a colossal mistake to me." Mrs M said, raising her voice above the noise of the motorway traffic.

I lifted her mobile up, so it was nearer her mouth.

No one said a word.

"Why are you so quiet?" I asked, slightly irritated by their silence.

"Hi there, Nicholas here, we're not ignoring you. The truth is we're unsure. I've been working in criminal law for forty years and I've never known anything like this to happen. Yes, I've known people to get out on Appeal and I've known innocent people to be suddenly released from prison, but there's always a very specific, and very publicly announced reason. Remember, there is a really important principle that justice must not only be done, but it must also be seen to be done. The MoJ's decision to release you without a meaningful explanation defies that principle. It's a first and quite frankly, Christopher, we don't know what to make of it. Come and see us tomorrow, will you? In the offices at Moorgate, you know, you've been before. Shall we say ten?"

I agreed. I then thanked them. I wasn't sure why but it felt the right thing to do, and terminated the call.

'Come and see us tomorrow' – such an easy thing to say. Yet the thought of travelling up to Moorgate in only a few hours' time, in a crowded underground train carriage, packed with strangers, made me feel sick. That horrible feeling in my chest, the one where I could feel absolutely every heartbeat, returned.

Chapter 30

Before I'd been sent to prison, I'd only lived at Mrs M's for nearly four years, but when I walked through the front door, carrying my holdall and five carrier bags, it felt like I was returning to my lifetime home.

I went straight upstairs and into my old room, I dropped the bags just inside the door and collapsed on the bed. I was completely and utterly exhausted, not physically but emotionally.

I lay there for twenty minutes, just listening to the silence, so different to the relentless noise of a prison.

In the space of just eight hours, I'd been given my life back and, quite frankly, the whole thing was almost too much to take in. I'd woken up in my prison bed, looking forward to moving pads, Mrs M's visit and another twenty-two years in jail. Here I was, while the last vestiges of the same day's sun streaked through the net curtains, lying on my bed in Buckhurst Hill, a free man, with a life of days full of endless opportunities stretched out before me. I felt every bit as anxious and nervous as I had in prison. I knew I wasn't mentally well. In my former life, my real life, I'd been one of the strongest people I'd ever known. I'd survived an IRA bombing and been kidnapped. I'd even killed a murderer in cold blood, without losing so much as a second's sleep about blowing his brain across the walls. But here I was, an absolute and total wreck. Sometimes, in prison, I was so nervous I would just start to shake. Somehow, some way, I had to find the old Christopher Pritchard again. I wanted to be him. To be fearless and respected. To be me.

I could hear Mrs M turning the taps on in the bath and then I heard a light tap tap tap on my door.

"Come in." I called.

Mrs M had brought me a tea in my old pint mug. I rolled over and smiled.

"Thank you, Mrs M."

"You're welcome."

"I'm not talking about the tea. Thank you."

"You're welcome."

I didn't say anymore. I was thanking Mrs M for fighting my cause, for believing my innocence and for never giving up on me but I didn't have to say all that.

She sat on the bed.

"How are you, really?" She asked.

This was difficult because whenever Mrs M had come to see me in prison, I'd always put on a brave face so she didn't worry any more than she had to. I'd never admitted or alluded to the struggles I was experiencing. When I was burned, I'd even tried to convince her it had all been an accident; not that I think she believed me about that for a second. I realised however that if I was going to get through this, I'd need her help more than ever.

"Not good, Mrs M." I said.

"I was so worried about you. You were so ill."

"Did you realise? I did my best to hide it."

"Oh Christopher, my darling, of course I knew. I was so worried I couldn't sleep. I wrote to the Governor about you. I begged him to make sure you got the help you needed. I told him I thought you were going to kill yourself. I went ballistic when they did that to you."

She pointed to my neck.

"I wanted to know how they could possibly allow such a serious assault to happen to someone over whom they had complete charge. I wrote to our MP. I wrote to the Minister for Justice, and the Home Secretary. I told them all what had happened to you. Oh, I'm running you a bath, darling, you're a bit smelly."

Her sudden and complete change of subject, half-way through her sentence, made me laugh out loud.

"I missed my shower today and I trained late last night so the sweat must be encrusted." I replied, by way of an explanation.

"I don't care." She said.

"I know you don't, but I don't want poor Pippa to see me like this. Where is she?" I replied.

"She's buying you some scotch and a welcome home card; she'll be back soon."

The house phone started to ring.

"Now, you'll have to let me know who you want to see and when. When news gets out, everyone, and I mean everyone, will want to see you, but I suspect you'll want to take things slowly?"

I nodded.

There was a knock at the front door. My bedroom was at the front of the house, so Mrs M walked over to the window to see who it was.

"It's the police, a senior officer, I think." She said.

"It's not your boyfriend?" I asked.

Mrs M was seeing an Assistant Commissioner called John King.

"I spoke to John a few minutes ago; he suggested we lie low for a while."

I nodded. John was married and he probably thought, with the storm of publicity that was about to arrive, it might be wise if he and Mrs M took a short break. It was the sensible thing to do.

"I'll get the front door; can you check the bath?" Mrs M said, as she hurried off down the stairs.

***

I made Deputy Assistant Commissioner Simon Morley and his Staff Officer wait until I'd had a bath, shaved, cleaned my teeth and dressed. It was only half an hour and Mrs M kept them going with tea and biscuits. It was a small but important thing for me to do, to keep them waiting; it afforded me a tiny bit of control and I hadn't had that for a long time.

I didn't know or recognise either of the officers. The DAC looked about twelve, but his Staff Officer was pretty. I shook their hands politely. Mrs M delivered a second round of hot drinks and snacks and then sat down next to me. Clearly, my protector wasn't going to be excluded and I didn't blame her. Besides, I needed someone by my side and couldn't think of anyone better. With that said, there was a tiny bit of me that felt I was holding onto my mum's apron strings.

"Mr Pritchard; how would you like me to address you?"

The question caught me off-guard. I frowned and had a flash of inspiration.

"Nostrils, you can call me Nostrils."

The DAC smiled.

"That was my nickname, when I was in the Job." I explained.

"I know. I read your personal file on the drive from the yard. The reference to the name appears several times."

"On my personal file?" I asked, with surprise.

He nodded.

"I've never seen a thicker one." The pretty Staff Officer added.

I looked at her and then back at the DAC. It was hard to let such a comment go unmolested, but I did.

"Ok, Nostrils it is. Nostrils, this is, as I'm sure you might appreciate, a difficult conversation but it is nonetheless, a very necessary one. For example, I want to congratulate you on your release, but that hardly seems the appropriate thing to do. As we now know you didn't commit the offence, offering you congratulations for your release seems obtuse. Nonetheless, I want to say I am delighted that the right outcome has eventually been reached."

I nodded. He was right. Congratulating me would have been the wrong thing to do. I thought he handled that well. The DAC may have looked young, but he spoke with clarity and, I have to admit, I took a liking to him.

"I cannot imagine what you have been through, not for a second. And there will be lots for you to think about and consider over the coming weeks and months. I'm not looking for anything today, but I have a very personal message to deliver from the Commissioner, on behalf of the Metropolitan Police. That is the reason I am here today.

"I see." I replied.

"The Commissioner has asked me to convey his genuine and profound sympathies to you for, what is now recognised to be by the Avon and Somerset police, a miscarriage of justice. He acknowledges the terrible events which you have had to endure and assures you that, should you wish, and once the formalities are completed, you would be most welcome back in the Metropolitan Police to resume your distinguished career in a role and at a rank of your choosing."

I looked the DAC straight in the eye.

"Do you know why my conviction has suddenly become unsafe?"

"No" He replied.

I didn't say a word, just let the silence hang.

Nothing.

"Sorry, Nostrils, I really don't." He said, after about twenty seconds.

I could feel my right arm starting to shake. I suddenly couldn't cope with this situation. Mrs M jumped to her feet.

"Thank you, please leave. Christopher is very tired." She said, curtly.

Chapter 31

Before Mrs M had shown my visitors out, I was back in my bedroom. I felt safe there.

Mrs M left me for an hour and in that time neither the house phone nor her mobile, stopped ringing.

I could hear a growing commotion and when I looked, noticed half a dozen news vans, including the three that had been at the HMP Bankside earlier in the day, parked on the street outside.

I didn't have a mobile phone. Avon and Somerset Police had one and I'd lost possession of another shortly before the day of my conviction. I found an old mobile phone and charger and plugged it in. It would take hours to charge but, even then, I didn't have a SIM card. And another thing, I didn't know anyone's phone numbers anymore. As they were always stored in the phone you didn't have to learn them like you did in the old days.

I put the radio on and checked the time. It was just before seven, so I tuned into Radio 4 to listen to the headlines. The lead story was about the London Olympics, an event which I'd followed closely from my prison cell and had got really excited about. I'd decided to watch every possible minute of television coverage, an activity which would break the boredom. Now I'd been released, I found with abject curiosity, that the event had suddenly lost its magic.

The second news story was about me, but it was very short.

"Former Metropolitan Police officer, Christopher Pritchard, was released from jail today pending an appeal against his conviction last year for the murder of Mrs Eileen Armstrong in Bath, Avon, in 1982.

Mr Pritchard had served just seven months of a life sentence.

Although a representative for the Ministry of Justice claimed information has recently come to light which casts grave doubts over the safety of the conviction, details of exactly what that information was, have failed to emerge. More information is likely to be revealed at next week's Appeal Court hearing, at which it is anticipated Mr Pritchard's conviction will be formally quashed."

About an hour went by, during which time I lay almost motionless, staring up at the ceiling and trying to calm the fuck down. I'm sure, if someone was watching me, they'd have thought I looked like a person who didn't have a care in the world, but nothing could have been further from the truth. In that hour I was in absolute turmoil. My heart was pounding; my breathing was rapid and shallow; and I was sweating profusely, as if I'd been training rigorously. I had achieved a level of anxiety that was worse than anything I'd known before. If I could have ended my life there and then by, for example, simply pushing a button, I would have done, no doubt about it. I didn't want to live like this, it was too painful, too hard. I wanted to die.

At some point I started to cry. I was so unutterably unhappy. I know it sounds absurd as this was, after all, the day of absolution. I was free; free to carry on with my life, free to meet people, free to have a relationship, free to go shopping, free to drink, free to stay up all night, free to do whatever I fucking wanted – and all I wanted to do was end my life.

Mrs M came in with another cup of tea and a plate of sandwiches *'just in case I was hungry'.*

I should have stopped crying and pulled myself together, but I couldn't. I couldn't even try. I just sobbed like a baby and Mrs M sat on the bed and pulled me into her, like a young child. She cuddled me and rocked me back and forth and I cried until I fell asleep. As I drifted off, all I could hear from downstairs was Mrs M's phones ringing, almost constantly.

When I came round, Mrs M was sitting in the chair in the corner of the room reading a paperback.

"Feeling better?" She asked.

I nodded.

"How long have I been asleep? What time is it?" I asked.

"Just gone one." Mrs M replied.

I was still fully clothed, but Mrs M had put a blanket over me and turned the main light off.

"I'll phone the lawyers in the morning and cancel the meeting." Mrs M said.

"Thank you."

"I'll also get the doctor out. You need some medical support, Chris."

"I know." I replied.

"You're having a mental breakdown; you know that don't you?"

I nodded.

"It's completely understandable. If you can, don't fight it, go with it. It's the only way. It's a horrible ride, but you will come out the other side."

Mrs M was speaking as if she knew.

"I had a breakdown after Dawn died." She replied, to my unspoken question.

"How long did it last?" I asked.

"A year, maybe fourteen months. When I first met you again at the cemetery, when was that? Back in the late summer of eighty-four perhaps, I can't remember now. Anyway, about then, that's when it started to ease off."

"I can't live like this for another year." I said, incredulously.

Mrs M smiled kindly, like only Mrs M could.

"You can, darling. I'll be here for you. We'll get you through this, I promise. You will be normal again, if you ever were!"

She smiled.

"Who was on the phone earlier?" I asked.

"The Prime Minister." She replied.

"You're kidding?" I said.

"Oh sorry, I thought it might be easier to tell you who wasn't on the phone. The answer is David Cameron, he wasn't on the phone. Everyone else in the whole world was."

I laughed.

"The thing is, Chris, since you were convicted, I've been giving my contact details to absolutely everyone in an attempt to solicit their support and to get them engaged in my campaign. Today, I'm starting to pay the price for sharing my telephone number with quite so many people."

Mrs M put her book down.

"In order of importance. Jackie and Trudy rang from Australia. They were just screaming down the phone. It was lovely. Jackie said she'd be over on the next flight."

I suddenly felt worried, I didn't want Jackie and Trudy to see me in this state.

"Is Trudy coming, too?" I asked.

"I don't know; I got the impression just Jackie."

"Julie called, said she got my number from the book 1 or something. She said to send you her congratulations, to tell you they all knew you were innocent, and that she'd come and visit as soon as you were ready for her."

"Did you tell her anything?" I asked.

"About you?"

I nodded.

"I said you were going to take a little while to adjust. I've said that to everyone."

"Wendy called."

"You've never spoken to her, have you?" I asked.

Mrs M shook her head.

"She said to tell you she'd keep her promise, and that you'd know what that meant."

"I do." I said.

I started to feel just a little bit better as Mrs M went through everyone who had called. It started to dawn on me that those who did really love me might understand why I'd fallen apart.

"Matthew's mum called; Sarah is it? She said you'd given the landline to Matthew last year. She wanted me to tell you that there hadn't been a day gone by when she hadn't been thinking about you and that she had written to dozens of people protesting your innocence. She sounded lovely, Chris."

"She was, I mean, is. She used to be a model, then she set up her own agency." I replied.

"I meant lovely as in personality, Chris. You men are all the same."

She laughed.

"Who else, who else?" I asked.

"Well, that completes your list of female admirers. No, I lie. Another woman did call for you. Strong northern accent, Lee or something? She said she'd heard the news and would love to meet up, now you're out. She really wanted to talk to you, but I said no. Who is she?"

I realised immediately that must have been Chloe and she must have got my number from my records. She was taking a big risk calling me.

I shook my head, and put on my best, *'I'm mystified'* expression. I doubt it fooled Mrs M, but she didn't push it.

"As you'd expect, there's been a load of media vying for an exclusive on your story. And some guy who wants to ghost write a book for you. I'll keep them all at bay, for the time being. Is there anyone you'd like to see, Christopher?"

I thought for a few moments.

"I want to see Brucie, boy." I replied, definitively.

Chapter 32

Brucie and I had only known each other a few years. We first met when we worked together on the Marcella Parker case. He was appointed as the Financial Investigator, but he was much more than that. He was a good, old school detective – I could give no one a higher accolade. Brucie was also smart. Like many of us, he might have joined the police with less qualifications than a pot wash required, but in his early forties he'd got a first-class law degree from the Open University in his own time. I understood that a first-class degree from the Open University was rarer than rocking horse shit.

When we were working together, we used to meet up at a café in High Beech, so I asked Mrs M to make the necessary arrangements and at eleven o'clock the next day, she dropped me off. I didn't have a car, mine had sat in the garage for eight months and now had a completely flat battery and a fully deflated tyre.

Brucie was sitting on a horizontal tree trunk, smoking a roll-up and sipping piping hot tea from a polystyrene cup. He smiled and held up a second cup to indicate he'd already bought me one.

"Hello prisoner Pritchard." He said, as I sat down.

"Hello cunt face." I replied, as I took the tea from him.

"They let you out then?"

"A brain the speed of lightening. Nothing gets past you, does it?" I replied.

He laughed.

"I bet you're going to sue them for every penny they've got?"

"Hadn't really thought about that yet. Give me a chance, I've only been out twenty hours." I replied.

"And the Job will have to re-instate you, and give you back pay from when they dismissed you."

"I don't know if I want to come back." I said.

"For fuck's sake, Nostrils, that doesn't matter. They'll have to reinstate you, then you can decide whether to come back or not. You could go sick straight away. Hell, you could go sick for a year. No one's going to blame you. Then resign. Take the money and run. How long have you got left?"

"Not long; less than two, now."

"Let me give you some advice. I don't care how you do it, complete your thirty. You'll get a DI's pension, that's two grand a month plus your commutation."

"They said I could come back to whatever job I wanted." I replied.

"Who did?" He asked.

"A DAC came to see me yesterday afternoon. He delivered a message from the Commissioner. Apparently, he said I can choose my job and my rank - that can't be right, can it?" I asked.

"Can be. The Commissioner has the authority to promote in the field. It's happened a few times that I know of. There was that PC in the Embassy siege, he got made the same offer. Obviously, I doubt they'd let you be the next Deputy Commissioner, but as a DI, you could certainly get a promotion to Superintendent. And that's pensionable, you lucky cunt! That's three grand a month."

I smiled.

"This is why you were the first person I wanted to meet. I knew you'd give me the right advice." I replied.

"Ask for a promotion to Detective Superintendent and a nice cushy administrative job at the Yard, or something. You'd be mad not to. Go and work for our old mate, the AC, the one that's knocking off Mrs M. He can find you a job somewhere. Not too much stress."

'Not too much stress', the words reverberated. Is that really what I wanted for the end of my police career? I mean, the Job itself had rarely got me stressed. Yes, being wrongly convicted of a heinous crime had caused me stress, but that wasn't the Job, was it? Was I ready to be put out to pasture? Like an old racehorse, well beyond his best.

"What was the fuck up, then?" Brucie asked.

"Sorry, what fuck up?"

"What was the problem with your conviction? You know, the recent information that they received that made them realise it wasn't you, after all?"

I shook my head.

"I don't know. I don't think my lawyers know, either. Even the DAC said he didn't know."

"Did you believe him?"

I thought for a few moments.

"Yes; he's a DAC, if he wants to, he can just say *'I do know but I've been directed not to tell you'*, can't he? There's no need for him to lie. But he flatly admitted he didn't know."

"Doesn't that worry you? Don't you think that stinks?" Brucie said.

"Not really because it'll come out at the Appeal Court, won't it. I'll know then." I replied.

"I suppose so." Brucie said.

He reached into his pocket and pulled out a Café Crème tin from which he retrieved a previously prepared roll-up.

"Good news about Kitty Young, though. Her career is down the toilet and her alleged perjury is looking even more serious, what with your release. I bet she's shitting it. I hope she gets charged and goes down for the full seven. Good riddance to bad rubbish." Brucie said.

Since my release, I hadn't even thought about her.

"I bet the team investigating that will want to interview you, now you're out."

I nodded.

"Strange thing was, when you were first charged, people in the Job that didn't know you, they were saying *'well, like, he must be guilty because of the DNA'* but when Kitty gave evidence against you, and it was so dreadfully bad and clearly a complete lie, everyone was like *'I reckon he's innocent'* – she was so hated by just about everyone."

"That's interesting." I said.

Stupid though it may seem, I was hurt that some had thought me guilty, even if they were people that didn't know me.

"Where are you working now? I'm sorry, I should have asked earlier."

"That's the problem with you, it's all me me me! Just because you spent six months in jail, you think the whole conversation has got to be about you."

"What can I say? And it was seven months, anyway." I said, apologetically.

"Potayto, Potarto. I'm working at Operation Athens, the Olympic Command. We're based at ESB and there's a team in Kensington. It's alright, a nice change to be doing something different."

Brucie's gaze suddenly lifted and he frowned. Instinctively, I turned around. Emerging from the forest was a while female in her mid-forties who was holding a dog lead. She looked terribly dishevelled, as if she had been rolling on the ground. She was crying, shaking and stumbling as opposed to walking.

"Help me, I've been attacked." She said.

Brucie went to stand up, his coppering instincts immediately kicking in.

"Hang on!" I said, urgently.

"Look!"

I'd seen a white male in his mid-twenties come out of the woods sprinting towards the car park and, with his right hand, he appeared to be holding his trousers up. It didn't take a detective to work out what had gone on. In a matter of seconds, the male was approaching a line of parked vehicles dipping his available hand into his pockets, clearly looking for a key.

The woman was only a few yards from us now.

"The suspect, we need to go for the suspect." I said.

Immediately we started running towards Brucie's car, which was an almost new and pristine white Audi A1.

Even in an emergency, two unfit, overweight white men in their mid-forties, aren't especially quick. The suspect, on the other hand, despite the handicap of having to hold his trousers up, moved like greased lightening. His car was parked between two others, so it was difficult to make out the make and model but before we were even at our car, there was a dramatic wheel spin and the sound of sand and small stones being thrown violently away from the rear of the car. When it emerged, we were only just opening our doors, but in his haste Brucie pushed the remote control several times and the doors relocked. I gave him some important advice.

"For fuck's sake, Brucie, open the fucking doors!"

He ignored me but did as he was told.

At first, the suspect's car was difficult to make out because of the cloud of dust behind it. He was off and right, towards the Robin Hood roundabout. As it turned, I got a quick glance at our adversary, sitting in the driver's seat, and years of police training kicked in, as I committed just the briefest glance of the right side of his face to my memory.

After what felt like an age, Brucie eventually got going.

"Which way's he gone?"

"Right, towards the A11. We gotta get there Brucie or we'll lose him at the roundabout."

"No shit, Sherlock. What's he driving?"

"It's a Saab, a blue Saab, the bigger one, the 95, not the 93." I replied.

We swung right out of the carpark without even looking for other traffic, the back of Brucie's car drastically oversteered which he controlled instinctively.

"Where's your fucking traction control?" I asked.

"I disabled it. It slows you down." He replied.

We drove towards the roundabout so quickly I was convinced we were going to die. What's more, because of the nature of the driving, I couldn't get my inertia seatbelt on as every time I pulled it out, it locked.

At the roundabout there was no sign of the Saab.

"Want to guess?" Brucie said.

"Go all the way round; if he's gone left or right, we'll see him. If we don't, it means he's gone straight over to Loughton." I replied.

Brucie slid the car round the roundabout with such precision I was deeply impressed. At the third exit, I saw the Saab about two hundred yards west and overtaking several London-bound vehicles.

"He's gone right. A11 towards London. Fuck me, he's a way away already." I said.

Brucie did another circle of the roundabout and then exited. We could still see the Saab but there were three or four vehicles between us on this long straight road and I'd estimate the distance was now half of a mile.

"Did you get the index?" Brucie asked.

"God, no." I replied.

I clocked the speedometer. Brucie was doing ninety-five and I still couldn't get my seatbelt on! We were rapidly approaching the first vehicle ahead of us, a Ford Fiesta but there were oncoming vehicles preventing an overtake.

This is a very straight road which runs without variation for about two miles. Epping Forest is on both sides and at some point, a yellow sign flashed by which informed us that *'In the last 10 years – there had been seven fatalities on this stretch of road'*.

"I reckon this road is wide enough for three vehicles." Brucie said.

Without slowing down, Brucie swept majestically between the slower moving Fiesta and an on-coming Range Rover. As we passed, I heard the Range Rover driver honking his horn furiously. I didn't blame him; it was an outrageous overtake.

"Please tell me you're a police driver?" I asked.

"Of course, mate, class one; you're in very safe hands.

We swept past the next car, with less stress, but the oncoming Mondeo driver flashed his headlights to indicate his annoyance at having to slow right down.

Ridiculous as it sounds considering the manner of Brucie's driving, learning that he was a class one Metropolitan Police advanced driver was reassuring. They were, quite simply, the best pursuit drivers in the world. We were closing in on the Saab, now held behind an articulated lorry, behind which there was a stream of slow traffic. The Saab was about fourth in line, but there were options to turn off coming up, both on the right and then the left. The latter would take him to Chingford along a fast, dipping road and I thought that would be the option he'd take, as long as the lorry didn't go that way too.

"Get on your mobile and call this in." Brucie barked, as he passed another car.

"I ain't got a mobile. Where's yours?" I asked.

"In my trouser pocket but I can't get it out now." He shouted.

"How can you not have a mobile, you cunt." He added.

We had slowed down now and joined the end of the line of traffic behind the lorry. Brucie pulled behind the car in front, into what police driver's call the contact position, which meant he was sitting only a few feet behind a Mini's boot but half-way into the middle of the carriageway. It was aggressive and no doubt the poor driver of the Mini felt intimidated, but it afforded Brucie with all the available options. It did mean I was temporarily unsighted, only able to see the Mini's back window.

"I think he'll go right; I think it's called Rangers Road."

"He's signalling right. Not that that means anything. Do you think he knows we're chasing him?" Brucie asked.

I'd assumed he had but now I thought about it, he might not. I mean when he got to the roundabout and turned right, he wouldn't have seen anyone behind him and then, as he drove along the A11, he'd have probably been too focused on overtaking to pay much attention to his mirror.

"Maybe he doesn't. But he will if he clocked your overtakes." I replied.

"He's turning right." Brucie said.

Waiting to get to that junction and then turning right ourselves seemed to take an age but in reality, we were probably about thirty seconds behind him. When we did turn, there was no sign of him.

"There's loads of little places and carparks in the forest that he can disappear into so don't drive too quickly. I'll try and check them out as we go by." I said.

Brucie ignored me and floored the throttle.

"This is quick, Brucie? What is it?"

"Two litre turbo diesel. One seventy horsepower." He replied.

Within about ten seconds we were doing ninety. It was thrillingly terrifying and reminded me of my younger days in the area car at Stoke Newington.

"Got him." Brucie said, as we cornered a left-hand bend which afforded him first sight as the road straightened.

"Fuck me, he's motoring. I didn't realised those big Saabs were that fast. Grandad's armchair cars." He added.

The Saab was dropping down into North Chingford now and would soon be in the busy High Street. We were a few cars behind him. Everyone slowed down as the traffic increased and I thought the suspect might be looking for somewhere to park. Then we came to a complete standstill as several buses were either pulling into or out of the station on our left. The Saab was only two cars ahead but getting out and trying to open the car door and drag the occupant out was risky. What's more, it would show our hand, as it was becoming increasingly likely that he didn't know we were following him.

Brucie took the opportunity to drag his phone out of his right front jean pocket and unlock it. As he did so, he threw it at me.

I dialled nine nine nine.

"Emergency, which service do you require?

"Police"

"One moment, putting you through."

"Police. Please tell me your name and telephone number."

"Christopher Pritchard, I'm calling from a mobile, but I don't know the number."

We had started to drive on at about twenty miles an hour.

"What's the nature of the emergency?"

"We are following a suspect who we think attacked a woman in Epping Forest, probably about fifteen minutes ago now. The attack took place near the Robin Hood roundabout on the A11."

"When you say following, what do you mean? Are you walking, running or driving?"

"Driving. He's in a Blue Saab index T202 AGF and this vehicle is currently west in Chingford High Street, right in the middle of the High Street. The driver, there are no other persons in the vehicle, is a white male, 5'10' and an apparent age of twenty-five."

We were approaching a T junction. I knew the area well. Right would take us to Chingford police station and left towards Woodford Green.

"We're coming up to green ATS and he's turning left, left, left onto the A110."

I clocked the road number from a green direction sign.

"The vehicle has no current keeper. What's your call sign?" The operator asked.

"No call sign, we're in a private vehicle. The driver is a serving police officer and I'm a former police officer." I replied.

"Stand-by. I'm going to try to find a call to the original incident. Did you say fifteen minutes ago? In High Beech?"

I hadn't said High Beech but that was the one.

"Yes, yes." I replied.

"We do have a report of a serious assault on a female. Can you confirm you are chasing the suspect?"

"Yes, yes."

I was aware that Brucie would not be allowed to pursue a suspect, even a rape suspect, in his own car. He wouldn't be insured and it would also be against every police driving regulation, so I quickly added.

"We're not chasing him. We're just following him at a discreet distance; he doesn't know we're here."

"Current location please?" The operator asked.

"North on the A110 towards Woodford Green. Speed 30 mph. We have one car cover. Driver still unaware that we are here."

I wasn't entirely sure that was true, but as the pursuit had gone on, and the suspect had put some distance between himself and the scene, he did appear to be slowing down and driving quite normally, which would suggest he was unaware we had been following him.

"Caller, we have units on way. Please maintain the commentary." The operator said.

"We are approaching Woodford Green High Street. Hang on, he's just turned left into a car park, I think it's at the back of the school here, Bancrofts."

"What's he doing, matey?" Brucie asked.

"No idea." I replied.

"Hello?" I said, into the phone.

"The suspect has driven his vehicle into what might be a car park at the rear of Bancrofts School. Stand-by, we're driving in."

We drove slowly into the turning which did, indeed, lead to a car park, with numbered parking spaces, surrounded by several two and three-storey buildings. The Saab had pulled up and the suspect was alighting. He looked around, as if he was getting his bearings. No one else was about, it was clearly lesson time and, apart from the sound of several controlled voices coming from afar, the school was quiet and peaceful.

"He doesn't know where he is." Brucie said quietly.

He locked the car and started walking back towards the entrance where we had stopped.

Brucie jumped out and I followed.

"Can we have a quick word, mate?" Brucie said, politely.

"Who are you?" He asked, nervously.

"I am a police officer ..."

Brucie produced his warrant card.

"... and this is my colleague."

Obviously, I didn't have a warrant card to flash.

"Do you work at the school?"

I could see Brucie edging closer to the suspect. The thing was, as you got older as a police officer, it came to the point where just about every suspect could outrun you, so you had to get hands on them before they realised and bolted. Bottom line was, if this twenty-five-year-old, slim male had it on his toes, neither Brucie nor I were going to catch him.

"No, I'm just visiting." He replied, nervously.

I had got out of the passenger's side and walked back behind the car to come up beside Brucie.

What happened next, happened very quickly.

Brucie reached out with his right hand and caught hold of the suspect's left arm. The suspect pulled away hard, and from his facial expression, he suddenly realised it was all about to come on top. Brucie lost his grip and found himself slightly off balance. Not a second later, with his right fist the suspect punched Brucie squarely in the face. There was an audible thud and poor Brucie fell forward and to the ground, his glasses smashed and blood was already pouring from his nose.

Before I could even respond, the suspect had turned on his heels and run. He was running back into the school car park and over towards the left. I set off, more in hope than expectation. I hadn't run for years, let alone tried to sprint. After about twenty yards, the suspect turned right through a short passage between two buildings. I followed but, as I entered the same passage, I felt a muscle go in my right calf. My brief sprint was coming to a rapid close.

As I emerged from the passage however, I came across a large sports field, probably the size of two rugby pitches, but this was the summer term and that afternoon, the field was a cricket ground, and a game was in full swing. In fact, it looked like the players, all young men in their late teens, wearing immaculate whites, were changing ends between overs.

The suspect ran straight across the cricket pitch and was just short of the wicket area when the players started to stop what they were doing and look at him.

I stopped a few steps over the boundary rope and shouted as clearly and calmly as I could.

"I am a police officer. Stop that man immediately!"

For a few seconds, no one moved. In just that short time, the suspect had made another twenty yards and was clearly making for the forest on the far side of the pitch.

"Please stop him." I shouted.

One of the umpires, clearly older and therefore a teacher, barked.

"Catch him, boys. Go, catch him, now!"

Their response was instantaneous, and not two seconds later, about twelve young men set off in pursuit of a rapist. When I replayed the scene in my mind later, I had to laugh. Several of them were wearing pads and carrying cricket bats and lumbered like they were going for a cheeky second run to short mid-wicket.

The pride of Bancrofts School caught their prey just as he was about to climb a gate into the woods. The first boy to get to him, I was later to learn, was a county rugby player who was just walking to third man, and he brought him down with a traditional tackle of which his coach would be rightly proud. The boys did a grand job and they handed him over in one piece. I was so very grateful.

Chapter 33

The suspect was taken to Harlow police station, as the offence had technically taken place in Essex. Brucie and I made our own way, but all we had to do once we were there was make a couple of short statements providing the continuity between the person we saw running out of the forest and the person arrested at Bancrofts School.

What was really nice was that no one noticed who I was. So, just for a few hours whilst I was at Harlow nick, I was busy writing and chatting to everyone and it was like I'd never been to jail, that the whole nightmare had been but a bad dream. My anxiety reduced too, not to zero but to just twenty percent of what it had been only a few hours earlier.

Brucie had a badly swollen nose but his pride was hurt more than his body, and his glasses were damaged more than his pride. I didn't realise just how blind he was without them, and at times he had to ask 'who was that?' or 'what's going on?' but we muddled through the day.

Late in the afternoon, I used Brucie's mobile to check in with Mrs M. I told her what had happened and apologised for not calling earlier. She was fine, but she had been fielding calls and people knocking at the door all day. From the stressed tone in her voice, I realised something I should have seen a while back. Mrs M was also under a great deal of pressure. Not just since my release but also whilst I was in prison. I should have realised sooner.

Mrs M said, in between calls and other demands, she had bought me an IPhone and compiled a list of all the numbers I would need. She was also quite insistent that we had to sit down as soon as possible and decide who I was going to speak to and under what conditions. Finally, she told me that my hearing at the Court of Appeal was set for Monday next week, in three days' time, and that the lawyers were desperate to see me before then.

"They are proposing coming here, on Saturday, tomorrow. What do you want to tell them?" She asked.

'Yes, okay. I do need to find out what's going to happen at court." I replied.

I had a sudden terrifying thought that the court might decide to send me back. I started to break out in a sweat and I needed the toilet.

"Mrs M, you don't think there's any chance they'll change their mind, do you?"

"No, not at all. I asked the lawyer, the Scottish one, the same thing and he assured me no, they don't release people like this and then send them back. That just wouldn't happen."

"Good" I replied.

"Oh, and Wendy wants to come round this evening. I thought you might like to see her. I can go out for a few hours, if that would assist."

The question took me completely off guard. For some reason I hadn't even considered the Wendy situation. I wanted to say no, because I needed more time, but I also felt awful turning her away. She had, after all, come all that way to visit me every other month.

"Yes, tell her to come round. You don't have to go out, in fact, please don't, it might make things easier for me. But I'm going for a drink with Brucie boy first, so I won't be back until later. Please tell her to come round about nine, that'll give me a chance to have a shower."

A few minutes past six, Brucie and I were sitting in the Horse & Well public house in Woodford Green. It was the first pub I'd visited in seven months. The Guinness tasted better than anything I'd ever drunk. Brucie ordered a lager and we took two seats near the window.

"How's the nose?" I asked.

"Fuck off." He replied.

It was the perfect response of a seasoned copper.

"I'm getting too old to roll around with these kids. Policing is a young man's game. Didn't I notice you limping earlier?"

I nodded.

"I did a muscle in my right calf, when I was chasing him. It's quite sore. I can't remember the last time I ran."

"See, we're getting too old."

"At least your injury was in the line of duty, I'm not even in the job." I replied.

Brucie looked up and straight into my eye.

"You are coming back though Nostrils, aren't you?"

"What? After today? After arresting a suspect for a nasty stranger rape on a lovely forty-five year old, perfectly normal and respectable lady, who did nothing but exercise her right to take a dog for a walk in Epping Forest, after all that, you expect me to come back to this pile of shit? To be an underpaid, never believed, often hated, regularly assaulted …

I indicated his nose.

" … police officer, who is constantly and remorselessly castigated by Britain's middle class – Oxbridge educated, media elite? You think I want more of that shit? You must think I'm some sort of cunt!"

Bruce stood up and put out his hand. He knew I had made my decision.

I stood up and shook it.

He held onto my hand.

"Remember, when ill of us they speak, we are all that stands between the monsters and the weak."

"I'm back." I said.

"Welcome home.' Brucie replied.

***

It would have helped if Wendy hadn't looked quite so good. She'd clearly remembered what always did it for me, and dressed accordingly. I was pleased she hadn't done this when she'd visited me inside, but doing it now wasn't quite as great as it should have been because I was frighteningly aware that it might cloud my judgement. The thing was, while Wendy was undoubtably the love of my life, she now came with someone else's children, a distraught ex-husband and goodness knows what other baggage. Besides, even if it was going to be Wendy, I needed a little space first, to catch my breath and settle my anxiety. Everything was happening too quickly and somewhere, at the back of my brain perhaps, a warning alarm was going off.

"Tight leggings and long high heeled black boots? Did you really have to come in battle dress?" I asked.

We were sitting in the lounge and Mrs M had taken a tray of hot drinks and biscuits to the reporters outside. She would chat to them and leave us alone for a while.

"A girl is entitled to play all her cards. If you're impressed with this, you should see what's underneath."

"Don't do this to me; and what about Mrs M?" I replied.

"Don't worry about Mrs M; we've had a girl-to-girl chat and agreed a night of passionate animal sex is exactly what the doctor ordered. Mum's got both my boys overnight and I've no intention of leaving this house until we've done just that."

I did appreciate the idea, I really did, but there were a couple of problems. These were, in no particular order; I wasn't in the mood, at all. Secondly, I'd been having regular sex for months and had had a very recent encounter with my favourite prison guard, so, even if I was in the mood, I certainly wasn't anywhere as desperate as Wendy would be expecting me to be. Thirdly, I wasn't quite sure anymore whether I wanted to commit to Wendy. I mean I might do, but I would need time, and if I slept with her now, that would be sending out all the wrong signals. Fourthly, I was quite pissed. I'd had three pints with Brucie, which wouldn't normally be a problem, but I hadn't had a drink in seven months, so it went straight to my head. Finally, I doubted with all these things rushing through my mind, I'd even be able to raise a smile, let alone an erection. Wendy clearly sensed something wasn't right.

"What's wrong, darling?"

"I'm sorry, I'm a bit fucked up at the moment."

"That's hardly surprising is it, Chris. You've just been released from a life sentence; you must be in shock. I'm really sorry, I should have thought. This is my fault entirely."

I smiled, kindly.

"Thank you for understanding. I'm just a mess."

We'd been sitting at different ends of the long settee, but Wendy relocated and put her arms around me. We hugged, a proper 'I love you so much' hug, that whispers a thousand words of affection. I genuinely couldn't bring myself to let go and we stayed in the same position for what must have been three or four minutes. When we parted, I wiped my eyes dry and Wendy did the same.

"Time, you need time." She said.

I nodded.

"I'll tell you what. Go and have a shower and I'll come up and give you the best massage you've ever had. I'll focus on your feet: I know how you love that. No strings, no happy endings, no pressure, my darling."

When we were together, Wendy often used to rub my feet. I loved that more than just about anything else. Her offer was impossible to turn down.

As I went upstairs, Mrs M returned and mouthed something to me. I frowned to indicate I didn't understand but I assumed she was referring to Wendy and I getting it together. Wendy was still in the front room. Mrs M repeated the gesture. I really wasn't in the mood to play guessing games.

"Come upstairs and tell me." I said.

When we were in my bedroom, Mrs M closed the door and, before I could say a word, said.

"There's a woman outside, says her name's Chloe, she wants to see you. Of course, Wendy's here, so I didn't know what to do, or what to say. Who is she, Chris?"

I was completely gobsmacked. Chloe lived in Doncaster! This was two hundred miles away, so what in god's name was she doing here? The day after I'm released from her prison?

Chapter 34

I got Mrs M to arrange a meeting for me the following day with Chloe and Mrs M, bless her, took her to a new Travelodge just at the top of Queens Road. She made up some story about the doctor having prescribed me a sedative and saying I should go straight to bed. I was very grateful.

Of course, I spent the night with Wendy, which was lovely, but as soon as I woke up in the morning, I had the most dreadful feeling that I'd made a really big mistake. I think half of me was so worried that I'd fall in love with her again, only to end up broken hearted once again. It had taken me three years to get over her and now, it seemed to me, I'd just set the clock back all that time.

I was pleased when she got up and left, saying she had to collect her boys and take them to swimming lessons at ten o'clock. Apparently, the father, who usually had them at weekends, had done a disappearing act for the last two. She thought he had probably gone on holiday and not told her, but she was worried about him on behalf of the boys.

Mrs M was cooking breakfast, a *'full English freedom fry-up'*, she called it, but as soon as Wendy left, she wanted to talk about Chloe.

"Oh my god, Christopher, who is that Chloe? She's as mad as a box of frogs. She says she's your girlfriend, she says you've been having an affair for the last six months, she says she loves you and if you end it with her, she's going to kill herself. And she's a prison officer at Bankside! Am I missing something? That's not allowed, is it?"

"No" I replied, meekly.

"So, she's telling the truth? You have been having a relationship with her?"

"I'd hardly call it a relationship, Mrs M." I replied.

"Explain that one to me, please."

This was as cross as I'd ever seen Mrs M. It was unsettling. I started to feel anxious.

"She was a prison officer in the Segregation Unit at Bankside. That's where I was, as you know. Actually, she was my personal prison officer."

"What does that mean? She was responsible for having sex with you?"

"Apparently" I replied, cheekily.

Fortunately, Mrs M saw the funny side and burst into laughter.

"Jesus Christ, Christopher! What were you thinking?"

I gave her a look, it said *'For fuck's sake, Mrs M, what do you think I was thinking?'*.

"It's just, well, you always knew you'd be released when they realised, they'd made a mistake. Doing that could really mess everything up. I mean, will they have you back in the Met if they know you were doing that …"

She paused.

"… to her?"

We both smiled because Mrs M's dramatic pause was quite brilliant comedy, timing wise.

"I didn't know I was going to get out. I thought I was there for the rest of my life. Having sex with Chloe was the only nice thing to happen to me; everything else was simply horrendous. For goodness sake, Mrs M, I was locked in my cell twenty-three and a half hours a day. Then along comes

Chloe, who doesn't just have sex with me, oh no, she teases me terribly for a month, gets me to the point where I get an erection just hearing her voice on the landing, and believe me, when you're well into your forties that really is something – so how on earth was I going to react? I deny any man in my position to do anything else. No, I know, sitting in your kitchen on a lovely spring Saturday morning in the outside world, it was wrong. But this is not where I was when it happened. I was a billion miles from here, with an eternity of fear, confinement and desperation ahead of me. I make no excuses or apologies for what I did, any more than I would for breathing."

"I'm sorry." Mrs M said, as I concluded my diatribe.

"That's all right. I love you, Mrs M." I replied.

***

The last thing I wanted to do was to meet Chloe at her hotel room but, without a mobile number for her, I didn't have any other choice. I accepted Mrs M's offer to wait outside for me. I was really nervous, and noticed that when I got nervous, my anxiety returned. That feeling in my chest was like someone had just crept up behind me and shouted boo. I didn't like it at all. I'd hoped the problem was purely a prison phenomenon but apparently it wasn't that easy to turn off the anxiety switch.

Seeing Chloe for the first time not wearing her uniform was weird. She looked nice, because of course, her hair was down, and she was wearing a pair of tight-fitting jeans not baggy black trousers.

She stepped back from the door, indicating that I come in, and I sat in the corner on an uncomfortable orange chair.

"You can sit on the bed with me, I won't bite." She said.

"How are you?" I asked.

I felt the anxiety rising in my chest; it was grippingly debilitating. The sight of Chloe took me straight back to my prison cell. I didn't know whether I was going to be able to hold it together. I started rocking back and forth. Chloe was talking but I couldn't focus on her enough to listen.

"I can't do this." I said, still rocking.

I started to focus on my breathing; trying to take in a deep breath through my nose and exhale through my mouth. I did this a dozen times, then another dozen. I could feel every beat of my heart. Somehow and slowly, I pulled myself back from the brink.

When I became conscious of my surroundings, Chloe was kneeling down beside me stroking my back and holding my left hand. The first thing I noticed was her perfume, strong and sweet. Then I could feel her touch and finally her breath, gently against my cheek. She wasn't speaking.

"I'm sorry, I'm really fucked up."

"Your mum said the doctor had been out last night and given you a sedative. Perhaps, it's worn off. Is there anything I can do?" She asked.

"I'm sorry but I can't do this." I said.

"Can't do what?" She asked, incredulously.

"Can't see you. It reminds me too much of being inside. I don't think I'm very well, mentally, Chloe. I think I'm having a mental breakdown. I can't cope, at all. It's not you, it's me. I'm really fucked up. Besides, couldn't you get in trouble?" I asked.

Chloe let go of my hand and returned to the bed.

"I don't believe this. You can't be serious. I've driven all this way to see you, I've even had to go sick to get the time off work, and you're dumping me."

I didn't know what to say, so I said nothing.

"Well, you're not getting rid of me that easily, Christopher Pritchard. You bastard. Didn't mind me sucking or wanking you off. Didn't mind me sitting on your cock when you were in prison, did you?"

I got up to leave, I couldn't handle this, but Chloe jumped up and put herself between me and the door.

"Oh no, you're not fucking leaving."

"I'm not leaving, I need the toilet; I'm going to be sick." I lied.

She stepped to one side and moved back towards the bed. As soon as her arse touched the sheets, I ran to the door, opened it and was off. What a complete fucking coward I had become.

Chapter 35

I met my lawyers at home later that afternoon. The main guy was Nicholas Cousins, a senior equity partner at the law firm, and he had with him a younger lady, Meriel something, who I hadn't met before. Nicholas did all the talking. He was really bright but more importantly, throughout my bail and the trial, I really got the impression he believed me when I said I hadn't done it. Nicholas had a habit, before he said anything, of taking a deep breath and thinking. You could almost hear his brain ticking over, and when he spoke, he did so with such clarity and precision of thought, that at times it left me spellbound. His only downside was that he sported a ridiculous Bobby Charlton comb over when he really should have accepted, he'd lost most of his hair.

During our meeting, it became abundantly clear that my legal team had absolutely no idea as to why I'd been released which, Nicholas informed me, was unprecedented. I asked him whether it was possible that there'd been some mistake and I'd end up back in prison? He assured me that was highly unlikely.

I took the opportunity to ask Nicholas about the situation with Chloe and whether I'd done anything wrong. He assured me I hadn't, that as a prisoner, I was a vulnerable person and that as a prison officer, it was Chloe who had taken advantage of me – not the other way around. He asked me whether I'd ever spoken to her from a mobile phone, because apparently that would be a problem, but I assured him I'd never possessed a mobile while I was in prison. Nicholas's counsel was that I should make an allegation against Chloe, to protect me in case she made anything up, like saying I'd indecently assaulted her. Although his advice was no doubt sound, I just couldn't do that to the girl, and so I said no. I hoped I didn't live to regret that decision.

Mrs M had sat in on the meeting, which was fine, and it was in fact at her instigation that I'd told them about the problem with Chloe. Of course, there wasn't any risk in me doing so, because everything I said to them was protected by client privilege. As the meeting was drawing to a close, Mrs M asked me whether she could ask a few questions.

"You don't need to ask, of course." I replied.

"Nicholas, what do we do about the gaggle of reporters camped outside? They're after an interview and I don't think there's any sign of them taking no for an answer and packing up. Is there any reason why Christopher shouldn't talk to them, you know, answer some questions? Perhaps they'd go then. It's terribly restricting having them outside, you feel like you've got no privacy, at all."

"Don't say anything to them yet. Being practical, Christopher may wish to sell his story, or to write a book and anything he says or does now, will devalue that. I'll tell you what, and I'm only saying this because you brought it up, I would never have mentioned this overwise, my brother Stephen runs a reputable PR company and I could ask him to reach out. He will advise you on how to handle the media. In fact, he'll probably just do it all for you."

"Perfect" Mrs M replied.

I wished Mrs M had spoken to me about this first but I knew she had only asked because she had my best interests at heart.

"I'm not sure, Mrs M. I'm going to re-join the Met; not sure they'd be too happy if I started selling my story."

"You're re-joining the Met? You're not well enough, my darling." Mrs M said, incredulously.

"Let's have this conversation later?" I said.

"Just some legal advice on that point, Christopher. I am confident my litigation colleagues would advise against returning to the police. Quite simply, I am sure you will be initiating an action against the State for damages, including loss of earnings and countless other hurts and wrongs. If you return to work, it might undermine your loss of earnings claim. We're talking a lot of money, Christopher, potentially hundreds of thousands of pounds, may be even more."

"Gosh, isn't there a lot to think about?" I said.

***

I had rarely seen Mrs M so distressed.

The moment the door closed behind Nicholas and Meriel, she went into one!

"You can't be serious about going back!" She asked, incredulously.

"You know what happened yesterday with Brucie. We caught and arrested a rapist. I realised then I can't give it up. And they've offered me any role at any rank; it's too good an offer to turn down." I replied.

"After what they did to you? After all you've been through? You're not well, Chris. You're ill. You need help, counselling, time to heal."

"I need a meaningful life, Mrs M."

"You heard what he said, you could be in line for hundreds of thousands of pounds, you don't need to work, not ever. You deserve it, Chris."

"I have to." I replied.

It was unnatural and very hard to think I was hurting Mrs M.

"I've already lost one daughter to the Job. Now you're going to go back out there! Please don't do this to me. Please, don't. Please don't."

"But it's who I am, Mrs M. Being a police officer is my life, it's in my soul. I'm sorry."

The last two words told Mrs M that I'd made my mind up. She looked so sad, but then she smiled and said.

"Even after all this, you're still blue through and through."

"The deepest blue." I replied.

A single lonely tear ran down her cheek.

Chapter 36

I took a black taxi to the Royal Courts of Justice. From Buckhurst Hill the cost was forty-five pounds, which was ridiculous, but my brief had told me to keep the receipt and assured me that would be just another cost we would be claiming back from Her Majesty.

As directed, I went in through a back entrance, far from the madding crowd of reporters and photographers in the Strand. I met my solicitor, Nicholas Cousins, and his assistant Meriel. I also met my new barrister, Dennis De L'Arcy. Dennis was well over seventy, but his eyes sparkled with enthusiasm. His junior counsel was a young Chinese lad, who looked barely old enough to drive, but that was probably a sign of my own advancing years, rather than his youth. Still, he looked like he was out for a day with his grandfather.

We found an interview room, really only suitable for two, which we all huddled inside as if it was a game of sardines.

"I thought it would be useful to explain what's going to happen. Unusually, for the legal profession, these events have all come about very quickly. It has certainly taken everyone by surprise. A week ago, I don't think we were even anticipating leave to appeal, where we, Nicholas?"

Nicholas shook his head.

"Now, it seems, the Crown is very keen indeed to get this matter resolved. Does anyone know why?"

I was astounded by the question. I thought this was where and when I was going to find out what had happened. Did this De L'Arcy fellow really not know?

A silence hung in the small room. I decided, for once, to speak into it.

"Listen, guys, I have said this a million times before, but now I know you will believe me. I didn't do this crime. That I have been released, while a great surprise on one side, is entirely in keeping with what should have originally happened. Let's not forget that. Just to be clear, Dennis, you really haven't got a clue what's happening?"

I deliberately used his first name, just to level off the playing field a bit.

"No, and yes." He replied.

I frowned, clearly frustrated by such an obtuse answer.

"I don't know why the Crown has suddenly learnt of your innocence, but I do know there was an ex-parte P.I.I. hearing last week, the day before your release."

An *'ex-parte public interest immunity hearing'* was a meeting between one party in a criminal matter and the judge, without the other party being present. They were unusual but I'd been involved in several as a police officer. When I had, it was always to do with withholding sensitive evidence from the other legal team.

Things became just a little clearer.

"Is it possible that an informant has provided credible evidence that I'm innocent?" I suggested.

I immediately jumped to that rather ridiculous idea because, whenever I'd personally done an ex-parte P.I.I., it had always seemed to be with informants, or to give them their proper title, covert human intelligence sources.

"After thirty years? I doubt it." Nicholas said, firmly.

"I know. I'm an idiot, ignore me. But it could be something off a line?" I suggested.

"After thirty years? I doubt it." Nicholas replied, repeating himself.

"Not necessarily. They might have picked up a telephone conversation, prompted by my recent conviction, where one person has talked about knowing a different guy did that murder. Of course, legally they can't refer to that conversation because of IOCA, but they'd still have to evaluate it and see whether it undermined their case." I said.

"I like the way you're thinking, Mr Pritchard. But I don't think that, alone, would be enough to get you out this quickly. I mean, that would be hearsay, anyway." Mr De L'Arcy pointed out.

I nodded.

"But I believe you're thinking along the right lines. Something must have come to light to cast the gravest doubt, but it's something they can't put into the public domain. Perhaps, somehow, it's a national security issue."

"What if, and just go with the flow, the scientist that falsely analysed my DNA sample, because the guy's analysis is wrong, I wasn't there. What if that scientist also did the DNA work on a load of bombing cases and they're worried that releasing me would undermine all these prosecutions to the point where they'd have to release all terrorists, too?"

I looked at Mr De L'Arcy and he smiled.

"Nicholas told me you were smart. He also told me you were innocent."

***

The actual hearing was in camera and only lasted about twenty minutes. We did, however, learn a great deal in that short time. None of which, frustratingly, brought us any nearer to finding out why I'd been released.

The Crown's barrister was first to address the court.

"Your Lordship is aware that this is a highly complicated, multi-faceted matter, and I beg his indulgence. For the record, the Crown concedes the Appellant's conviction under which this matter is listed here today, is unsafe and will, at the appropriate time, be quashed, either by Royal Pardon or the offering of no evidence by the prosecution at a subsequent retrial. For reasons with which His Lordship was recently fully acquainted, the Crown is not in a position to reveal in open court the rationale for this decision. The Crown does, however, fully understand that His Lordship has agreed to this, almost unprecedented, course of action only on the condition that the Appellant concurs, and is prepared to sign a non-disclosure agreement, to that effect.

While I open discussions with my right learned friend Mr De L'Arcy, we will require additional time to address the several other matters irretrievably linked to the Appellant and therefore, to this case. May I respectfully request an adjournment for a month? During this time, the Appellant will be remanded on unconditional bail.

"Do you have any representations Mr De L'Arcy?" The judge asked.

"My Lord. I feel like the proverbial mushroom. I know nothing about the *'complicated and multi-faceted'* matters to which my honourable friend alludes. Perhaps more importantly, neither does my client. All we appear to know for certain is that there are the gravest doubts in respect of his convictions. Convictions, may I remind the court, that he fervently denied both during his trial and every day since. We may, I think not unreasonably, now accept that he is innocent and there has been the most dreadful miscarriage of justice. My client requests, no, my client demands an end to this nightmare. He wants to return to his former job, as a police officer in the Metropolitan Police, he also wants to return to his former life. The life he worked so hard to attain. Yet with this case in limbo, and hanging, like the sword of Damocles, over his head – he must yet suffer even more. I object to this application for a remand and respectfully request this matter be resolved now."

The Judge retired for a few minutes and then returned.

"Before adjourning this case, which I have decided to do, I would like to explain something to the Appellant and his legal representatives. I am sighted upon matters which you, shortly, will also be sighted on. As a consequence, I am able to make a decision which is in both your best interests and the interests of justice. You will, I am afraid, for now, have to trust me. When the fog clears, I am confident you will understand. The case is adjourned for one month."

The Judge stood up and walked out.

Chapter 37

I felt sorry for Mrs M. She'd only gone and put up a load of decorations for my return. The house was covered in balloons and 'congratulations' banners. She opened an expensive bottle of champagne, the one normally kept in the Killer Queen's 'pretty cabinet'. I wasn't in the mood because I had thought that when I returned, I would no longer be a convicted murderer, but I was.

We opened the bubbles, nonetheless, and I took her through the day's events.

"It's clearly only a matter of time. They're obviously going to quash the conviction. I know you're fed up, Chris, but we're very nearly there." Mrs M reassured me.

"I know, you're right; and, of course, I'm a lot better off than I was only a few days ago, when I was still inside. But I am disappointed."

"What did your barrister make of it?" She asked.

"He's got a meeting with the Crown's legal team on Thursday, so we'll know more about things after that. He's perplexed, yes, but he's pretty certain we're talking about issues of national security. I honestly think I'd worked that one out before he did. This guy, he's got the most wonderfully pompous name of De L'Arcy, and he specialises in appeal cases and said that, as a junior barrister in the late 60s, he was involved in an appeal case which had the potential to compromise a senior member of the royal family. Basically, they threw out the rule book and the case was heard in secret. They were able to do deals and come to agreements which would not have normally been allowed. He said, he thinks this case has a similar feeling to it, he used the expression, *'a similar stink'*. I asked him if that was a good thing or not? He wouldn't commit but I got the impression, he rather thought it gave us some leverage."

"But you are innocent. Obviously, they now know you're innocent. There's nothing complicated or difficult, just release you, which they've done, and acquit you." Mrs M said.

"It might be to do with how they know I'm innocent. It might be that they can't reveal that source because to do so would completely compromise, say, an undercover operation that's been running for years and is about to come to fruition."

"Is that likely in your case? It happened thirty years ago?"

"Well, no, but I'm trying to give you an example of something that, hypothetically, might be happening. I know, Mrs M, it doesn't make sense. I'm gutted. I'm not acquitted but I am free and that's the main thing. I see the number of reporters has diminished significantly." I said, trying to change the subject.

"I noticed that, too. Must be a bigger story elsewhere. That reminds me, I need to make them some hot drinks."

"How are you doing without your fella?" I asked.

I was referring, of course, to Assistant Commissioner John King with whom she'd been having an affair for the last couple of years.

"I miss him, Chris, but he calls every couple of days. It's just, with such press attention here, it's not safe for him to come round."

"I've never asked before, but do you know anything about his family?"

"Of course. He's been married for ever. He met his wife, shortly after he joined the army. Her name's Emma. They have five children ..."

"Five!" I interjected.

"Five children. The oldest is twenty-six, the youngest ten. She's a stay-at-home mum."

"Well, he earns a fortune, so she can be, can't she? He must be on a hundred grand, maybe more, maybe one ten." I said.

"And I think his family have got money. They live in Epping in an old barn conversion. Anything else you want to know?"

"Does Emma know about Jennifer?" I asked.

"She does. She asked him, once. He always said he wouldn't lie to her, so he told her the truth."

"And she's okay with it, I mean, you?" I asked.

"No, I don't think that would be the right way to explain it. She accepts that he needs some 'freedom'. That's what she calls it."

"Will he ever leave her for you?" I asked.

"That's the wrong question, Chris."

Mrs M was right, of course.

"Do you want him to leave Emma for you?"

"No, Chris. I'm perfectly happy the way it is."

I took a call from Wendy and spent the next forty minutes telling her about the day's events. Like everyone, she was equally mystified.

"If I can get a baby-sitter, would you like a night out this week?" She asked, as the conversation about the court case gradually waned.

"Yes, but keep it simple, I'm still very jaded. Do you just want to come round? We can get a take-away." I said.

"I thought we could go to the Green Man in Toot Hill." She said.

That was where we'd had our first date, back in 2003. She'd sent me an invitation to dinner there, but she hadn't signed it, so it was all a bit of a mystery. I still remembered, as vividly as if it was only yesterday, seeing her walk in that evening. I don't think that before or after, I'd ever been more physically attracted to a woman. Even, all these years later, I could describe exactly what she was wearing. We'd ended that evening in my bedroom in Loughton and Jackie, who by the way had left me, decided to walk in on us having sex, just as I was about to end, if you know what I mean.

"That's a nice thought, let me think about it." I replied.

The truth was it was all happening too quickly for me. I'd only been out for five days and I needed time. I wasn't even sure I wanted to commit to Wendy; it was way too early to decide. What I didn't want to do until I knew, was to fall back in love and to become emotionally reliant on her. That would cause a pile of pain and grief. I needed to keep some sort of barrier up. I was still suffering terribly from anxiety. No one saw. I kept it really well hidden but, to me, it was constantly boiling just under the surface. It stopped when I went to sleep, but often returned when I woke up in the middle of the night to use the toilet; that's how omnipresent it was. I wasn't quite sure how long I could take it.

Chapter 38

I got a call from Brucie the next morning. He wanted an update on yesterday's events and, when he discovered that I was still not a police officer and likely to remain as such for the foreseeable, he asked me whether I'd be interested in a piece of work with his friend, Steve Kibble. I'd met Steve a few years ago when Brucie and I were investigating the Marcella Parker case.

"Is he still at the auditors?" I asked.

"No, you peckerhead, they made him redundant, remember?"

Of course, I knew that, so I felt somewhat foolish.

"Steve took their money and set up a small private investigator's outfit. He employs ex-old bill. He's always looking for people. Nothing full time, just the odd bit of contract work; you know, a week a month, something like that. Are you surveillance trained?"

"Many years ago." I replied.

"Foot and mobile?"

"Both" I replied.

That was a lie. I'd only ever done the foot course but who was ever going to find out? Besides, over the years I'd been involved in enough surveillance jobs to blag it.

"He's looking to put a team together. Just four of you. He's got some big client in the city who's given him a job. I said I'd see how you were fixed. If you're interested, give him a call, I'll send you his number."

***

While I'd been on my phone, I'd heard the house phone ringing and as soon as I hung up to Brucie, Mrs M came in.

"Remember that policeman who came round last week?"

"Deputy Assistant Commissioner Simon Morley?"

"Yes, his office called. If it's okay, he wants to come and see you again. In fact, he's in Loughton this evening on a personal matter and wondered whether he could call in, on the way through. I said yes, but I've got a number to call if it's not good for you."

I agreed. I was intrigued to see what the latest development was in this, to steal a phrase from yesterday's court case, complicated and multifaceted matter.

***

I had to smile. DAC Morley arrived dressed in a dark black suit, white shirt and black tie. Either he had just gone to a funeral or he was, a suspicion which was confirmed when I clocked his square and compass handcuffs, on his way to a masonic meeting.

We shook hands and Mrs M disappeared to make some hot drinks.

"I have a rather delicate matter to discuss with you."

"Go on, Simon." I replied, deliberately using his first name.

I saw the tiniest flash of unease cross his face.

"Until I return to the Met, I shall address you by your first name." I said, with a smile.

He nodded.

"Fair enough. As I said, I have a delicate matter to discuss."

He paused, as if he was waiting for me to say something.

"Miss Kitty Young, well, umm, as you know, as you may know, she's being investigated for perjury in connection with the evidence she gave at your trial."

"I understand she offered to resign but that her offer has been refused until the investigation has been concluded. Please don't tell me you've come here today to tell me that she's been found to have done nothing wrong and is being reinstated. That would be the last fucking straw. I mean, it is now acknowledged that I was wrongly convicted and remember she was the one that told the court I'd apparently confessed to this murder years before."

He was shaking his head.

"No, please listen. As part of the investigation, they need to interview you. They require a statement, your account of that meeting where she claims you admitted the murder, the murder you've now been found not to have admitted."

"It's not looking too good for her, is it?"

He shook his head.

"Not now you've been found to be innocent, no."

"I haven't yet, the Court of Appeal have adjourned the case for a month."
I replied.

"There is no doubt where this is going, Christopher – sorry Nostrils." He
said, quickly correcting himself.

"I'm going to tell you something in confidence. I'd rather you didn't
repeat it but, I know, as long as you're not in the Job, I can't enforce your
silence."

"Go on." I said.

"As you know, Kitty Young is currently suspended. We have it on good
authority she has written a book. Apparently, the moment her
relationship with the Metropolitan Police ends, she's going to publish.
Ostensibly, it's an autobiography but in it she makes some pretty serious
allegations against the Met and just about everyone she's ever worked
with. It could do us irreparable damage and set race relations back a
decade." He explained.

"Has anyone seen a draft?" I asked.

'Only the odd chapter." He replied.

"Am I mentioned?"

He frowned.

"Curiously enough, no. It's more focused on other senior officers, ACPO
rank."

"Is she using the book as leverage?" I asked.

"You are smart." He said.

"Not really, it's obvious." I replied.

"Can I ask you, not as part of any investigation but just off the record, why would she make something like that up? I mean, honestly Nostrils, that part I don't understand."

"You do know, we have a long and unpleasant history, don't you?" I asked.

I realised that there would be no earthly reason why he should know anything about that.

"No, I knew you'd worked together previously but not the details."

"You haven't got long enough before your meeting for me to tell you the whole story …

My reference to his 'meeting' brought forth a wry smile from the Assistant Commissioner.

" … but we first met at Stoke Newington where she accused me of racism and sexism – that ended up at the High Court. She stole and then doctored my notebook, which she produced at the trial as evidence of my racism. Then ten years later, at Tottenham, our paths crossed again. This time she planted racist material in my desk and then sent racist letters to other black and ethnic minority officers on the division. Fortunately, I managed to sidestep that Exocet missile by finding the material before CIB2 did."

"Gosh. I had no idea. Of course, I'm only getting your side of the story." He replied.

"I know, but we are not friends. In fact, we hate each other. I think she honestly believes I'm a male chauvinistic, racist pig. I'm not, by the way. But holding that belief justifies why she's so determined to destroy me."

"But giving perjured evidence, in a Crown Court trial, for murder! That's just such a risk." He replied.

"Yes and no. Not if she genuinely thinks I've done it and let's be brutally honest Simon, with the DNA evidence, you all thought I was guilty. Didn't you?" I asked.

He nodded. I appreciated his honesty.

"But I wasn't. I'd never, ever hurt an old lady like that."

I suddenly got really choked up. I couldn't talk. It suddenly hit me that for the best part of a year, the whole world had thought I was a monster. I gathered myself. It took a few moments, but Simon sat there patiently and politely, and with just the right empathetic expression on his face.

"Anyway ..." I said, after about a minute.

"... you want me to give evidence against my arch enemy?"

"We do. Are you all right with that?"

"Of course. It may have looked like I was down for the count, but I got up at nine, and dug in my heels. In this bout, Simon, only one of us will come out alive. It's going to be me."

Chapter 39

The following day and so early that I was still in bed, I got a call from Nicholas Cousins, my solicitor. He told me that they had now received more information about the meeting on Thursday with the Crown legal team. He was, he said, surprised to learn that the meeting was also to be attended by the Permanent Secretary of State to the Ministry of Justice and a senior representative from the Attorney Generals office.

"What the fuck is going on?" I asked.

Nicholas had got used to my swearing, but I still sometimes wished that I could stop myself.

"We don't know. I've spoken to counsel and he is as perplexed as we are." He replied.

"But he's an Appeal expert, isn't he? He must have some idea."

"Christopher, he hasn't got a clue. What's more, we got this information yesterday and he spent the day making phone calls and speaking to colleagues. No one's ever heard anything like it. It's simply unprecedented for there to be such a high-level interest in what, ostensibly, should be a straight-forward case. Either they think you committed the murder, or they don't. And they clearly don't because they've released you. They should merely quash the conviction, pay you a few hundred thousand pounds in compensation, and everybody can move on with their lives."

"Something else is going on, isn't it?"

"Yes" He replied.

"What if it was what we said, like the intelligence had come off a line?"

"It shouldn't cause this much stir." He replied.

We agreed a meeting for Friday morning, but I told him I wanted to know what was going on as soon as they wrapped up on Thursday. He promised to call.

***

While I was on the phone, I got a text from Wendy asking me whether I'd had time to think about it, and should she book a table at the Green Man. I felt under pressure. I needed a few days to mull it over, not a few hours. Still, it was nice to feel wanted.

Before I'd even finished reading the end of Wendy's text, the phone rang again. It was Steve Kibble, Brucie's mate.

"Hello, Chris. They let you out then?"

I laughed out loud. Only old bill could say that to another old bill who had just been released from a life sentence, and get away with it.

"No prison's ever been built than can hold old Pritchard!" I replied.

"Good. Then I've got some work for you, if you're interested?"

"Tell me more and I'll tell you whether I'm interested."

"Oh, I do love banter." Steve replied, sarcastically.

"Me too, you're a big, fat cunt!"

"Being honest, mate, prison's not sharpened your wit, has it?"

I laughed again. It felt like a long time since I had such a ridiculous, pointless but relaxed conversation.

"Right. It's seventy pounds a day, cash in hand. Doesn't matter whether you work an hour or twelve hours." He said.

"Fuck me, three hundred and fifty pounds a week! However will I spend the money?"

"Alright, eighty. Do you need to know anymore?"

"Well, if it's not too much trouble, and assuming you haven't forgotten the other details."

"We've got quite an interesting job on. It's part of a much larger operation and my little outfit has been sub-contracted to keep an eye on one specific member of the Russian Olympic team. Officially, he's a coach, or technical advisor, but he's suspected of being one of the key players in assisting their athletes to avoid getting caught using performance enhancing drugs when the games start in a couple of months. We've got to find out who his associates are, you know, who he's meeting."

"Lifestyle then?" I asked.

"Yeah, lifestyle. As I said, this is part of a much wider job and he's just one of half a dozen targets."

"Who's paying you? The International Olympic Committee?" I asked.

"The answer to your question is the name of a well-known world-wide detective agency, you would have heard of them. As I said, our works being sub-contracted, but ultimately, I think the U.S. might be behind this.

It's also tied into a large bribery and corruption scandal that involves the FIFA World Cup, as well as the Olympics. They've obviously got a source who's coughing his guts up."

"You're right, it sounds interesting." I replied.

"Every week, I have to submit a report on our target's movements to the detective agency. I am required to undertake a minimum of sixty hours surveillance a week, so I need a small army. Would you like to join up?"

"Go on then, Steve. I'll give it a go." I replied.

"Brucie said you were fully surveillance trained, is that right?"

"I am, but I've done very little over the years."

I desperately wanted an excuse for not knowing as much as I would have known, if I had been fully trained.

"Did you do the Met course or the one at Wyboston?" He asked.

"I did the foot course from Beak Street when I was on the Stoke Newington Crime Squad. Back in '86." I replied.

I knew I was avoiding the question and waited for him to push me for an answer.

"If Brucie says you have, that's all I need to know." He said.

I wasn't sure I hadn't bitten off more than I could chew.

Chapter 39

I hadn't done any surveillance for years and forgotten just how mind-numbingly boring it was, most of the time.

I was paired up with a chap called Luke Pollack, who was ex-job. I'd never met him before; he was at least ten years older than me. In policing terms that was kind of two generations apart, but his name did ring a bell. It was only when he said that he was the older of three brothers who all joined the Metropolitan Police, that I realised where I knew him from, or, more to the point, how I knew his brothers.

Simon, the middle brother, used to work at Chingford and, way back in the 80s, I'd done a job with him. He was a lovely guy, and I always thought he was something to do with me getting into the CID when I was so young in service. The younger brother was Paul. I'd had an affair with Paul's girlfriend, the lovely Sarah, and when Paul found out he committed suicide by blowing his brains out in the basement toilets of Stoke Newington police station.

There really was no reason why Luke would know I was connected to his youngest brother's suicide. I thought it wise though not to say a word about Stoke Newington and the bad old days. What's more, Steve had asked me not to tell anyone that I was the police officer who had just been released from jail. I was discretion personified and carefully negotiated Luke's questioning about my previous police career, focusing my answers on the murder squad and staff officer roles, the latter being enough to bore anyone to tears.

With two other vehicles, we were parked up in the vicinity of a hotel in Earls Court where the target was currently residing. Someone called Dave had eyeball on the front door and we were waiting for him to give us the signal when he spotted the our man.

Police surveillance teams were much bigger than this, but clearly even this resource commitment, there were six of us, was going to prove expensive. We did have excellent technical equipment though, much more modern than the last I'd seen in the Met.

"This guy's really hard work." Luke said.

"Why's that?" I asked.

"He uses black cabs. They're a nightmare to follow because they can use the bus lanes and other cabbies always let them into traffic. We try to get a footie into a second cab and then deliver that infamous line *follow that cab* to the driver. It's really the only way. If Dave picks him up, that's what he'll try and do and we'll make ground, as best we can. Of course, it's not like the old days; when you're in the job you can get away with red lights and speeding tickets, but this is obviously different."

"It sounds impossible." I said.

"It's a challenge." Luke replied.

"Were you surveillance when you were in the job?" I asked.

"Last fourteen years. I did my training on the old SPG, then moved to C11." He replied.

"When did you retire?" I asked.

"In 1999, went on an ill-health with twenty-eight in."

I did some quick mental maths and realised Luke must have joined in 1971, meaning he was at least sixty! I thought that was quite old to be playing this game.

"Contact, contact. Subject is out and off, waiting to hail a cab. Wearing his usual blue suit and white shirt, carrying his brown duffel bag. Stand-by. Black cab livered green, Harrods. West towards Brompton. Stand by..."

We set off. I kept quiet. This was no time for idle chatter.

"I'm in a cab, directly behind him. Continues west. Cab is signalling left at ATS. Yes, that's a left, left, left onto the B317 towards Putney."

I was impressed. Although small, this was one slick surveillance team. Despite all the challenges of being privately operated, they were simply outstanding. We stayed behind the subject all day while he met contact after contact, in about half a dozen locations, all within a few miles. I had an absolute whale of a time. I hadn't had so much excitement in years.

At five o'clock the subject went into a pub right next to the Thames at Putney and I was deployed to enter the pub to see what he was up to. I gave him a few minutes and walked in, ordering a pint of Guinness.

He was sitting at a table, deep in conversation with another white male, and I sat at the bar and turned my back towards them, as I remembered I was trained to do, all those years ago. After a few minutes, I used the taking off of my jacket as an excuse to get a quick glance in their direction. They were nearly finishing their drinks and, from their body language, I anticipated they were about to leave. I gave several rapid clicks on my handheld transmitter.

"Chris, is that you?"

I gave three clicks, the signal for yes.

"Are you able to talk?"

Two clicks, the signal for no.

"Do you wish to communicate a message?"

Three clicks.

"Do you require someone else in there?"

Two clicks.

"Is the subject still there?"

Three clicks.

"Is he about to leave?"

Three clicks.

"All units stand-by, stand-by. The subject is about to leave the Boatman. Chris, rapid clicks when he moves towards the door please."

Three clicks.

"Chris, please remain and try to identify anyone the contact has met. Perhaps, by following them off to a vehicle and getting the index, or any

other innovative means. If we lose you, make your way home and call in on the way."

Three clicks.

I turned back to the bar, ostensibly to order another drink, but in reality, to get a better view of the subject.

They were both standing up now.

I looked more closely at the other man, conscious that I would have to give a detailed description of him later. He turned slightly and our eyes almost met, always the worst possible scenario when you're doing this role.

Fuck me, I was looking at Tristram Parker. He was the husband of Marcella, the woman who went missing four years ago. I'd interviewed him for days and met him at the airport after his release from custody.

I looked away immediately but whether it was quick enough, I didn't know. The thing is, I could have compromised the whole surveillance operation. If he saw me, he might still think I was old bill, although it was equally possible, he now knew me as *'the policeman that raped the old lady, who also dealt with my case'*. And besides, what the fuck was he doing out of prison? I'm sure he got six years for money laundering. A remarkably short sentence for what he'd done, but no doubt reduced because he cooperated with the police.

A good thirty seconds had passed and he hadn't come over. When I looked up, he'd gone and by the time I left the pub, so had the surveillance team. As instructed, I made my way home. It had been a great day. At times, my anxiety had almost disappeared. It was just like being in the Job again, only the pay was a lot worse. And fancy spending a day with Paul Pollack's older brother, all these years after that dreadful day at Stoke Newington.

I got the rattler home, a journey from south-west to north-east London which involved four changes on the underground and countless stops. It didn't matter. It was nice to be free and the trains weren't too busy, so I could get a seat.

Before the train went underground, I sent a text to Steve telling him everything that had happened, including the identity of the subject's meet in the pub. I explained candidly that there was a small risk I'd been compromised. I suspected Steve wouldn't be able to use me again on this particular job. It was a shame but that would be the right decision.

Chapter 40

When I was in the Job, I loved going to barristers' chambers. It was like going back in time about two hundred years. Mr De L'Arcy's chambers were right in the middle of the Temple, in what must have been one of the oldest buildings in this unique part of central London.

The three of us, Mr De L'Arcy, Nicholas Cousins and myself, were in the main board room, somewhat lost sitting at the large, aged conference table, which could accommodate at least twenty people, probably more.

I was a little surprised that the mood was so sullen. After all, this was the big reveal, where I would find out why the powers that be had changed their mind about my conviction. I would have thought the atmosphere would have been upbeat and positive, but I detected an air of caution and that worried me. Were things not quite as straight forward as I'd hoped they would be? Was there some final twist in this perverse saga of wrongful conviction?

A young man brought in three black coffees and he left the tray on the table before us. Both my barrister and solicitor each carried a blue notebook upon which they'd recorded their meeting the previous day. As soon as the young man had closed the door behind him, Mr De L'Arcy put his notebook down and started speaking.

"Where were you born?" Mr De L'Arcy asked.

The question caught me completely by surprise.

"Bradford-on-Avon, Wiltshire." I replied.

What a strange question, I thought.

"My apologies, as a barrister I really should have known to ask a more specific question. Were you born in a hospital, did your mother ever tell you?" Mr De L'Arcy said.

"Umm, no, no, Mum said it was a homebirth. She used to say, *'you were born in this house. Dad died in it, I'll die in it and you were born in it'*. I'm sorry, why? Are you going to tell me I'm not who I think I am? Was I adopted? Because I've seen, well I've got, my birth certificate unless that's a forgery?"

"No, you are Christopher Pritchard, Christopher."

Mr De L'Arcy paused. I could almost hear the cogs turning in his brain, working out how to phrase what he was about to say next.

"Does the name Jeffrey Hampshire mean anything to you? Think carefully."

I racked my brains. Jeffrey Hampshire? Nope. I shook my head.

"Well ..." Mr De L'Arcy went to speak but I interrupted him.

" ... hang on. Mum had a friend called Hampshire. Hen Hampshire, Hen was short for Henrietta. She had a son; his name might have been Jeff. Fuck me, I'm stretching the old grey cells, here. Hen and her son used to come round quite a lot when I was little, I mean, really little, like four, five, maybe. Didn't see them after that. I don't think I noticed particularly, they just stopped coming round. Mum might have said they moved away. Mum was drinking heavily by then so perhaps they just couldn't put up with her anymore."

"Christopher, listen carefully. Jeffrey Hampshire is your brother, he's your identical twin brother. Well, he was, he died a month ago. Alcoholism and drug addiction. They took his fingerprints at the morgue and they linked him to numerous outstanding burglaries ..."

"They also took his DNA, didn't they?"

I was ahead of the conversation; the reality of the situation and what was being revealed, washed over me like a wave.

Mr De L'Arcy nodded.

"It matched the Royal Crescent crime scene, didn't it?"

He nodded again.

I put my head in my hands. It was all too much to process but it seemed to help a bit if I rocked back and forwards. No one spoke for a few minutes. Eventually, I looked up.

"There was absolutely no record of the adoption. Your mother must have quite literally given Jeffery to her friend at the time of the birth and kept you. Mrs Hampshire died last year, so we'll never know the full details, but Jeffrey, her son and your brother, went through his life without a birth certificate. She never claimed child allowance for him. I mean, he went to school, so he did exist on some registers, but not others. More amazingly considering his lifestyle, Jeffrey seems to have avoided arrest his whole adult life."

"Which explains everything." I said.

"Indeed. Jeffrey grew up in a place called Keynsham." Mr De L'Arcy replied.

"Exactly half-way between Bath and Bristol. Talk me through the sequence of events then."

For the first time, Mr De L'Arcy referred to his notebook.

"On 2nd April, Jeffrey Hampshire died in his sleep at a YMCA hostel in Bristol. It appeared that he had taken a heroin overdose, there were no suspicious circumstances. On 4th April the post mortem identified the causes of death as heart failure due to alcoholism and drug abuse. He had a raft of other medical conditions including hepatitis and HIV. His fingerprints were taken to confirm his identity and submitted to NIB. On 11th NIB identified a number of matches to crime scenes, burglaries going back decades, both domestic and non-res, and made a request to the Coroner for a sample of DNA. So far, procedurally, everything was quite standard. The DNA sample was taken on 14th and submitted to NIB the following day.

On 17th April a forensic scientist at NIB matched the DNA to the Royal Crescent crime scene and notified Avon & Somerset police by telephone. The following day, the case was formally re-opened and urgent enquiries commenced to ascertain exactly who the deceased was, and whether it was possible he'd actually committed the murder and rape. Over the next two weeks, the investigation interviewed friends, family members, teachers, social workers and neighbours. Their enquiries were hampered because Mrs Hampshire was deceased, but her sister did eventually, and under some pressure, reveal the true story.

By 26th April, Avon & Somerset police had learnt your brother was a heroin user from the age of fifteen, lived close to the murder scene and was funding his drug addiction through burglary. They also discovered family rumours that suggested, as a young child, Jeffrey had been repeatedly sexually assaulted by an elderly couple who were neighbours and used to babysit him while his mother went out to work. Photographs taken at the time also showed he had really long hair, like the suspect in the photofit."

"Fuck me." I said, almost without knowing I had spoken.

"That day Avon & Somerset formally notified the Crown Prosecution Service that their enquiries revealed the gravest doubts about the safety of your conviction."

"And that's it. That's where we are? If it's that straight forward, why wasn't my conviction quashed on Monday?"

Mr De L'Arcy took a deep breath and exchanged a quick glance with Nicholas Cousins, my solicitor.

"What? What is it? What's up?" I asked.

I could feel panic rising.

"Christopher?" Nicholas spoke for the first time.

"Yes" I replied, impatiently.

"What do you know about the murder of Barry Skinner?"

Chapter 41

Obviously, I'd seen people faint. The occasional soldier during trooping of the colour, maybe a couple of pupils during a hot assembly at school, even the odd hysterical female in an old movie, but I'd never fainted myself. Well, not until I heard the question which I feared most coming from the lips of my earnest solicitor.

Apparently, I went very limp and fell gracefully to one side, slipping off my chair and onto the carpeted floor. On the way, I caught my cheek on the corner of a chair next to mine breaking the skin, causing a cut of sufficient length and depth to, very nearly, require stitching.

All I remember is the sudden onset of tunnel vision which increased until I couldn't see. The very next second, I was coming to, surrounded by people, all fussing and running hither and thither with cold flannels and a make-shift ice pack for my face. I was flat on my back with my legs raised on something soft, perhaps a pouffe.

I felt a bit sick and my heart was pounding, and it took me a few moments to realise what was going on and why. Then the realisation hit me. Nicholas had asked me about Barry Skinner.

I suspected by fainting, I'd probably answered his question, but I needed to think quickly and, if possible, coolly. I shut my eyes and concentrated.

If they sent me back to prison, I would definitely kill myself. I knew that for sure. After being unexpectedly released in such a dramatic style, there was no way I could serve more time inside. I would simply go mad. I'd rather be dead. But I had to force myself away from these thoughts. Though valid, at this precise moment in time, there were more important issues I had to focus on.

How in god's name did they know about the murder? The only answer to that was that it had been brought up yesterday during their meeting with the Attorney General office, the CPS and everyone else representing the

Crown. If the Crown knew I was responsible, how long had they known? It was inconceivable that they'd only just found out, that was too much of a coincidence, so they must have known for some time. If they'd known for some time, why hadn't I been further arrested and, at least, interviewed about my involvement, if not charged?

And how did anyone find out I was involved? The only other person who knew was Mrs M and she would never betray me. Besides, the Real IRA had claimed responsibility, so why did anyone start looking elsewhere?

Of course, it might well be that they knew I did it but couldn't prove it because their case was based on intelligence rather than evidence and, as we all know, sometimes you just can't use your intelligence in a criminal prosecution.

I thought the fact that I wasn't already in prison for Barry Skinner, was a very good indication that all might yet not be lost.

My most pressing decision was how to play the whole thing with my legal team. Although, my fainting might suggest my guilt, it wasn't a confession. I wanted to tell them the truth, and of course, anything I said to them wouldn't be admissible in evidence because of client privilege. Once I'd admitted my involvement to them however, if the case then went to trial and I pleaded not guilty, ethically they wouldn't be allowed to represent me. If they didn't represent me, you might as well tell the world that I'd admitted it to them.

Half an hour later, I was sitting back at the large conference table. The well-meaning first aiders had departed, leaving just the three of us again. I was holding a damp cloth to my face, but the bleeding had stopped.

"Do you want to come back tomorrow? If you're not feeling up to it?" Nicholas asked.

"No" I replied, perhaps a little too curtly and without looking up.

"What do you know about the murder of Barry Skinner?" He repeated, quietly.

I shook my head.

"No" I replied, firmly but less brusquely.

"Sorry? You don't know anything?" Nicholas asked.

"No, that's not what I mean."

I looked up briefly.

Both Nicholas and Mr De L'Arcy exchanged glances.

"What do you mean, Christopher?" Mr De L'Arcy asked.

"That's not how we're going to do this." I replied.

"What do you mean?" They both said, almost in unison.

"I'm not saying a word. You two are going to tell me absolutely everything you know before I say fuck all about fuck all."

"Give us five, will you Christopher?" Nicholas said.

I nodded and they both got up and left the room.

As soon as they were outside I took my mobile out and pressed the home button. There were numerous missed calls, from Mrs M, Wendy, Brucie and Steve and a voicemail from my doctor's surgery. I listened to the voicemail which told me I was no longer registered with them, their allocations were full and, as they weren't taking on new patients at the moment, I'd have to go elsewhere. This was a big problem. I desperately needed a repeat prescription of the anti-anxiety tablets I was on while I'd been in prison. Without them, I was really struggling and that was before today's little revelation. I wondered when anything would go my way.

I started to wish that I hadn't been released. I was, after all, just about coping inside. Being set free and then locked up again would be more than I could bear. I felt absolutely terrible.

Chapter 42

"At our meeting yesterday, the Crown concedes, without equivocation, that your convictions in respect of Mrs Eileen Armstrong are unsafe and they will quash the conviction through the Appeal process. They claim, however, to have irrefutable proof that you were responsible for the murder of Barry Skinner in June 2007. They wanted us to take instructions from you in connection with that matter and then contact them again."

To my surprise, Nicholas stopped talking.

"Go on." I said.

"That's it." He replied.

"You can't be serious?" I said.

They looked at one another and nodded.

"That's not how it works, is it? They should arrest, interview and charge me. In the police, I wouldn't have said to a defence brief, off you go and ask your client if he did the burglary and tell me what he says. That's not how it works. Surely, you're as amazed as I am, or am I missing something?" I asked.

"Christopher, let me tell you something that might help to explain what's going on. It's not about you, but it will illustrate what might be happening here." Mr De L'Arcy said.

I nodded. I was confused, I had no idea what he was going to say.

"As you are aware, Her Majesty's Government operate one of the most effective security services in the world. Mostly, these operatives act within the same laws as you and I do. They have to comply with the Regulation of Investigatory Powers Act, the Human Rights Act and all the other statutory and common law. Very rarely, and in the interests of national security, an operative may have to act outside of the law. When he or she does so, I am asked to represent them because I am one of a few Queens Council cleared to the highest level of vetting. While my legal responsibility is, of course, to protect my client's interests, my role is usually one of negotiation and agreement. In the twenty years I've been doing this type of work, I have never had to go to court.

A month ago, I was contacted by someone, it doesn't matter who, and asked to pick up your case. That was before you even knew you were being released. It was why your last barrister stepped aside, to allow me in, so to speak. Do you understand?"

My mind was racing. What was Mr De L'Arcy telling me? That HMG knew I was guilty but was going to come to some kind of negotiated settlement? Why, why would they do that? I hadn't been operating for the Queen when I killed Barry Skinner, so why would anyone in power care what happens to me?

"I think so. Basically, when James Bond, in a car chase, crashes and takes out a couple of innocent bystanders at a bus stop, you get involved and make sure he just gets a conditional discharge."

"Something like that." He replied, and I detected just a hint of a smile at the edge of his lips.

"And the fact that you were asked to represent me. Hang on." I said.

I suddenly realised the vital importance of a small but crucial piece of the jigsaw.

"When, when exactly were you asked to take this case on?"

Mr De L'Arcy smiled.

Mr Cousins smiled and said.

"I told you, didn't I?"

"Was it before they knew I was innocent of the Armstrong murder or after?"

"It was at the end of March." He replied.

"My twin, the Hampshire guy, he didn't die until 2nd April, did he? This predates that."

They both nodded.

"Any idea what the *'irrefutable evidence'* is?" I asked.

Mr De L'Arcy shook his head.

"It could be a bluff?"

"It's not." He replied, definitively.

"Does the fact I was wrongly convicted strengthen or weaken our hand?" I asked.

"Strengthen."

"You're telling me there's some kind of deal here? One that'll keep me out of prison? Please note that I haven't admitted anything."

I added the second thought quickly, just so there was no confusion.

"I think so." Mr De L'Arcy replied.

"What is it?"

"We haven't got to that stage, yet. In order to get there, I need you to indicate both your guilt and your willingness to resolve the issue. Once I have those two assurances, I can start negotiating."

"What will your negotiations include?" I asked.

"Whether you stand trial for the murder of Barry Skinner. Whether you receive compensation for your wrongful conviction; whether you get your QPM reinstated; whether you can re-join the Metropolitan Police; the details of any non-disclosure agreement; what the media are going to be told about your release. And most importantly of all, if you aren't prosecuted, what mechanism will be used to facilitate the process because everything still has to be done lawfully. Quite a lot really." Mr De L'Arcy replied.

"Have you any idea why they don't want to just prosecute me?" I asked.

"Officially, no. Unofficially, yes, because I read the newspapers and understand the politics. The latest Northern Ireland peace process is at a crucial stage. Her Majesty's Government has always been in a stronger negotiating position because the Real IRA murdered Barry Skinner, something they can hardly deny, as they claimed responsibility. If you were now to stand trial for his murder, they would lose that advantage. What's more, they would look stupid. Even worse, as you were a police officer, it might look to some like a state sponsored assassination. Another example of the *'shoot to kill'* policy, which the UK government has so fervently denied.

What's more, having acquitted you after a grave miscarriage of justice, it would be politically difficult to put you on trial again and almost impossible to get a jury to convict you.

Thirdly, I suspect they don't want DNA evidence undermined. The credibility of the forensic science is the reason so many offenders are behind bars, can you imagine the raft of appeals that will fly in, after the reasons for the miscarriage of justice become clear.

Finally, I think those right at the top have no problem with what you did to Barry Skinner. I suspect they're looking for a way to help you." Mr De L'Arcy replied.

"Me? I didn't do nothing."

My use of the double negative was deliberate, my response, as a consequence, ambiguous.

Chapter 43

The more I thought about it, and the more I turned over everything Mr De L'Arcy had said, I realised I had a strong hand. In poker terms, I was holding a full house, aces full of kings. Like most police officers, however, I'd played enough poker to know that the only thing worse than a shit hand, was having a great hand beaten by a better one. If the government had me bang to rights, and I was in fact staring down the nostrils of a doubled barrelled life sentence, then my full house might not be as strong as it appeared.

I'd agreed that Mr De L'Arcy could go back and open negotiations. By so doing, I was admitting my involvement, but informally only. My legal team had assured me that such an admission was *'without prejudice'*, meaning, they explained, it couldn't be used, or even referenced, in any future trial.

I realised both how lucky and unlucky I'd been. Of course, my twin brother's timely death was a great stroke of fortune. Had he not died, I would have spent the rest of my life in solitary confinement in a cell no more than eight feet by five. I was pretty convinced I would have gone mad, because after only seven months, my sanity was hanging by an ever-weakening thread. I'd also been remarkably unlucky to have a secret twin brother so mentally deranged as to do such a terrible thing to an old lady. Maybe the mental illness was hereditary? Was it possible that now I was similarly suffering, I too might be capable of terrible deeds? I thought about that briefly and dismissed it. I might be on the verge of a breakdown, but I was no more capable of raping and murdering an innocent person than I was of flying.

I did wonder how they'd discovered my involvement in the Barry Skinner murder. It then dawned on me that, if everything about the murder was so damn sensitive, why not simply let sleeping dogs lie. Why did they go looking for something they really didn't need to find? What's more, why did it take them four years? If I'd been discovered by DNA, that would only take a matter of weeks at the most to come through. If a decent CCTV image of me had been my undoing, that might have taken a few weeks to find and analysis, but no more. The four-year delay didn't make any sense, at all.

Then the penny dropped.

While I was in prison for murder, it wasn't in the public interest to prosecute me. I mean, I was serving life anyway, adding a second life sentence would have been somewhat meaningless. The problem only arose when I was released. At that point, my previous murder suddenly became a live issue.

No, no, no. That didn't make sense either because I'd only been in the frame for the Bath murder for the last year.

I prided myself on being able to work things out, but I can honestly say these events totally perplexed me, especially their sequence and timing. It didn't matter which way I turned everything over, there was no possible explanation why this should be playing out in this way.

When I got home, I was grateful that Mrs M was out. I suspected she was at the cemetery. I really didn't want to have to try to explain what was going on. Well, with the exception of the bit about my twin brother.

As I was taking off my suit, I emptied the pockets and came across the calling card from Louise Lusher. Gosh, what a lot had happened since I'd last held that in my hand. I vaguely remembered that I'd called her, and she'd suggested some sort of threesome with her husband. That was at a time when I hadn't had sex for years and, had I not been about to go off to the Old Bailey to stand trial for murder, I'd almost certainly have given the idea a go. Ironically, going to prison had improved my sex life no end. That's not something many straight men would want to admit. But for a few months, Chloe had sorted me out at least once a week. More often than not, it wasn't full intercourse, but I can honestly say it made every time she was on duty, an absolute thrill.

I'm pretty certain some of the other staff knew what was going on, but they never interfered. On a normal wing the other prisoners would have eventually latched on, but prisoners were only on the Seg for a few days, or a couple of weeks, at most. Personally, I think Chloe enjoyed the first couple of weeks of our little fling the most, the teasing stage, where she used to flirt outrageously but actually do nothing. I don't know now, but perhaps I did, too. I was flabbergasted when she turned up at my house a couple of weeks ago. I thought it was nothing more than physical but clearly, she saw more into it, which is ridiculous, as I was at the time doing a life sentence.

Holding Louise Lushers's calling card between my thumb and forefinger, I twisted it around several times, before I made my mind up.

I got my phone out and sent her the following text.

You won't remember me, but I am the policeman from Heathrow. We spoke a while ago, but I got rather taken out of the game. I keep finding your calling card in my pocket and thought 'what the hell!'. Feel free to ignore my text but otherwise, I'd love to meet up.

I never expected to hear anything but no sooner had I gone to the toilet and come back, there was a text for me.

I do remember you, Mister policeman from Heathrow. When you say taken out of the game, have you been terribly unwell? Nothing catching I hope because that would certainly spoil my plans. xxx

Play it cool, Pritchard, I thought. Leave it a while to respond.

I don't really know why I was interested. On some levels, it didn't really make any sense. I mean I had the love of my life, Wendy, available on tap. When I say, *'on tap'* I meant *'babysitter availability allowing'*. Wendy was ten years older than when we'd first met, but she was still *'top totty'.* Despite this however, I was curious. I think perhaps I'd come to realise just how transient life was. Was I put off because it wasn't just her and me? Ther husband was part of the arrangement? No not really. Like all men, I looked at internet porn and what I enjoyed wasn't especially one on one sex, it was often situations involving multiple partners. I mean, I wasn't interested in men at all, but the thought of two men sleeping with one woman wasn't unappealing to me, though, nowhere near as exciting as the thought of two woman and just me.

Several texts later, we'd agreed to meet for Sunday lunch at a pub in Surbiton, which was a bit of a trek from Buckhurst Hill but what the hell! I had no idea what the plan was after lunch, I thought I'd just go with the flow.

Chapter 44

The following day, I got a phone call from Steve Kibble. I hadn't heard from him for a few days, in fact, not since I'd texted him on the way home from Putney on the day I did the surveillance for him.

'Hello, stranger." I said, in reference to his lack of communication.

"Hello, mate. Listen, we've had a bit of a result. There's good news and bad, which do you want first?" He asked.

"Bad, give me the bad." I replied.

"I can't use you again, not on this job. If you know this Parker guy and he knows you were old bill, obviously that ain't going to work."

"I understand. I thought you'd say that." I replied, with a degree of resignation.

"But the good news is …"

"Go on."

"Our employeer are absolutely delighted with the Tristram Parker identification. Apparently that's the missing piece in the jigsaw. We've practically solved the case and it's all down to you."

"I thought he was in jail. I worked on him years ago, you know, during that case you helped us with."

"I know who he is, Nostrils. I couldn't believe it when you texted that through. He got sentenced to six years for laundering and served just three and a half; he was released six months ago. He's still got all the Russian connections." Steve explained.

"But didn't he rat them all out?" I asked.

"No, just a select few and the others, of course, just moved in to fill the gaps."

"What's his role in all this? I mean, he doesn't know anything about performance enhancing drugs, does he? And surely he lost his money to the Confiscation Order?" I asked.

"I don't know, matey …"

"You're spending too much time with Brucie, that's just what he would say." I said.

"Probably right. No, I don't know what his exact role is, we're only doing the surveillance, but I tell you what, the Americans were stonkingly happy with the result. Apparently, they've been trying to identify him for months and we've done that for them. They've rewarded us with a bonus and I'm happy to compensate you accordingly. Two grand all right?"

"Sounds great, Steve, are you sure? It was only a day's work? That is good news." I replied.

The money would come in really useful, as I had no income coming in.

"That's not the actual good news, Nostrils." He said.

"Go on." I replied.

"We've got another job on."

"Oh, and you want me working on that?" I said.

"No, you can't work on that, either."

"Why's that good news then?" I asked, a little miffed.

"I thought you might like to know the target of that operation is our currently suspended Deputy Commissioner. I'm telling you this in confidence, right?"

"I won't say a word. Is it to do with the investigation into her committing perjury?"

As soon as the words left my mouth, I realised that was a really stupid question. Any investigation into Kitty Young would be undertaken by the IPCC and not subcontracted to some smallish local private investigation company.

"Of course not, Nostrils. No, I've been contacted by a production company who are making a documentary programme about her." He explained.

"What's the gist? It is about my trial?" I asked.

"For fuck's sake, Nostrils, the world doesn't revolve around you."

I felt slightly embarrassed.

"Sorry" I said, meekly.

"Apparently, they've been approached by an ex of hers who wants to spill the beans. She's been using her Met Police credit card for her own expenditure, like for years, and no one's realised. She even had some cosmetic surgery and charged it to the card. That's not all. I understand she has a very interesting personal life, you know, quite promiscuous."

"Really? I'll be honest, promiscuity doesn't sound like the Kitty Young I know. Besides, she's the Deputy Commissioner, how would anyone not recognise her? That sounds like bollocks."

"It's what the ex is saying. He reckons she's a right little goer!"

"A right little goer? For fuck's sake! Good luck to her. Is that really the best he can do? As for using her job credit card for personal expenses, honestly Steve, I think they're all at it. Some of the expense claims I used to see pass through the Assistant Commissioner's office were frankly staggering. She must really have pissed her ex off, if he wants to put the knife in that badly." I said.

"Well, I thought you'd be interested." Steve said.

He sounded a little hurt.

"I am, mate. I truly hate the woman but the fact she used her Metropolitan Police credit card to purchase a black mamba, isn't something I can get terribly excited about." I replied.

"Anyway, we can't use you on that job, either." He said.

"It's alright. I'll survive. I've got some savings and I'm hoping the Job is going to reinstate me." I replied.

"They'll have to, won't they? Promise me you'll show me your wage packet when they do, because they'll have to backdate your pay. It'll be the biggest pay packet anyone has ever seen!" He said.

"I don't know about that, I used to do the Miner's strike back in '84." I replied.

We both laughed.

"I'll be in touch if we ever get a job where you don't know the subject." Steve said.

"Cheers, mate." I replied and hung up.

I had two missed calls from a London number, which surprised me, as I'd been really careful about who I gave my new mobile number to. When I returned the call, it was the switchboard for the BBC. I hung up. As soon as I did, a voicemail notification came through.

"Hi, I'm leaving a message for Christopher Pritchard. This is Terry Downing, the deputy Commissioning Editor here at the BBC. We'd like to meet you. We're interested in making a TV documentary series about your life."

Chapter 45

As I walked into the small Italian restaurant about two hundred yards from the beautiful art deco station, for the first time in a year I felt nicely anxious. I was met at the door by an elderly waiter, a heavily accented dark skinned Mediterranean male, who immediately told me they were fully booked. My eyes darted about, but I couldn't see Louise Lusher anywhere. My mobile rang, I mumbled an excuse and stepped outside.

"Chris, it's Louise. Turn around."

I did as I was told.

"I can see you. We're in the pub opposite, come across the road. What do you want to drink?"

Five minutes later, I was sitting at a raised table with Louise immediately to my right, a pint of Guinness directly in front of me on the table and her husband, who's name I had already forgotten, sitting opposite me. Louise looked exactly how she had at the airport, immaculately turned out, everything about her was perfect. Her nails and hair had just been done, her make-up perfectly but discreetly applied, and her clothes designer and expensive. She looked classy. If Louise was in her early forties, her husband was a good ten, maybe even twelve, years older than her. He was a good-looking guy, and I rarely say that about other men, with short salt and pepper hair, an excellent physic and a square, rugged, handsome face. His skin however was dreadfully pitted, like he'd suffered from terrible acne as a youth.

"Sorry about the little restaurant trick, but it gives us a chance to look at you, make sure you're on your own. Gives us a chance to get a feel for the type of person you are, you know, like were you on time? Did you dress appropriately? Things like that." Louise said.

I smiled and nodded.

"Makes sense, I suppose."

"Got to be honest, I've never done anything like this before. I'll be honest, I don't even really know what 'this' is. I'm starting to feel like I might have made a mistake."

They looked at each other and grinned.

"It'll be fine. You don't have to do anything you feel uncomfortable with. You can get up and leave at any second." Louise's husband said.

It was the first time he'd spoken. His voice was deep, calm and reassuring.

"Why don't you just ask us whatever you want?" He said.

"Do you do this often?" I asked.

It sounded the most insipid, stupid question and I was immediately embarrassed.

"We have done this three times. One time it didn't work out at all, twice it was simply wonderful." She said.

"And when was the last time you did this?"

They looked at one another and silently agreed.

"Two years ago."

"And what do you look for in the other person?" I asked.

"That's an interesting question." Louise replied.

"Is it always a male?" I asked.

"Yes, always. That's the dynamic we're seeking. We want someone who's confident, someone who has a presence and a bit of charisma; and please don't take this the wrong way, someone who isn't drop dead gorgeous with a fantastic young, fit body." Louise replied.

I laughed out loud; and droplets of Guinness went up my nose.

"None taken." I said, with a broad smile.

"Someone like that would be too intimidating, for both me and David. "

This time I clocked his name.

"I'm a little older than Louise; although I keep myself in shape I really don't want to feel, well, you know ..." David said.

He sipped his glass of white wine and, for a second, I just detected a little apprehension. Was it possible that I wasn't the only one sitting at that table who was a little nervous? I changed the subject.

"What do you do for a living?" I asked.

"I work for a multinational insurance company." He replied.

"David's being modest, he's a very senior executive." Louise added, with just a hint of pride in her husband's success.

"I'd love to know a little more about you. I know you're a policeman but what are you in to?" Louise asked.

"Well, I'm divorced and have two daughters ..."

"Do you have a partner?" Louise interrupted me.

"Sort of, her name's Wendy." I replied.

"Does Wendy know that you are contemplating a deep, meaningful, exhilarating and exciting sexual relationship with another couple?"

Louise looked me squarely in the face and held my eye.

In that second, I was completely aroused but I suddenly felt very much in control.

"No" I replied, confidently.

"When I asked, 'what you're into', mister policeman, I meant in the bedroom."

Thoughts of Wendy and Chloe flashed through my head.

"Do you like to dominate, or submit?"

Under the table, she put her right hand on my thigh.

"... do you like it rough or romantic? Do you like to be watched or to watch? Do you want me to dress as a whore or a lady?"

'Yes, to all those." I replied.

The truth was, I suddenly started to realise what a boring sex life I'd had. I knew what she was asking, and probably deep down inside I had answers to all her questions, but I'd only ever had sex one-on-one, in private, with a woman, where we were both emotionally pretty equal.

"Is there anything you won't do?" Louise asked.

She adjusted her position again, and out the corner of my eye I saw her right leg reach across towards David's body.

"I am completely straight …"

"Good, so am I." David added quickly.

"… and I don't want anyone or anything going anywhere near my bottom."

"Okay …" Louise replied.

"… I'll leave my buttplug exactly where it is for now."

Chapter 46

We ended up spending nearly three hours in the pub in Surbiton. After the first awkward thirty minutes, we started to get on well. We consumed way too much alcohol and I still wasn't entirely used to drinking after my seven months at Her Majesty's pleasure.

They were a lovely couple, very upper middle class but also quite down to earth. They had the perfect life, lived in a beautiful house on an island in the middle of the Thames. They showed me photos on their phones of two beautiful children, who were looked after by a live-in nanny, and they had enough money to do anything they wanted. They had been married for twenty years and had just got a little bored with their sex life, so they decided to spice it up. They discussed various options and decided to invite another man into their bedroom. They didn't do it often, two to three times a year was just perfect for them, they didn't want any emotional attachments forming, although they wanted the third party to be a friend, too. Strangely, I got the impression that David was the driving force behind the concept. With that said, Louise obviously took control in the bedroom. She hinted that she liked to be in charge and on two occasions David joked about *'doing exactly what I was told'*, which I thought, although said in jest, was wrapped in truth.

After the fourth pint I really opened up, probably too much, and told them that I was the police officer who'd just been released from prison having been wrongly convicted. They had both heard about the case and even discussed how terrible it must have been for the poor man. Louise said she'd seen my picture on the news but hadn't put two and two together and linked the article to the policeman she'd met at the airport.

We agreed to meet the following Saturday and go to a party at a house near Heathrow airport. They said they would book a couple of hotel rooms locally and I could drive over in the late afternoon and get ready in the room. We would then get a cab to the party and back to the hotel afterwards, which meant we could all have a drink. They mentioned the party was at a friend's house. I didn't ask any more as I'd had too much to drink by then and somehow the whole proposal made perfect sense.

***

Time was starting to drag. Without any work or quite frankly, much else to do, I spent way too much time lulling about the house getting under everyone's feet. Since I'd got out, the anxiety had eased but not as much as I'd hoped it would. Of course, I still had the sword of Damocles hanging over my head, as Mr De L'Arcy and Nicholas Cousins were busy negotiating my future with the powers that be. I was in purgatory, neither in heaven nor hell. I noticed the Job had suddenly gone quiet about having me back, but with that said, they probably needed me to be formally acquitted first, before the wheels could start turning.

Seeing Wendy had become tricky because her husband was refusing to look after her boys, and I wasn't quite ready to meet them yet. I needed to make a definitive decision and to do that, I needed time. I was terrified of losing Wendy again, and that fear even outweighed getting back together with her.

One thing was positive. I had a lovely letter from Chloe apologising for coming down to see me and thanking me for keeping quiet about our relationship. She said she'd been keeping a secret from me, she was married with children, and now she had got her 'head in the right place', she wanted to stop being so stupid and try to make her marriage work. I wished her well, I really did. In my darkest months, she was a rare ray of sunshine. Truth be told, she had informed me about her husband, but had clearly forgotten doing so.

* * *

It was on that Thursday evening when I had one of the nicest surprises of my life.

When I think back, it was obvious something was going on, but I can honestly say, I never realised.

Mrs M and Pippa had said they were going late night shopping in the West End and left about four in the afternoon. On Thursdays, the shops in Oxford Street stayed open until eight, so there was a credibility to their story. They never went shopping in the West End, but usually went over to Bluewater, in Thurrock, and that was very much a once a year, pre-Christmas event. I didn't pay a great deal of attention other than to appreciate how great it was that both of them got on so well.

At about half-eight, I heard Mrs M's car pull up and the front doorbell ring. I assumed they were asking for some assistance to carry the shopping in, so I pulled on a pair of shoes and opened the door. Mrs M and Pippa hadn't been to the West End, they'd been to Heathrow to pick up Jackie and Trudy, who had flown all the way from Australia to see me. I was completely overwhelmed with happiness. I hadn't seen Trudy in years, well only via a pixelated internet picture, and she'd grown into the most beautiful young woman. She jumped up into my arms and wrapped her legs around me. Tears were streaming from her face and she was sobbing with joy. Next, Jackie hugged me long and hard, like only long-lost friends can do. It was lovely. I was so happy I was shaking.

I will remember that evening as the best few hours of my life. Although they were shattered after their thirty-hour journey, Jackie and Trudy showered and changed and came downstairs for supper. We sat up until two in the morning, or in the afternoon for them. I spent half of the time laughing and the other half crying my eyes out.

'We always knew you were innocent' was said about a million times.

When everyone except Jackie and I had gone to bed, we decided to have just one more glass of wine.

"Why don't you come back with us?" Jackie asked.

It wasn't a bad idea. It would give me some time and space to get my head together.

"How long are you over for?" I asked.

"Ten days. As soon as I heard you'd been released we booked the time off work and came as soon as we could. Trudy misses you more than she'd ever say. So do I." Jackie said.

"I need to sort everything out here first." I said.

"Like what?"

"Well, I still have to be acquitted. Then I need to get my job back."

"For Christ's sake, Christopher, you can't be serious! You're going back to the Met?"

I nodded.

"it's all I know. It's my life." I replied.

She shook her head from side to side.

"I give up." She said.

Chapter 47

I was fast asleep when Mrs M woke me up, she was sitting on my bed shaking my arm.

As soon as my eyes opened, I realised I had the mother of all hangovers.

"Chris, Chris, look!" She said, handing me her phone.

I rubbed my bleary eyes and sat up but as soon as I took the phone, I must have touched something because the screen went blank. Mrs M snatched it, entered her passcode and handed it back to me. It was open on a page from the BBC News App.

News Flash

Murderer of Queen's Favourite Uncle Identified.

New information has just come to light to suggest that the 1981 murder of the Duke of Durham, a close confidant and advisor to Queen Elizabeth the Second, was the responsibility of the now notorious former IRA terrorist, Barry Skinner.

Barry Skinner, who under the Northern Ireland Agreement had pleaded guilty to two bombings on mainland U.K., was assassinated by the Real IRA in 2007.

The Press Office at Buckingham Palace confirmed that the Queen had been informed but declined to comment.

I put my finger to my lips and mouthed *'don't say a word'* to Mrs M. I was worried this was a trigger. A deliberately placed news story designed to solicit a conversation between Mrs M and myself, which would be picked up on probes and used as evidence against me.

The Duke of Durham was killed, along with his two teenage sons, when he was piloting their private plane on a flight from Hampshire to Derbyshire. The plane had just taken off from Blackbushe Airport when the IRA detonated a bomb which had been hidden in the luggage compartment. All three were killed instantaneously. The Duke had been something of a second world war hero. He fought in the Battle of Britain and rose to the rank of Air Vice Marshall. After the war, he was made Governor of Hong Kong. He was also a member of the Order of the Garter. At the time, the murder shocked the nation and the Queen's sister was reported to have publicly referred to the IRA as *'murdering bastards'*, which was, in itself, a bit of a scandal. It was reported by everyone that Her Majesty and her husband were absolutely devastated. The Duke was afforded that rarest of tributes, a state funeral, only the third non-head of state after Lord Nelson and Sir Winston Churchill, to get one.

"Shall we have a chat about this later?" I said, loudly.

Mrs M nodded and took her phone back. She put her mouth to my ear, so it was touching.

"Are they trying to get us to talk about stuff?" She whispered.

I nodded and mouthed the word *'probably'*. The only upside to this development was, if they were indeed trying to get us to say something, it could only mean they didn't have enough evidence.

I spent the next hour searching every inch of my bedroom for a probe. I did a full POLSA search, like I was taught in the police. I found nothing. If it wasn't a trigger, then it was true. If it was true, then what did it mean for me. As I mulled over these several thoughts, my mobile rang. It was my solicitor Nicholas Cousins.

"Hi Chris. We need to meet."

"Today?" I replied.

"Today, come to my office."

"Will Mr De L'Arcy be there?" I asked.

"He's here already. Get a cab. See you in an hour."

* * *

Mr De L'Arcy was pacing the room like a caged animal throughout our meeting. Nicholas Cousins was more sedate, sitting quietly, rarely speaking, making notes.

"Why didn't they tell me?"

It was a rhetorical question, so neither Nicholas or I felt obligated to respond.

"I've been with them for the best part of three days!"

228

"It's a good job I've got legal aid." I commented.

"They can't have known this was going to come out." He continued, ignoring my reference to his ridiculously high salary.

"Does it change much?" I asked.

"I think it changes everything." He replied.

"That's good?" I asked.

"I think so. Only yesterday they were suggesting quashing your conviction, not proceeding *sine die* with the second murder charge, you signing a non-disclosure agreement which also included a clause where you waivered your right to sue for wrongful conviction. That was it. That was as far as they would go."

I was quite pleased. I would have agreed to anything, as long as it didn't include another trial and conviction for murder. I wasn't bothered about suing them, besides the prosecution looked sound to me, even though I had been on the wrong side of a miscarriage of justice. How was the state to know that forty-eight odd years ago my mother had, illegally by the way, given away my twin brother at birth?

"Bollocks to that." Mr De L'Arcy boomed.

I was quite taken aback by his use of an expletive.

"You weren't happy with that?" I asked.

"No, Mr Pritchard. You deserve significant compensation and the reinstatement of your QPM; and, most importantly of all, I wanted more than a *sine die*, I wanted an assurance never to prosecute."

"And how have things changed now?" I asked.

"I think they must have been bluffing. I think we're in a stronger position now. The whole country was outraged when they killed the Duke and his children. No jury in their right mind will convict you, especially after what they've just done to you." He replied.

"Besides, I didn't do nothing." I said, remembering that, technically at least, I'd never admitted any involvement.

"Ummmm" Mr De L'Arcy replied.

I looked at him and he smiled.

"I think we both know that's a big lie." He said.

I didn't respond. I just looked at him. Clearly, he knew something, but what could he possibly know? Suddenly, I wanted to find out.

"Go on then, don't fuck me about, what makes you think I had anything to do with it?"

"What, apart from the fact that you had the motive?"

"Apart from that?"

"And that you fit the picture of the suspect on the pedal cycle perfectly?"

"Apart from that?"

"And that whoever committed the murder had an unparalleled awareness of forensic evidence and in particular, Locard's Exchange Principle. Apparently, the Scenes of Crimes Officer had never collected less evidence at a scene."

"Apart from that."

"Apart from all that?" Mr De L'Arcy asked.

I nodded.

"Oh, the photograph of you entering Barry Skinner's front door on the morning of his murder."

Chapter 48

At about the same time that I'd discovered Barry Skinner's address, so had the Real IRA. Barry had told his daughter who lived in Derry, where he was living, and she, in turn, had told her partner. Her partner told his contact in the terrorist organisation and within a few weeks they had managed to rent the house opposite Barry's. From there they were able to set up a camera on his front door. By regularly reviewing the recorded footage they were able to corroborate that he was, in fact, residing there, and then to plan the most appropriate timing and guise of his assassination.

Only I beat them to it.

During the latest round of peace negotiations, when Barry Skinner's murder became an issue, they produced the photograph and denied responsibility. Of course, it didn't afford them much high moral ground, because by admitting that they were watching him, they were also acknowledging their intention to assassinate him, making all those concerned guilty of conspiracy to murder.

I also realised that it would be difficult for the Crown to produce the photograph as evidence. To do so, they would first have to establish provenance and continuity, both of which would be almost impossible to do under these circumstances. Would a republican terrorist really be prepared to go into the witness box on behalf of the country they so hated? I very much doubted that.

What I desperately needed to know was what other evidence the Crown had managed to amass as a result of this enormous steer? Mr De L'Arcy had hinted that they hadn't recovered any forensic evidence from the scene. What's more, I knew Mrs M would alibi me. So what did they have which was tangible? I could understand why putting me on trial was going to be a real challenge but, still, I would agree to almost anything if to do so would guarantee my freedom.

I went home from the solicitors confused. I'd thought everything through so much, my brain was simply addled.

I got the rattler back. The idea of going everywhere by black cab seemed decadent but the reality was the journey was quicker using the underground. When the train came above ground at Leytonstone, I turned my phone on and picked up a raft of messages and voicemails. They arrived one after the other and there were so many, the other passengers near me started to look a bit pissed off at all the bleeps and alerts. What had happened in the last few hours to make me in such demand?

The first voice message was from the guy at the BBC, Terry something. He was, he said, calling again to ask me whether I would agree to be interviewed as part of a programme he was making about my life. I noticed immediately that this time, unlike the first, his message contained the definite inference that they were making the programme whether I liked it or not. That worried me immensely; I had way too many bone men in my clothing box. I really wished I'd mentioned the BBC thing to my legal team, but I'd completely forgotten about his first call.

The second message was from a woman called Lauren at Sky News. She spoke quickly and with a Scottish accent. I pressed the phone harder against the side of my head. She asked whether I had any comment to make about the suggestion about something, but I just couldn't hear it.

While I was looking to press the 'replay message' button, I got an incoming call alert from Nicholas Cousin's office number – I couldn't have left there more than fifty minutes ago – I pressed the green button.

"Have you seen the latest news, it's on the BBC and Sky?" He asked.

"No, mate, I've been on the underground …"

With that the phone signal cut out because the train had briefly gone underground again. I looked at the screen but there wasn't even one bar! I waited patiently. My phone rang again.

"It's me." Nicholas said, he sounded exasperated, and I guessed he had been trying desperately to contact me.

"I haven't seen the news, what's happened?" I asked.

"The BBC are reporting that the UK and Irish governments are negotiating a new peace deal, which will effectively end the sectarian violence which has rumbled on since the Good Friday Agreement, even the Real IRA are under pressure to become part of the process."

"I don't understand. Does that mean I've been sacrificed? That the Real IRA has only agreed to join if I'm put on trial so that they can be exonerated of his murder?"

"That's not what we think. We suspect they called a truce on the whole Barry Skinner affair and have drawn a line under it so that they can move on. We think this is a very positive development. We've just been invited to another round of meetings with the Attorney General over the next couple of weeks."

"Are you honestly telling me this could drag on and on?" I asked.

"Hopefully not, Chris. I think they'll want this matter put to bed before long."

I was nervous. I knew I had somehow become some sort of bargaining chip in the peace process, but what that involved, I really had no idea.

Chapter 49

I didn't know whether this was my first real weekend of freedom or my last. Next weekend, would I suddenly find myself back in jail? Or would I be on bail for the murder of Barry Skinner? Or most exciting of all, would I be free?

So, although all week I thought I'd probably find an excuse to not to go to the party with Louise Lusher and her old man, the uncertainty of my future prompted me to do something which was kind of adventurous. As a consequence, late that Saturday afternoon, I drove over to a small hotel, the Adelaide or something, which was literally in the shadow of Windsor Castle. There I met my two drinking companions and new best friends, from last Sunday, who suggested we had a walk around the town as we had plenty of time before the party started. I dumped my bag in my room and joined them in the lobby. I did notice that my room, which was up several floors and located in the attic, was really small, with only a three-foot single bed in one corner and the smallest toilet imaginable. I could hardly say anything as Louise and David had booked the room for me and had make it clear they were paying for everything. They were just the same as they had been last week; friendly, good company and quite amusing. When I asked about who's party we were going to, they were a bit vague, saying they think a chap called 'Paul' ran the place, but they weren't sure.

"What kind of party is it? Someone's birthday?" I asked, as we walked along the shorter part of the Long Walk towards the castle.

"Not really, it's just a party." Louise replied.

"Will there be music? I warn you I hate dancing. Do we need to take alcohol?"

Apparently, we did but David had brought enough for all of us and I needn't worry.

"Is it far from here?"

"No, about ten, fifteen minutes by cab. It's right at the end of the Heathrow runway." He replied.

"So, you go regularly to this guy's party?" I said.

"Once every couple of months. We've been on our own recently and that's nowhere near as much fun." Louise replied.

"What time do we have to leave?"

"It starts at ten but doesn't really get going until midnight, so we'll leave the hotel at eleven." Louise replied.

"Eleven? I'm normally tucked up in bed by then." I replied.

Louise and David shared a private joke between them. They didn't say anything, but they looked at one another and laughed.

"I won't know anyone there, so please don't leave me alone. I can't remember the last time I've been to a party." I said.

"I promise we'll look after you." Louise said.

As she said this, she walked into me in a sort of comforting gesture, our shoulders gently touched, and then she held my hand. It was all perfectly natural, or it was at first, because she didn't let go of my hand as we walked along. It was just as if we were the couple and David the third party.

David didn't seem to notice, let alone care. He pointed out the absence of the royal standard, explaining that this meant the Queen wasn't in residence at the castle. Something which I knew but I pretended not to. Then he went on to talk about the history of the castle, first commissioned in the eleventh century by William the Conqueror, and a heap of other interesting facts. I think he must have swallowed the guidebook. All the time he did, his wife held my hand and occasionally squeezed it. It was weird but not unpleasant.

By late afternoon, we were ensconced in a pub right next to the castle and having a few drinks. I realised we were not drinking at the rate we had the previous weekend, and it was clear Louise and David were pacing themselves. Once again, I was having a really nice time. As I didn't really know them, I could relax and at times that afternoon. It felt like it was the first time I'd really unwound in years.

At one point when David was at the bar, Louise reached into her purse, a really expensive Mulberry purse, and took something out which she pressed into the palm of my hand. It was only when I opened my hand that I saw a small brown tablet. I immediately assumed it was an ecstasy tablet and was just a little shocked. I quickly glanced around to make sure no one else had witnessed this supply of a controlled drug.

"Take this just before we leave this evening, it'll help you to keep going all night." She said.

"I don't do drugs." I replied, trying to hand it back.

"What?" She replied.

"I don't do drugs, I've never taken an E. Honestly, I don't need it but thanks anyway."

"It's not an illegal drug you fool; it's a Levitra." She replied.

"I've never heard of it." I said.

"Well, on one level, that makes me quite pleased. But take it. It's not illegal and it'll mean you can have an erection for hours upon hours."

"Ok" I replied, popping the pill into the small hip pocket on my jeans.

"Does David take one?" I replied.

"He takes two, which is a waste really, because I'm never going to let him have an orgasm this evening."

***

I may not have had any sex between Wendy dumping me and going to prison but over the years I'd watched a fair amount of internet pornography. The biggest danger of such activity, and perhaps its biggest attraction, is that it allows you to explore not only your own fantasies, but everybody else's too. As a consequence, I wasn't completely naïve and had a good idea what was going on in this little, and very private game of three, that I was playing with Louise and David.

Did I care? Not really. Did it disgust me? No. Did it interest me? A bit. Did I want to play? One hundred percent.

When we arrived back at the hotel, the game stepped up a notch. Whilst standing in the reception, Louise asked for my room key. I took out the wooden key fob and handed it over, without any idea why she wanted it. She clicked her fingers at her husband, who did the same, taking their room key out of his jacket pocket.

"Give it to Christopher." She said.

David handed it over and in turn she handed him my key.

"Now go and get Christopher's bags and bring them to our room."

From David's body language, he was suddenly adopting a different persona.

He shot off, up the stars like a very well-trained dog.

Louise smiled and held my hand.

"Let's go to our room. It's the honeymoon suite, it's absolutely beautiful. And just the two of us have got it all. It's even got a hot tub, so we can relax when we come back tonight." She said.

Chapter 50

It was all quite strange. I mean, we didn't see David for the next three hours and I lay on the bed watching TV while Louise spent most of the time getting ready, starting with a long soak in the enormous bath. We chatted easily and she told me all about her life, her husband and her kids. She was lovely, and in a different time and place, I could have quite easily fallen for her. But not under these circumstances. She made no effort to conceal her nakedness, as she went about the suite, like a soldier dressing for battle.

"How long will you need to get ready?" She asked.

I looked at my watch and made a great fuss about trying to work out all the timings.

"Fifteen at most. Shower, shave, clean teeth and dress; yes, fifteen will be perfect."

"I'll give you the nod." She said.

I kind of knew what was going on with David, but I thought I'd ask, just to make sure I wasn't missing anything.

"The idea sort of grew. His ultimate fantasy was to watch me with another man, which I don't think is as unusual as you'd think. We did that for a while, it was fun, we used to call them *'take-aways'*, you know, *'shall we have a take-away this weekend?'*. We would have a threesome in a hotel, it would last an hour, but as time passed, I think we both wanted more.

David wanted to be immersed in the scenario, he wanted more than to just watch another man have sex with me. Strange as it may sound, Chris, he wanted me to reject him, to treat him badly, and to completely take control of his sex life. Of course, this isn't really us. We are in fact, when we're not playing our game, a completely normal couple. But just occasionally, we like to leave reality behind. It's harmless, it's fun and sometimes, it's absolutely fabulous."

"Is it what you want too?" I asked.

Having taken a new pair out of their packaging, Louise was just unrolling a black stocking up her right leg, a gesture I have always found extremely erotic.

"Yes. What's not to like? David is very successful and in every other respect of our marriage and for the last twenty years, he has been the boss. As such, he makes all the important decisions. I don't mind, I really don't, I'm kind of old fashioned. When we play this game, for once I get to be in charge, completely in charge. What's more, I get to have fantastic sex with men I find attractive. Then come Monday morning, we resume our almost perfect life. The kids, our parents, our friends and neighbours, no one knows any different."

Louise gave me the fifteen-minute warning, in which short time I did my ablutions and dressed.

***

When we arrived at the party, I discovered it was being held in a large bungalow somewhere between the M25 and the west side of the airport. I soon realised it wasn't anybody's party in particular, but rather what they'd have called in the nineteen seventies, a swingers' party.

By the time we arrived the place was busy without being full and I'd have guessed there were about two hundred people, all couples or groups. Apparently, singles men could only go on a Friday night, but single women, couples and threesomes were welcome anytime. Most of the men were formally dressed in trousers and shirts but the women dressed provocatively either in lingerie, or short skirts and revealing tops. The surprising thing was the variety of people. The youngest couples were in their mid-to-late thirties, most in their forties and fifties, but quite a few well into their sixties. Although most were white, there were a few Asian couples and three black ladies, who I only caught a glimpse of, as I was putting my stuff into a locker.

It was very apparent that Louise and I were a couple and David the spare. Louise held my hand and led me on a tour. David followed behind but at a distance.

The bungalow was enormous, with perhaps twenty bedrooms of varying sizes around every turn; a large covered swimming pool; half a dozen jacuzzies spread randomly about the place; a large outbuilding which had once been a stable block; six or seven log cabins; a large bar; a cinema room that could seat thirty and an impressive dance area. Each building and area was connected by covered walkways and marquees with hot air blowers and patio heaters everywhere to make sure you didn't get cold.

Louise had clearly been before because several of the other guests chatted to her, opening their conversations with *'we haven't seen you here for ages'* and similar observations.

While every so often you saw a couple, who looked hopelessly unsure and very nervous, *'virgins'* Louise called them, the majority of people were really friendly and chatty. Some of the rooms had windows, and there was an open invitation to watch those inside have sex. In one large room, a bed was surrounded by a cage. On the bed a couple were having sex and around the cage others stood and watched, occasionally reaching in through the bars to touch or caress the couple.

There were a dozen party goers in the pool, all completely naked, and interacting with each other.

As the minutes became hours, the pace picked up until you could barely go anywhere where people weren't having sex. It was surreal. It was like watching a film. It was all very erotic, although it felt like a dream. We wandered from place to place, always holding hands, David in tow, and watched everything. At times, Louise seemed almost in a trance as she studied couple after couple, and group after group copulating.

One of the rooms had a huge and heavy curtain across the door and a complete absence of any lighting inside. This was called the dark room and it was into this room, after ordering David to wait outside, Louise took me to finally get to know each other intimately. The place was pitch black but no sooner had we taken two steps inside than I felt strangers' hands starting to touch and caress. I was immediately unnerved but only because I didn't know whether they were male or female digits. Don't get me wrong, I'm not homophobic but I only ever want sex with a woman. I expressed my unease to Louise but loud enough for everyone to hear.

"Don't worry. I promise you all three of us are girls." Said a female voice to my right.

Louise had dropped to her knees and the women, I guessed there were three, were kissing me and touching my upper body, as Louise gave me head. For a few seconds I had to ask myself whether this was actually happening.

Maybe ten, but probably five minutes later, the first half, so to speak, was all over. I had at least fulfilled one of my fantasies, to be seduced by a group of women. It was the dark room, so for all I knew the three of them might have been in their sixties, but I put that thought to one side and simply enjoyed the moment. Louise too, had received some of the female attention from the two taller girls, which she didn't seem to mind at all.

It had been so dark in there, when I got back outside, it took a minute or two for my eyes to adjust to the light. Sitting at a table, a few yards away was David, looking eager and excited. I smiled, a little awkwardly. Louise walked over and whispered in his ear, then kissed him full and deep, took him by the hand and led him away. I guessed he was going to get his reward and sat down where he'd been sitting.

An attractive young couple decided to explore the dark room but as they entered there was a small kerfuffle because they almost collided with several people coming out. The first to emerge was a tall, very attractive black lady, about forty, who was wearing hooker shoes and a short black leather skirt and black basque. I smiled at her, in deference to the moments of intimacy which we'd just shared, before realising that was a pretty stupid thing to do, as she wouldn't recognise me. Next came someone who I can only assume was her twin sister as she looked so similar. As they walked away from the door, they parted slightly; stepping into the gap between them was the third of the trio, a person I had known for nearly thirty years.

Neither of us looked away, we held one another's stare, looking the opponent firmly in the eyes. I think I almost stopped breathing; I was that taken aback. The girl to the left mistook the situation and said to me.

"I think my friend wants you again."

Then she frowned and asked.

"That was you in the dark room, wasn't it? A few moments ago."

I nodded.

"That was great fun, but personally I preferred your wife. Kitty here, however, likes her cock way too much to become a lesbian, don't you darling?"

Kitty ignored her.

It was hardly surprising that I didn't recognise my adversary. Normally, Kitty had short hair cut in a very masculine fashion, but tonight her hair was long and full, which completely changed her appearance. When I looked closer, I saw she was wearing a wig. What's more, Kitty was 5'4" at most, but with five-inch heels, she had a completely different outline. And another thing, Kitty always wore round glasses, now absent. It didn't help that throughout the party the lighting was dimmed, like a night club. If I hadn't been only a few yards from her and looking her straight in the face, I would never had known who it was. Kitty had lost weight, perhaps two stone, probably through the stress of being suspended.

After what felt like an age, Kitty walked off and her two friends followed. I was left trying to work out exactly what had happened and with whom, but in the dark room who would ever know who'd done what to whom?

Chapter 51

Putting the Kitty incident aside, I enjoyed my Saturday night party. When we got back to the hotel room, Louise and I had the most amazing sex I'd ever experienced. I don't think I've ever been with a woman that was quite as aroused as her that evening, or rather, early morning. While we made love she left her phone open on a call to her husband, in his tiny room up in the attic, so he could hear everything. Every so often she would talk to him and tell him exactly what was happening. They both enjoyed the game, so who was I to judge?

I didn't get up until gone eleven and then made the long trek back to Buckhurst Hill around the M25. I wasn't entirely sure I'd left it long enough for the alcohol to get through my system, so I drove slowly and with extra care. I sobered up pretty quickly when I pulled up at home to be confronted by Wendy, who demanded to know where I'd been all night.

"I've been here since nine! Mrs M has no idea, or she's covering for you. Have you got someone else? Just tell me!"

And that was before I'd even got out of my car!

I couldn't help but feel a bit sorry for Wendy. She was in a right state and had clearly been crying, but I was also a little annoyed. I didn't need this. I was stressed enough as it was and surely I was entitled to come and go freely?

"I didn't realise I was back in prison." I said, as I stood up and walked to the boot to retrieve my small suitcase.

"Where have you been?" She asked.

"With Dave and Louise, some friends, over in west London." I replied.

"Who are they? I don't know them."

"Well, you wouldn't, would you? You haven't been any part of my life in years. You dumped me, remember? I got on with my life, didn't I? You finished with me a few months after Jackie threw me out. Just when I really needed you. What you did to me in 2007 destroyed me, Wendy. You never called me to see how I was doing. You never texted or wrote.

You treated me like I was dead. You showed no compassion or interest in how I was getting on. You knew my family had emigrated to Australia. You might even have learned I was living on a small boat in the Thames because after my divorce I had fuck all of fuck all. But not one single word in four year, until, completely out of the blue, you turn up in the Visits Hall in Doncaster. And now you have the front to start demanding to know where I've been! You have no right to ask. You gave that right up when you finished with me. You treated me badly. You treated me without any regard for all the love we had shared. You were a cold-hearted bitch. Now fuck off and leave me alone."

What had started as a frustrated diatribe ended up as a good, old fashioned rant. Wendy walked back to her car sobbing, got in and drove off.

Mrs M, who'd obviously been watching from inside, came out immediately.

"Are you alright, darling?" She asked.

"No, not really." I replied.

"A cuppa and a chat?" She asked.

I nodded.

"Where's Pippa?" I asked.

"Out with her Mum and sister." She replied.

"Oh, that's good."

I was relieved they hadn't had to see my very public fall-out with Wendy.

We were in the kitchen, when Mrs M mentioned something which I'd started to turn over in my mind over the last couple of days.

"My darling, have you thought about going to Australia with Jackie and Trudy? Just for a few months, perhaps, you know, to get your head together?"

"But what about re-joining the Job?" I asked.

"The Job can wait. Besides, John was saying how, not only will you get all your salary back paid, you will also get back your annual leave, so you'll end up with two years' worth of annual to take in just twelve months. Why don't you re-join and then take a couple of months off?"

I had to admit, it wasn't a bad idea. I got thirty-five days a year, so I could easily go for two months and still have a week or two left for the rest of the year.

"It'll also give me a proper chance to think the Wendy issue through." I said.

"You were pretty awful to her just then, Chris." Mrs M said.

"I know." I replied.

"This is a woman who even though you were serving a life sentence for murder, stuck by you. Who travelled to Doncaster to visit. Who terminated her marriage, with all the impact that would have on her children, just on the off-chance that by doing so, you would choose to be with her. And she's beautiful. My god, those legs! That hair! That face!"

"Now I am confused. One minute you want me to go to Australia, the next, you're telling me I should be with Wendy."

Mrs M laughed.

'I'm not telling you anything, my darling. I'm demonstrating options. If you do go to Oz, there's a chance you won't come back and that would devastate me – but I'd never stop you. I just want you to be happy. When I lost Dawn, you filled a huge hole in my heart, in my life. Now I've got Pippa, too. She's so lovely, so beautiful, so like Dawn."

I'm not sure that was true, Dawn was a thousand times more streetwise than my own daughter would ever be, but I didn't feel the need to say anything.

"And now I have John, too, and that's thanks to you. I think the holiday would be a great idea. It would give you time to think about your future, you know, whether you go back to the Met, whether you give it a go with Wendy. Sometimes I look at you, Chris, and you seem so very lost. I want to help you but I'm not sure I can anymore, not since prison."

"Do you think I've really changed?" I asked.

She nodded slowly.

"I'm struggling. I've developed some sort of anxiety thing. I was seeing a shrink when I was inside, but I can't even find a G.P. who'll have me now. I was on medication, but I can't get that anymore. I thought now that I'm out, the problem would just cure itself, but it hasn't. It's there all the time. A feeling in my chest. It's horrible. When it's really bad, even my hands start shaking. Sometimes, even though I'm out of prison, I think *'I don't want to live like this for the rest of my life'*. I need help, Mrs M. I'm not sure I can cope anymore."

"You can, my darling. You are stronger than you know. Things like anxiety and depression don't just disappear overnight. They take time to work through your system." Mrs M replied.

I knew Mrs M was right, when had she ever not been?

Chapter 52

The next week, Jackie and Trudy flew back to Australia. It was truly wonderful that they'd come all that way to see me. Mrs M and Jackie had obviously been talking because Jackie offered me her spare room if I wanted to escape England for a month or two to get my head together. I was tempted but I had too many things to sort out here in the UK before I could allow myself the luxury of a holiday.

After my shenanigans at the weekend, I got regular text messages from Louise; these were usually flirty in nature and as the week progressed, she started to sound me out as to whether I'd like to go to their house on Sunday for a BBQ with a group of their friends. She did explain that this wasn't *'an event'* and that I would simply be introduced as a friend with whom David worked. I thought that was slightly strange but said yes.

Something about the whole bizarre affair sucked at my curiosity. Besides, after all that had happened, it was sometimes nice to be around people who knew nothing about the complications surrounding my every thought and action.

I had dinner with Julie one evening. She had been my partner on the murder squad for years and, along with Brucie, was probably my closest friend in the Job – or out of it, for that matter. It was the first time I'd seen her since my release, in fact we worked out it was probably the first time we'd seen each other in over a year. She seemed happy enough, and she'd put on about a stone in weight, but the closeness we'd once shared seemed to have faded and that made me a bit sad. Don't get me wrong, it was lovely to see her, but I thought at times she was slightly distant, or perhaps it was me?

Brucie called me every day, and we met up at least once a week, normally at the bikers' café in High Beech. None of those meetings however were as exciting as the time we caught the rapist.

And Wendy called me every day, too. We didn't meet up, but as the days rolled by, I started to realise as Mrs M had inferred, I owed it to her to at least give our relationship a chance. I also owed it to myself, too. The problem was, the Wendy I had known and fallen so hopelessly in love with was a single lady who, for the four years we were going out, had put me completely at the centre of her world. Not to put too fine a point on it, she had, sort of, worshipped me. Not as a deity but in the sense that everything she did was focused on making my life as perfect as possible and quite frankly, that was wonderful. The new Wendy had two children, both who would, and quite rightly, come before me, in every sense. I understood that completely, but these new circumstances would change our relationship dynamic.

After a couple of weeks of daily calls, I told Wendy about my mental health issues and warned her that, if anything, they were getting worse. I said that if she could put up with these, we should see whether we could work everything out between us. She was so happy she did what only a woman would do and hung up the phone on me! An hour later she called back, happier than I have ever known anyone. We agreed to take it slowly and that although I would meet and get to know her children, I wouldn't move in for at least a year.

Mrs M found me a mental health counsellor and had my first session the following week. Strange though it seemed at first, these were conducted by phone but, as it transpired, that didn't matter. The counsellor was a beautifully spoken lady called Dr Leana Austin, and her practice had a Harley Street address. Mrs M insisted on paying, so it must have cost her a fortune. The session helped but I was starting to accept that feeling anxious was now just part of my life. I'd rather not experience it but I could survive if I had to.

One day, just when I was giving up on ever hearing from my legal team again, I got a call from Nicholas Cousins and I was summoned to Mr De L'Arcy's chambers the following day, a Friday.

When I got up that morning, I opened a long letter from Matthew, which I put in my pocket to read on the way up to town. Matthew Starr was my son from a brief relationship I had with a lady named Sarah back at Stoke Newington in the mid-80s. His mother had always kept a scrapbook of my life, which she gave to him on his eighteenth birthday, an act which prompted him to find and meet me. About ten years ago, he'd spent a couple of weeks with me, during which he briefly flirted with joining the police, but the idea faded quickly, and he went back to his privileged life amongst Gloucestershire's elite.

After that, he visited me occasionally, but once a month soon became once a year and then not at all. I still sent and received birthday and Christmas cards and for years I would often text him, but he rarely replied, and the relationship effectively died. I was a bit sad, but not a lot. There's only so much one can be sad about.

I put my best suit on and jumped the rattler up to the Temple. I knew what happened this day would shape the rest of my life.

Whilst on the train I read Matthew's letter. He apologised for being such a poor son, said that when I was convicted, in a fit of anger and disgust, he'd thrown the scrapbook away but his mother, Sarah, unbeknown to him had retrieved it from the rubbish and hidden it away. Sarah, he said, had always maintained my innocence and, when I was sent down, wrote to her M.P. to share her concerns about a miscarriage of justice. Matthew asked after Wendy, said he would love to come and visit, and his mother would like to come too, but she wouldn't be offended if I said no. He asked me to call him, apologised for ever doubting me, and sent his love.

It was funny but as my Central Line train pulled out of Snaresbrook station, I suddenly felt that someone, somewhere close to me, had struck a tuning fork, and that my life was starting to come back into focus.

Chapter 53

We were, once again, in the conference room at his chambers, awaiting the arrival of hot drinks.

Mr De L'Arcy opened proceedings.

"As you are aware, Nicholas and I have been negotiating with the team, and it is a team, from the Attorney General's office for several weeks. We've come to a provisional agreement. We need to put the terms and conditions to you and then persuade you to accept it."

"Are you happy with it?" I asked.

They looked at one another and nodded.

"Yes; and we think you should be too." Mr De L'Arcy said.

"Do I stay out of prison?" I asked.

It was the only question I really needed an answer to.

"As long as you can keep your mouth shut, yes." Mr De L'Arcy replied.

"Where do I sign?" I asked, half seriously.

Mr De L'Arcy, who was still pacing around the room in his usual fashion, banged his fist on the table.

I jumped, but ever so slightly.

"God damn it, Christopher, I need your focus, not your jokes. Are you focused?" Mr De L'Arcy asked, with more than a pinch of aggressiveness.

I banged the table, just as he had.

"Of course, I'm fucking focused." I said, with considerable force.

I didn't like him treating me like a child. I was not going to be spoken to like that, even by my barrister.

My reaction took both men by surprise and, for a few seconds, no one moved or said a word.

"Very well. Sometimes, I underestimate you, Mr Pritchard, my apologies." Mr De L'Arcy said, quietly.

"That's quite all right." I replied.

"What's the deal, then?" I asked.

"We'll take it one section at a time. The first section of the contract deals with your current conviction for murder and rape. On Monday morning, the High Court will quash the conviction on the grounds that it is unsafe, and you will be formally acquitted on both charges. This will happen whether you sign this contract or not. The State now unequivocally accepts that you did not commit those terrible crimes."

"Next, the question of compensation for being wrongly convicted."

"Go on." I said.

"The Crown maintains that the prosecution was lawful and the conviction appropriate. It is not the Crown's fault that your mother unlawfully concealed your brother's birth, which she didn't register, and then illegally gave him up for an unauthorised adoption. The Crown will not compensate you. What's more, you will, as part of the settlement contract, forever forfeit your right to sue them."

I was more than a little surprised, but I just nodded. Was that the price I had to pay for killing Barry Skinner? If so, it seemed worthwhile.

"Next, the suggestion that you murdered Barry Skinner, which I would add, we have never conceded. If you admit the offence in writing, and for that purpose there is a document prepared in this paperwork, Her Majesty will exercise Her Royal Prerogative of Mercy and you will be pardoned for the crime. This will be done alongside a Section D notice, forbidding you, or anyone else, including the media, from ever discussing this matter again. You will not stand trial for the murder, nor will you ever be capable of being held to account for any action in relation to it by a criminal court. You could still however, and this is highly unlikely, be civilly sued by the victim's family, for compensation."

Admit the offence? That sounded terribly risky.

I breathed out heavily and asked:

"What's your advice, guys?"

"We have a long way to go, yet. Let us get through it all, first." Mr De L'Arcy replied.

I frowned, what more could there possibly be?

"Your QPM for Bravery will be re-instated, and the annulment voided. You will be reinstated to the rank of Detective Inspector in the Metropolitan Police and you will be deemed to have served continuously from the date of your dismissal until the date of reinstatement. You will therefore receive back pay and your annual leave entitlement will be carried over. The reinstatement will occur the day after you sign this settlement agreement."

"Sounds brilliant; apart from not going back to prison, that was my heartfelt wish. I don't care about any compensation, as long as they let me back in the Job." I said.

I was barely able to contain my excitement but then I saw the two men exchange a look and I knew that I was about to be stung.

"The day after your reinstatement, you will submit an application to apply for an ill-health pension, which will be granted. The papers for that are also here. You will then serve three months on sick leave, before retiring on a full pension. You will never physically return to work nor will your warrant card be returned to you."

My heart sank.

"No" I said, without even realising I had spoken out loud.

"You must." Mr De L'Arcy said, quietly.

I put my head in my hands, rubbing my fingertips across my eyes.

"Tell me about the pardon thing?" I asked.

"It's used occasionally, particularly when those acting for Queen and country have to do activities that are outside the law."

"You mean Box?" I asked.

"Christ, I haven't heard that term in twenty years. But yes, you're right, the security services. They're the main recipients of the royal pardon. As far as I am aware, you will be the first for a police officer. In fact, there's an informal term for this procedure, it's called purple cover." Mr De L'Arcy explained.

"But I can't stay in the Job?" I asked.

They both shook their heads.

"Can't I have a desk job, you know, non-operational?" I asked.

They both shook their heads.

"We did explore that possibility." Nicholas replied.

We sat in silence for a few seconds, but it seemed like longer.

"You must also agree not to pursue any criminal or civil grievances against the Deputy Commissioner, who will also be allowed to resign with a pension." Mr De L'Arcy said.

"She's not going to be prosecuted for perjury then?" I asked.

They both shook their heads.

"Never in a month of sabbaths." Nicholas added.

"What about that expenses scandal with Emu? Where she signed off the false accounts?" I asked.

They shook their heads again.

"Un fucking believable." I said.

"I think you're being something of a hypocrite." Nicholas pointed out.

Of course he was right.

"Anything else?" I asked.

"Apparently, the BBC were considering making a TV programme about your life." Mr De L'Arcy said.

"Some guy called Terry has been trying to get hold of me." I replied.

"I think the Director General has been warned off but just in case this Terry chap tries to go to an independent producer, do not cooperate with him."

"No problem, I wasn't interested anyway. Anything else?" I asked.

"Just the one ..." Mr De L'Arcy said.

"... Her Majesty wishes to confer on you the George Medal for your acts of great bravery at the Stoke Newington bombing. Her Majesty is of the opinion that at the time you did not receive the recognition you deserved."

***

This wasn't a negotiation, it was a choice, and the decision was stark and brutal - either sign the agreement and the myriad of accompanying papers and agree to everything, or, within a week, I would be charged with the murder of Barry Skinner.

I really needed to talk this through with either Mrs M or Brucie but that wasn't an option. Everything had to be carried out in the utmost secrecy. I even had to sign a consent form to allow them, whoever 'they' were, to place me under surveillance, at any time and without notice, to monitor whether I was complying with the agreement.

Nicholas and Mr De L'Arcy clearly thought they'd got me a fantastic deal, and in many ways, they had, but it would mean the end of my police career, and neither of them truly understood quite how devastating that would be to me. They spent the next hour trying to convince me. I spent that hour of my life feeling more anxious than when I was back in prison. At one stage, my nerves were so bad my hands started to shake, which I had to try to hide.

I was going to get my pension and not go back to jail, could I really expect more?

Then there was a nagging doubt because I knew they'd struggle to get the photograph of me at Barry Skinner's house into evidence and without that, I reckoned their case looked pretty weak. When I expressed that to Mr De L'Arcy he took a deep breath and replied.

"Even if you're acquitted, Christopher, they won't have you back in the police, they can't. Don't fool yourself; they'll get you on some technicality. You'll probably fail the medical or the eye-sight test, or something. Your police career is over, but you have the perfect opportunity to retire with your head held high, with dignity, with a decent pension and the highest award for bravery anyone can receive in peacetime. Can I be candid, Mr Pritchard GM QPM?"

I nodded.

"Don't be a cunt, sign the formal contract, sign the Non-Disclosure Agreement, sign the application for an ill-health pension, sign the confession, sign the surveillance consent form; sign the Official Secrets

Act declaration; sign the D notice, sign the whole damn lot and consider yourself the luckiest murderer that ever walked this fucking planet!"

I nodded, smiling inside at Mr De L'Arcy's sudden use of profanity.

"Okay" I said.

Mr De L'Arcy sat down immediately next to me, handed me a black fountain pen and took me slowly through each pencilled cross on the countless forms. I signed each one. It took several minutes. When the last signature was finished, Mr De L'Arcy said.

"Now you've done that, I am able to inform you, in complete confidence, that it was Buckingham Palace who leaked the story about Barry Skinner being responsible for The Duke of Durham's murder."

"Really? Why?" I asked.

"I don't rightly know but I do know Her Majesty's Government were furious because it really forced their hand in these negotiations." Mr De L'Arcy said.

I went to hand the pen back.

"Keep it." Mr De L'Arcy said.

I looked at it more closely.

"But it looks expensive, it's a Montblanc, isn't it?" I asked.

"It's a limited-edition Montblanc Meisterstuck, made for the company's 75th anniversary in 1999. That stone on the cap is a carat of diamond. It's yours now."

I was gobsmacked. A carat of diamond alone was worth at least two grand!

"Why?" I asked.

"Because in my forty-five years practicing law, I've never felt prouder to represent a client. It may only have been for a few weeks, but what an amazing time it has been! Being your barrister through this process has been the highlight of my career. What I have not told you up until now, is that my younger brother served with Two Para in Northern Ireland in the mid-seventies. He was killed by a roadside bomb, planted by the IRA. When you took your revenge after twenty-five years on Barry Skinner, you did it for all of us that lost a loved one to those cowardly murdering scumbags. The gift of my treasured pen is my way of saying thank you. Christopher Pritchard, you've got balls made of steel. I bow my head before you in deference and respect."

He stood up, came almost to attention and bowed his head, like he was entering a sitting court room. I was humbled.

Epilogue

Six months later

It's a bit like a school play, you're only allowed to invite a certain number of guests, so you have some difficult choices to make. The invitation to receive the George Medal stipulated that I could only take one, but one was all I needed. I asked Mrs Jenny Matthews to accompany me to Buckingham Palace and thereafter to afternoon tea at the Ritz. She was, she said, absolutely delighted to accept.

When the day came, it was a crisp but clear, perfect English autumnal day. Mrs M and I had both hired our outfits and the Metropolitan Police sent a car and driver for us to use. The car was fitted with blues and twos, so we slipped through the morning London traffic like royalty.

We arrived at the palace exactly at our allotted time. It appeared we were one of the first but over the next hour, hundreds of other recipients joined us. We were all being politely made to comply with a well-established routine to move us effortlessly from room to room. In each, we waited for ten or fifteen minutes before being moved onto the next. Gradually though, we seemed to be making our way to some kind of inner sanctum. In fact, the process was, to all effects and purposes, just a queue.

The person before us was a young lady, no more than twenty-three, and no higher than 5' tall and well under seven stone. She wore a dark blue military uniform which bore the insignia of a Lance Corporal. She had come with her mother whom Mrs M got chatting to, while the soldier and I smiled politely at one another. Both the older women were bursting with pride and keen to tell the other why they were there. My fellow recipient, I learned with unmitigated fascination, was about to be awarded the Victoria Cross for rendering lifesaving first aid to several colleagues while under sustained fire from insurgents in Afghanistan. During the episode she had taken two bullets in her back, but undeterred, she carried on. Her actions undoubtedly saved the lives of three of her fellow combatants.

I hoped Mrs M wouldn't try to compete with that, but she did, and she told how having been blown up and sustained life-threatening injuries, I'd crawled through broken glass to try to save her daughter. The fact was anyone of my colleagues would have done the same. I felt more than a little embarrassed being so close to the undiluted bravery this soldier had demonstrated.

At some point and just before we were formally summoned into the investiture room, a gentleman adorned in stately court uniform and standing on a stool, gave us instructions as to how to behave and what to say and do during the ceremony. The most important pieces of advice seemed to be not, under any circumstances, to ask Her Majesty any questions and to call her *'Ma'am, as in jam'*, and not *'Ma'am as in palm'*.

I hadn't realised, although perhaps I should have done, that the investitures were done in order of importance. The soldier who was receiving the Victoria Cross therefore went first. A gentleman who was standing to the far side of Her Majesty, recited the citation, which was almost exactly, word for word, the account her mother had told Mrs M. That made me smile because it meant her mother had read it so often, she knew it verbatim.

Her Majesty was dressed in yellow, complete with a yellow hat and shoes, and long white gloves. She looked just like your favourite grandmother.

The Queen asked the soldier several questions which I couldn't hear, very briefly shook her hand and smiled warmly. The soldier stepped back and away.

Next, I was called forward and it was indicated to me that I should stand on a small black cross on the carpet made of tape. I stood up straight and pulled my shoulders back, just like I used to do when I was on parade at Hendon.

"Her Majesty, may I present Mr Christopher Pritchard, formerly Detective Inspector Christopher Pritchard, of the Metropolitan Police."

The Queen took a few steps towards me, stopped and turned slightly to collect the medal which another courtier was holding in a presentation box.

A voice to the right spoke.

"The citation reads: On 24th May 1983 in Stoke Newington, the then Police Constable Christopher Pritchard and a colleague, Police Constable Dawn Matthews, were evacuating a shopping centre following the receipt of an anonymous but coded telephone communication claiming that a bomb had been planted at the location. While they were doing their duty to protect the public, the improvised explosive device detonated causing both officers the gravest injuries. Despite his own severe suffering and without regard for his own well-being, Police Constable Pritchard made his way through the debris to his colleague to render first aid. He then remained with PC Matthews to comfort her. Tragically, a few minutes later, PC Matthews died of her injuries while cradled in his arms. In recognition of his gallantry, Her Majesty is pleased to announce the award of the George Medal."

Her Majesty then took two more steps and pinned the medal on my chest. She shook my hand. It was just like being in a dream.

"We would very much like to thank you personally for what you did." Her Majesty said, her voice barely more than whisper.

"I only did what any police officer would have done, Ma'am. I went to help a dying colleague and friend." I said, honestly.

The Queen smiled, still holding my hand.

"I'm not referring to what happened in 1983, Mr Pritchard."

Her voice was low and slightly croaky. She smiled again and looked me directly in the eye, holding my gaze for just a few seconds too long. A moment of complete understanding passed between us. Then she gently pushed my hand away and let go.

In January 1983, on my first day at Hendon training School, I had taken an oath to Her Majesty. Now, twenty-nine years later, that royal validation brought my time in blue to an end. What a ride I'd had! Apart from Dawn's tragic death, being kidnapped in Thailand, suffering from a terrible heroin addiction and being wrongfully imprisoned for nearly seven months, I wouldn't have changed a single thing.

I thought I might write about my early years and particularly my time at Stoke Newington as a young PC. A kind of autobiography perhaps but hidden in the guise of fiction. It would also be a nice way to remember Dawn. I already had the perfect title - *'Puppy Walking Nostrils'*.

Printed in Great Britain
by Amazon

60191846R00149